Gotta Move On

A Novel

MickiMichelle

Moqa Books

Moqa Books
www.mickimichelle.com
8099 Lavender Drive
Baton Rouge, Louisiana 70818

Gotta Move On

For information on booking the author for book signings, interviews, and other speaking events, contact: MickiMichelle at mickimichel@live.com

Created & Printed in the United States of America

ISBN: 978-0-9828746-1-5

Cover by Michelle Foster

Dedication

To the most magnificent people in the whole world: my family.

1

Trying to mask the fear caused by the man whom I loved so deeply at one time was not only frightful, but also heartbreaking to say the least. Deep in the pit of my heart was the eternal affection that surrounds the man that I've loved all of my life, as in the back of my mind was the good sense to tell me that he was now a new creature.

I tried to think about all of the good times we'd shared before the infidelity; before the deception. When the strange behaviors began several months ago, I convinced myself in believing that he loved me too much to physically harm me. But indeed he had.

Many months ago I would have killed to be with him again. Going to the end of the earth with him was a journey willingly fulfilled had he asked. Instead he turned me away and turned away from me.

As I unwillingly occupied the same vehicle as the shockingly new Todd Taylor, the maniac who'd forcefully taken me from my bed, thoughts of my life danced energetically in my head. I reminisced, compared, fell in and out of a quiet depression, cried silent tears, and stared into the unknown sky trying to find the man I'd married somewhere inside of the heartless body that occupied the space next to me. I searched our database of memories and recollections to find a good answer to the questions that remained. I found nothing.

I guess as he drove he was thinking also. Thoughts were heavily in rotation. *Where did things go wrong?*

We rode in silence. The only sound was the wind beating at the passenger side seat where I lay curled into a tight ball like an unborn child.

The silence and the cool wind brought sleep to my eyes.

2

After what seemed like eternity, I was awakened to a cell ringing. I opened my eyes to see him look down at the number as he ignored the call.

The clock inside the car told me it was now 8:35 am. The sun was shining and the damp air that entered the car from the broken widow made me shiver. From the looks of it, it was going to be a beautiful day in wherever the heck I was. I had no idea.

"Good morning lovely." Todd chimed after noticing my movement.

"Where are we?" I said groggily.

"Don't worry your pretty head. I'm gonna take good care of you just like I used to."

"I wanna go home Todd. I'm tired of riding, I'm cold, and my head hurts."

"You'll be okay." He said as he gazed at me in the seat next to him.

"I need to use the restroom."

"We'll stop at the next gas station."

My cell started to ring from my bag that Todd had thrown into the backseat the night before. I'd totally forgotten about the purse that I'd picked up on my way out of my bedroom. Todd had immediately taken it out of my hand before I even exited the room.

I looked at him. He didn't take his eyes off the road. So I reached back to retrieve my bag.

"Uhm, I don't think so." He said grasping my arm to halt further movement.

"Todd you know people are gonna be looking for me."

He looked over at me in silence, and then reluctantly let my arm go.

In my attempt to reach over the seat, I made a quick movement and felt a sharp pain radiate in my side. My thoughts quickly went to the abuse I'd endured the night before. Sadness quickly slithered its way into my heart.

Though in pain, I somehow managed to get to my purse.

The distinct ring had already told me it was Ryan. I wondered why he was calling me so early. *Shouldn't he be at practice?* I thought.

"Is it okay if I answer?" I asked Todd. I didn't want to set him off.

"Is that one of your boyfriends?"

I wasn't sure if I should answer that or not. I studied his face for a reaction before I spoke.

"He's gonna get suspicious and will probably call all day if I don't answer." I said calmly as I continued to watch his face closely.

"Make it quick and don't try anything."

"Hello." I answered quickly.

"Hey sweetheart."

I didn't reply. I really didn't want to talk to him, but I just needed to hear from somebody, anybody to let them know I was alright.

"Krisha where are you?"

"Why?"

"I've been at your house for an hour, and you're not answering the door."

My house? Oh God. Just what I need. I thought.

"I'm not at my home."

"I know that now…so where are you?"

"What do you want?"

"I wanna see you."

"Well too bad."

"I came all this way to see you and that's all I get?"

"Sorry."

"I'll sit here until you get in."

"Well do that okay."

I hung up the phone.

I'd gotten mad at Ryan all over again. Almost forgotten that I was with Todd and being taken against my will.

"Call to check on the kids then turn that phone off." He demanded.

"I need to call Mia."

"Forget her."

"If I don't speak to her you know she'll have the FBI and half the country looking for me in no time."

"Your punk ass hero of a boyfriend probably already talked to her."

"No, I don't think so. She hasn't called yet so I doubt it."

"I'm sure he will. By that time we should be out of the country."

My eyes grew as big as doorknobs. "Out of the country? I can't go out of the country!"

"Relax boo." Was all Todd said as I looked upside his head.

He just didn't know the evil thoughts that lurked in my brain. I tried to remain calm, so I made my two phone calls as instructed.

I think Mia knew something was wrong. That girl knows me too well. I'll have to find a way to call her back. That's if my phone didn't die first. I had two bars left and no life support.

I realized a few miles back that we were driving through Alabama. My guess was we were headed to Florida. For what? I had no clue. But, I didn't ask questions. Instead I laid the seat back and allowed my thoughts to resume.

3

After arriving in Miami, Florida after sixteen hours of driving, Todd wanted to go shopping. He had driven sixteen hours straight but didn't seem to be phased at all. He said we needed some clothes and personal items so we shopped two hours before we went to get a hotel room.

At this point, I didn't know what to think about the situation I was in. *Was I being kidnapped?* It sure didn't fell like it anymore. I was definitely not here by choice, but who could resist Miami. It *almost* felt right. The only problem was I was sore all over and I had a bruise on my face from those licks I took. The memory of the fight with Todd brought tears to my eyes. We never fought while we were together, what sense did it make to fight while divorced?

That night in the hotel, I had plenty opportunities to use the phone, scream for help, anything to alert someone that I was taken from my home against my will by my deranged ex-husband. I chose to do neither of the above; though I felt threatened in the beginning. For some reason, I felt more comfortable now.

Todd wasn't gonna hurt anybody. He just wanted me. For whatever reason, he wanted me.

He seemed to mellow out and was like the old Todd again. The behavior that he expressed at my house was long gone. The behavior that I'd witnessed in the past with Kyra was uncharacteristic of Todd Taylor. Maybe he was stressed by recent events that had unfolded, maybe he was really dealing with issues he couldn't handle in his personal life or maybe he couldn't handle the fact that he'd given up the most dedicated and loving woman he'd ever come across, but one thing was for sure, he'd been dealing with something.

After dinner and a shower, separately of course, we laid down for the night.

Though exhausted, I lay awake trying to imagine what my life would be like now if Todd were still in it. At one time, I lived, breathed, ate and slept him. Right now I feel nothing less than resentment toward him. I kind of felt sorry for him knowing that his life was in total disarray. But what sense did it make to make my life just as crazy because of his selfish and stupid decisions? I couldn't see why he didn't understand this. He *is* a highly intelligent man.

4

Around 8:00 am, Todd was awakening me. I was instructed to get up and get dressed. So, I pulled myself up and did what I was told with no questions asked.

After a small breakfast and gathering the few things we'd acquired the day before, to my surprise we boarded a cruise ship to Jamaica intended for seven whole days. I was reluctant to getting on that ship and tried my best to talk Todd out of it, but he wasn't taking *no* for an answer.

After we were cruising for a day, I realized pouting and staying locked up in the cabin wasn't gonna help my situation. So I decided to try my best to go with the flow. He wasn't hurting me, and I wasn't uncomfortable. I'd see where all this would lead to, because regardless of anything, once we arrive back at home, things were gonna be the same as before. I still didn't want his ass. But I'd play the game because I didn't know what he was thinking. His crazy behind might throw me overboard. I was nobody's fool.

After a while, I began to have a better time than I thought possible. It was almost like old times between Todd and me. Sometimes I'd have to stop, think and look at him to remember the bullshit that he was about, the fight we'd had, and the hard strokes to my face that he'd given me.

He'd been a gentleman and very accommodating the whole time on the cruise. He'd bought me everything imaginable and would give me the world if I asked for it. But I don't think he realized that money could not replace the things he'd done to me. Nothing could erase our past.

On the third night, we partied, danced and had a really good time. Todd had never made a pass at me throughout the whole trip, even though we slept in the same bed. But tonight I think he saw something I prayed he'd forgotten all about.

He stared at me as we shared a table in the lounge. "You are beautiful Krisha." He said in his signature sexy tone.

"Thank you. You're not too bad yourself." I said with a smile.

He was sweet. I appreciated the gentleness.

"Thanks."

That's as far as he went. I was grateful because I was getting a little uncomfortable with the strange looks.

The champagne had me in a good way. I danced a slow song with a guy who looked to be in his early forties, maybe, tall, dark, sexy ass goatee; all man. I could sniff them out though, another pretty boy.

As his hands engulfed my lower back, I could tell that they were big, but soft. That was a turn off. No more pretty boys with soft hands for me. Spelled nothing but trouble. He was definitely a looker, so I know he didn't come alone. He whispered all kinds of BS in my ear including wanting to meet me for drinks. It was already ten o'clock at night, so I knew what ole boy had in mind for later.

After we were going for dance number two, Todd rudely cut in. This was okay because I was trying to get rid of "lover man" anyway.

"What are you trying to do Krisha?" He said as we danced.

"What?"

"Why are you all up on him like that?"

"We were dancing Todd."

"Looked like he wanted more than a dance."

"Well you know how you men are." I answered sarcastically.

"Don't disrespect me like that again."

I leaned away from his chest to look at his face. Not a smirk or smile that meant he was joking. He was dead serious.

I was shocked that he'd be jealous of a dance from a stranger. Especially since he and I were not together as a couple. At least that was my view on it.

When we reached our room it was late and I was tipsy and tired. Todd had had a few drinks too and he looked beat.

"Todd can I ask you something?" I said as I took off my shoes.

"Shoot."

"Why did you arrange this?"

"I thought I'd be doing something nice for you. Another way to say I'm sorry."

"The gesture was sweet Todd." I paused. "But I'm gonna keep it real. I love you because you were my first love and my husband for so many years, but we can never be together again."

"You should never say never."

"How can you say that after all that's happened? I had you and my boys and that's all I wanted and needed. Now if I want you I have to accept your other two kids and their mommas. I wouldn't settle for anything less than what I already had."

"The mothers won't be an issue to you. You had no problem with my kids before."

"Oh you think so? I accepted one child because I was so in love with you, but not two. I saw past your mistakes and loved you regardless of what you'd done. Our family was too important to me to just throw it away. But, I didn't have to throw it away, you did."

"And I regret that every day. I could kill myself for what I did."

"I couldn't just sit around and wait until you got your stuff together Todd. I finally moved on. You know how many days and nights I cried for you. And after Kyra…I thought I'd die at one point. That hurt like salt in an open wound. I had to save myself. I had no other choice than to move on with my life; for my children and myself."

I sat on the edge of the bed while he stood.

"I know I'm wrong for a lot of things. I caused all of this and to know that eats me up. And sorry about the other night I never meant for it to turn out like that. I didn't want to hurt you. I really just came there to talk and invite you to go away with me. Tell me how I can fix us?"

"I don't think you can fix something that's not there. There is no *us*. We've been over for a long time now."

I was very sincere in telling him the truth. I hated to see him agonize, but he cared less when I was agonizing.

"So do you love him?"

"I love myself and my kids. *We* are who's important in my life right now."

"Are you in love with him? If you say yes, I'll learn to respect that."

"Todd just…"

He cut me off. "Answer me Krisha."

I looked up at Todd with fear in my eyes. I wasn't sure if I should speak the truth, a lie, or nothing at all. Not sure of the outcome of either, so I followed my heart and told him the truth.

"I'm not sure if I'm in love or not. I'm not rushing anything."

"I want my life back. I admit that I can't accept my wife being with someone else."

"As long as I didn't have a man in my life you were happy. But now you know someone else is in the picture, you can't take it. So you thought I'd never get lonely? You thought I'd never get over you, or you thought I just down right couldn't get another man?"

I watched his face to find the answers to my questions.

"I knew you could get another man, I just didn't expect you to. Guess that was me being selfish. I'm sorry Krisha. I just can't say that enough." He said as he found my eyes.

"Well I'm sorry too." I spat as I sat on the bed with my arms folded.

"Excuse me." He said walking toward the door.

He quickly left the room.

I showered, and threw on a black tank and black panties and lay on the top of the covers thinking about the men in my life and the road that I was traveling. I didn't know what to think about Ryan or Craig. I cared deeply for both. The last night I spent with Craig had made me view him in a different light. *Could I be in love with both men?* One thing was for sure; I couldn't continue having a sexual relationship with both of them.

A couple of years ago I would have never been caught up in a situation like I was currently in. I always had one man and would talk about women that juggled more than one and were having sex with them all. Now here I was doing the same thing.

Then I thought about that damn condom that broke with Craig. I immediately felt sick.

I definitely wasn't ready for a baby or a relationship with Craig because of a baby.

If all is clear after this incident, I'll definitely make sure this doesn't happen again. I thought. *Maybe I'll just get rid of Ryan and Craig and start over.*

As I lay across the bed, my mind went to Ryan. Settled in on him. I missed that man so much. Wanted to be in his arms.

When I closed my eyes, I felt his strong hands on my skin as if I could feel his presence.

Within seconds, my mind traveled to the average heffa Ryan had in his apartment and that whole incident. So I switched gears and perused down Craig avenue. I could feel that expert tongue caressing each breast and gently moving over to my stomach in search of my sweetness. The thought of his fetish ignited a fire under my skin.

I jumped as I thought I heard Todd returning. Tried to cover my warmed body. Fortunately it must have been someone next door or in the hallway but I took the opportunity to get up anyway. Had to shake the feelings brought on by my thoughts.

Almost an hour had passed and Todd had not returned, so I decided to go check on him being he was upset when he left. I threw on a pair of shorty shorts that Todd had brought me on yesterday and left in search of Mr. Todd Taylor.

When I located him, he was standing on the deck looking over into the water. Sorrow warmed my heart at the sight of his pitiful stance.

I cared about his well being, so I didn't like seeing him all torn up and confused. But I was still mad at him for hitting me. I don't know, I guess impulse made me walk up behind him and give him a tight hug. He didn't turn around, simply caressed my hands that surrounded his waist.

Silence.

"I feel like jumping and just letting it end."

Shock came across my face.

"Don't say that Todd." I let him go and went to his side to look at him.

"I messed up Krisha. I messed up bad. I hurt you bad. I hurt my kids. Over the last few months, I just began to see how bad I messed up. I'm sorry it took this long to realize that. I've lost the most important thing I've ever had in my life... My family...I did you wrong. I did you so dirty. I see why you hate me."

"I don't hate you anymore."

"You should. I had no right going there and I had no right putting my hands on you or bringing you here without your consent. I just didn't know what else to do get to you. I felt I needed to be out of the area to get a breath of fresh air to be able to talk to you."

"We all made mistakes Todd."

"Mine are almost unforgivable and definitely unforgettable I know that now and I'm sorry. How could I ask you to ever want me after Kyra? Your friend. A bitch who doesn't mean anybody any good."

"This is not about her."

"I know it isn't. I'm to blame."

"Can I ask you about that and will you be honest?"

He nodded his head.

"How did it all start?"

"You don't wanna know." He whispered as he looked out into the ocean.

Silence.

"If I leave this earth tonight you would have everything I own. I've left all my kids a share in what I have, but everything would be yours. I never changed my Living Will and I never will. I'll never marry again, so what I have will be yours when I close my eyes. I owe you that and so much more."

"Stop talking like that, please. You're not going anywhere. There are four kids who need you."

He managed a smile.

"You know I have two girls and two boys."

That brought an even bigger smile to his face. He loved his children.

"No, I didn't know the other child was a girl."

He didn't speak. Just nodded his head.

"Do you have a picture of her?"

"Ah...Yeah!" He said quickly.

He took a picture out of his wallet of a little girl who did not have those eyes. She looked nothing like him.

"She's beautiful." I said with a warm smile.

She *was* cute. But a blind man could see that she wasn't his.

"Thanks."

Todd finally looked up into my eyes. He'd been crying. Something I'd seen only a few times throughout our relationship. Usually when he'd mess up big time.

"I'll always love you."

He leaned over and kissed me. I was so stunned I didn't move or respond. Lips as soft as I remembered. He kissed me again, this time his tongue licked my lips and softly pried them open.

He shifted over to me and stood in front of me as I stood with my back against the railing. As the waves rushed the water, Todd's tongue made love to my mouth under the moon light. He was a terrific kisser and even better than I remembered. I didn't know that I even missed that until now, but his tongue told me he'd missed me over the many months.

When I could no longer resist the sensation of his kisses, I took the back of his neck in my hand and reciprocated as his hands caressed my back and hips. Being in his arms again actually felt better than good.

"Open your mouth." He whispered.

I obliged.

The passion in his tongue was more than I could handle. I was in a zone that was stuck somewhere between stop and go; yes and no; do and don't. Todd pressed his hard body closer to mine and I could feel his desire to have me.

"Open your eyes." He whispered as he held my head between his hands, thumbs caressing my temples. A hypnotizing gaze captured my eyes; a forced surrender.

"I'll never stop loving you." A soft kiss to my temple. "I will *never* stop loving you Krisha."

Our embraced tightened; passion intensified.

"Can I make love to you Krisha?" He whispered softly.

I didn't answer. I couldn't if I wanted to. The dog had my tongue.

As he licked my lips and took my tongue deeper into his warmth, my lower body began to agree to the stimulation.

"I wanna love you." He said between kisses.

His middle had settled right where it was supposed to be. So good against me.

"Please, allow me to make love to you." He whispered.

I didn't offer a reply. I smiled and hugged him tightly. If I didn't say *no*, I guess that meant *yes*.

Taking my hand in his, Todd led me back to our cabin.

As soon as the door closed, I began to have second thoughts.

I don't need another annoying man in my life right now. Hell, if it was that good to him, he wouldn't have walked away before.

Before the other side of my brain could respond, I felt a moist tongue on the back of my thigh.

While he proceeded to taunt me into submission, expert hands slowly unzipped my shorts; got a grip on the waistband, brought them down to my ankles along with my bikini.

"Todd, wait." I begged softly.

The gentleness of his whispers and moans left my mind in disarray.

I'd missed him. It wasn't until this moment that I realized I'd missed all I'd ever known. The man who'd taught me to love. The man who'd taken me to the mountaintop in my youth.

My protests for him to halt his advances were really urges for him to continue.

His mouth never stopped its quest at ushering me toward satisfaction.

I moaned loudly as my body took me on an orgasmic high. I tugged at him in an attempt for him to have mercy on me.

Now I remember. I thought.

Todd Taylor. Hands down.

"Turn over on your stomach."

I obliged.

He went to his bag to retrieve a bottle of massage oil, took off his clothes down to his boxers and went to work on my back. The massage was magnificent. Just what I needed. He massaged my back, down to my feet. My body was beyond relaxed. I was in a good state.

I was then convinced he was trying to take my life. With each toe into his soft mouth, I thought for sure I'd leave the world.

He moved up my body while still using his mouth to satisfy me. Moans of pure satisfaction escaped my lips, leaving me breathless with each kiss.

Todd maneuvered up my body to look into my eyes.

He planted a kiss on my lips. I kissed him back.

"I need you Krisha." He whispered. Then followed with short kisses on my neck and breasts.

"I love you…" He whispered.

He moved to replace his hands with his gentle tongue. Heating me up once again.

"I'm sorry." He whispered as he loved me. "I'll die for you girl." He repeated his love for me, over and over. Told me his life didn't matter anymore if I weren't a part of it. Said he'd never let me go.

"Let me love you." He moaned.

The stimulation was so taunting and mind blowing that without thinking about it, I helped him slide on a life jacket.

He continued whispering his love for me as he settled into place. I closed my eyes tightly and shed a tear. The feeling of his body along with his confessions and whispers sent me over the edge. I was somewhere I didn't want to be but never wanted to leave. There had to be a sexual heaven somewhere. If so, I'd definitely found the spot. I opened my teary eyes to see tears streaming his face.

His compassion always got to my heart. That's why I could never leave him. He was always so sorry when he was wrong.

Todd moved slowly, stroking me the way I liked it. If I could get my mind right and stop crying I could love him the way I knew he liked me to. My heart ached, but my body rejoiced. I shed more tears.

"Do you want me to stop, baby?"

I shook my head.

He continued his rhythm.

"Tell me you love me. Nobody means it anymore. I know you always did."

I felt my heart bursting.

He's taking me there again. I can't go there. Not after all I've been through. I can't. I won't. But how can I stop? How can I stop loving this man?

I turned my head to stop the movement of his mouth on my ear. He stopped in mid-stroke. Turned my face to meet his.

"C'mon baby, tell me you love me."

Todd lifted my bottom by moving one arm underneath my waist. Making sure I remembered who he was. He was on that spot that no one but him has ever, and I mean ever, touched before.

This is unreal. I thought but remained speechless.

"Let me know if I'm hurting you."

I kissed him long. My mind was no longer in my head. It was somewhere in my ass.

After an extended love making session, I relaxed in his arms.

"You're body is so hot."

"It's always been hot remember?" *I said with a chuckle.*

He gave me a kiss on my forehead. "No I mean like, really hot. I've never felt you that way before."

"So that means it was good right?" I asked already knowing the answer.

"You ever heard of better than best?"

Todd pulled himself up to go dispose of the condom.

When he came back to the bed, I asked with a mischievous smirk. "You got some more?"

I was feeling cocky. I knew better. But the sad thing was, I didn't care.

"Condoms?"

"Yeah."

He pointed to his bag in the chair.

"Let me see." I reached in to retrieve three condoms, put them on the nightstand.

"Damn, girl what you planning on doing to me?"

I smiled. I'd already gone there, so hell, I might as well have some fun now. I wasn't married. He wasn't married. So, he could still be considered my husband, *right?*

We didn't use all those condoms that night. Actually we only used one more. But the next few days we used all he had. We ended up buying more. On my last night with Todd, one condom broke. I was driving really reckless these days. The killing part about it was I didn't know where the hell I was going.

5

Todd had turned the rental in before we set sail so we stayed in Miami over night when we got back. We continued our lovemaking in Miami. I almost didn't want to leave, but we caught a flight back home the following day. But not before he catered to my every want, wish, and desire. I had a load of gifts and a huge smile plastered on my face.

My abduction and ass whipping had turned into a very pleasurable trip with my ex-husband.

I was almost certain things were going to change and be back to normal once we got back to reality; home.

I'm sure all had turned out the way Todd had wanted. With the exception of my not saying those three magic words to him or agreeing to get back together with him.

I can admit that being with him brought back up some old feelings that I was sure were dead.

I've asked myself over and over, *"How could I sleep with this man after he'd taken up with my best friend for months?"*

Call me stupid but I do still love him. That's something that I just can't help. One thing was for sure though; he'd never hear me say it. It's inside of me most definitely, but it'll never come out. Not out my mouth that is.

I arrived home around two pm the next day. I checked my messages, charged my cell, and dialed Mia. I was exhausted but I had to check in with her. Though it was Sunday afternoon, I knew she would be at home in bed with either a man or a hangover.

Mia answered with sleep in her voice.

"Hey chick." I said.

"Krisha, where have you been?" She screamed frantically, immediately waking up.

"Long story."

"I aint got nothing but time."

"Who's with you?"

"Nobody. Why?"

"Where's Kyra?"

"She has her own place now."

"Where's Derric?"

"At his place. Why?"

"So, can I come over?"

"I'm about to get up and go to the store, so I'll come to you."

"Cool. I'll be waiting."

When Mia arrived, I explained to her everything that happened not leaving out one detail.

She sat and listened without saying a word the entire time.

When I finished, she was staring at me in disbelief.

"Tell me you just made that up."

"I wish I could."

"So he just took you against your will, beat your ass, you had sex with him, now he's forgiven?"

Mia made it sound worst than it actually was.

"No, I didn't say he was forgiven."

"You didn't have to."

"I'm not saying I want to be with Todd like that Mia. I just told you what happened. That incident wasn't what I asked for."

"You know what? It's your life. Do what you want."

With that said she got up and left my house slamming the door behind.

She was clearly upset with me. I sat on my couch feeling bad and looking stupid. *How can I get Mia to understand how I feel about this? How can I get her to see my side?* I did love Todd deeply, but I knew I could no longer be with him. *So what was the deal with her?*

About ten minutes after she left, I called her cell.

I know she knew it was me from my distinct ring, but she didn't answer. So I called her mean butt right back.

She answered on the first ring. "Bitch what do you want?"

"Mia, why'd you just leave like that?"

"Look, I don't have time for your drama today. I told you, *do you* okay!"

"Why are you acting like this?"

"Why did you sleep with him?" She spat angrily.

"Mia, it was just the moment. The situation I was in."

"Did he rape you?"

"No. Absolutely not!"

"Then go ahead and admit it, you wanted to."

"No I didn't."

"Bullshit Krisha!"

Silence.

I'd given my answer so I didn't know what else to say.

"Krish you know the hold that man had on your mind. You know his ass is of no earthly good. Why would you give in to him like that? He's gonna have you all twisted up again, or he's gonna bury you. I just don't know why you can't see that."

"I don't want Todd like that Mia."

"Tell that to someone who doesn't know your dumb ass…you are too weak for that idiot."

"I am not."

"Girl please. You don't know if you love Ryan and you're sexing him. You say you don't love Craig, but you sexing him too. And you don't want Todd, but you sexed him. What kind of crap is that girlfriend? You have slept with three men numerous times within the last couple weeks."

"You make it sound so bad."

"It's not good Krish! What is wrong with you? Look at what you're allowing him to do to you."

"Mia, I, I…"

"I, I my ass. That's why I left because I couldn't talk to you without going off. So, I gotta go. You're running my blood pressure up!"

Click. She hung up the phone in my face.

I stayed put to think for a while.

What is going on with me? I asked myself.

I know whatever Mia felt about the situation was probably right. Sometimes I needed her to make me see things straight. Whenever she gets over being so mad at me, she'll talk to me. That's nothing new. She could curse me out in Japanese, French, and Italian, and I'd call her back in five minutes or less or when I thought she'd calmed down, and we'll go on like nothing. I know she loves me and I love her. She just wants the best for me. Though she's only four months older, she's the only big sister I've ever had. I wouldn't know what to do without her.

6

Crying or feeling sorry for myself was not an option, so I decided to get up and clean my house.

My bedroom, to my surprise, was all cleaned up. I noticed that Craig had changed the sheets and made my bed. He'd cleaned the bathroom from where we'd showered and left towels. The towels and sheets were washed and neatly folded and sitting on my dresser. Guess he didn't know where to put them. Craig was amazing. After all that drama with Todd, he still cared enough to clean up the mess.

I noticed something over on my nightstand, that I know wasn't there before I left. I went over to retrieve the small package wrapped in lime green paper. It was a card in an envelope. The card inside was lime green and purple, my favorite colors. Someone definitely knew me. The inside of the card displayed a very romantic message. It read.

Love is beautiful
Love is a wonder
That no man shall put asunder
The love we have
The love we'll share
The love I'll give'
The children we'll bear
For my love for you will forever be true
And reign in my heart, when we're apart.
The day will come, when we'll be together
Together with you
Together forever.

That was so sweet. There was also a letter inside. I sat on my bed and eagerly opened the letter. Wondering why Craig would take the time to write me a letter after the fiasco of a night that we'd last experienced.

Krisha,

I came to see you to set things straight between us. If you would have let me explain things to you, none of this would be happening. I've waited for you just as I told you I would, but it doesn't seem you're coming home tonight. I didn't know what to think when your door was unlocked, car in the garage, and you were nowhere to be found. I decided to straighten the mess in your bedroom to surprise you with a romantic candlelit night when you came back. Thought maybe that'll get me some brownie points too. After the phone call I made to you, I ruled out foul play and realized that you had no interest in seeing me. But I waited anyway. However, I realized that I was doing more injustice to myself than justice for you because in preparing my surprise for you, I was the one surprised. Looked like you two had a really nice time considering all the used paraphernalia in the garbage can in your bathroom. What bothered me most is that you knew I flew in just for you and you didn't bother to come home to see me. Now I know why.

I can't explain what I feel right now Krisha but hurt will never describe it. You know as well as I know that women can come very easily for someone in my line of work. But I chose not to live that lifestyle. I only wanted you. I get the message. As for ole boy tell him he's a lucky man. Have a nice life. Love you.

Ryan

Now, I had reason to cry. I balled up under my thick comforter and cried.

I knew crying wasn't doing me any good, but I cried anyway.

I had no idea he was inside my home. *Why did Craig leave my door unlocked and why didn't he flush those damn condoms?* I pondered.

I wanted to call Ryan so badly, but I was too ashamed. Was that the reason my mind was on Ryan the whole time I was with Todd, because he's the man I really want or was it de ja vue because he was finding me out.

Lying in my bed feeling like a fool, I realized that I honestly did love that man. My heart hurt badly. *Why did I have to go through this to realize that I really do love him?*

I tried to sleep, but I couldn't so I tossed and turned for about two hours before I got the nerve to call him. It had been more than a week since I'd last spoken with Ryan. I prayed he would even talk to me.

I called his cell first. Got his voicemail. Then I dialed his home number.

"Hello." An energetic male caller said. Didn't sound like Jace.

"Hi, may I speak with Ryan please?"

"Hold a sec."

He laid the receiver down and started screaming for Ryan to get the phone.

After a few seconds, he returned to the phone.

"Sorry baby, he can't come to the phone right now. Can he call you back?"

I was at a loss for words. Couldn't think of what to say for a second. He always took my calls.

"Why can't he take my call?" I boldly asked.

"I don't know, but if you wanna talk, I'm available."

"Look, please go tell Ryan that Krisha said to get his black ass on the phone right now!"

I know I could have said that better and probably gotten the same response, but I didn't want to.

"I'm sorry Ms. Krisha. My bad. Hold a sec."

This time he didn't scream. He went to deliver the message personally. I didn't hear another sound until Ryan picked up the receiver.

Un huh. I thought. The games people play.

"Hello." He said enthusiastically.

"Hey Ryan."

"What's up?"

I heard the enthusiasm leave as soon as he heard my voice.

"I need to talk to you."

"Well I don't have much more to say to you."

"I think we have a lot to say to each other."

"Look, why don't we just let it be. Just leave it just like it is right now before someone really gets hurt."

"Ryan, I'm sorry. I need to explain. Can I come see you?" I was talking fast.

He laughed.

"Look, we've wasted enough money making these trips for nothing. You stay there and do you. And I'll stay here and do me. Okay Krisha."

I didn't respond, neither did he. We were so silent on the phone until I could hear someone whispering in the background.

"I'm leaving if you're gonna ignore me." A female voice said in a low whisper.

Ryan didn't answer her. He just held the phone.

I broke the silence.

"Look, I don't care about her Ryan." Letting him know I'd heard the girl.

"Ryan." I heard her call again.

She wasn't letting up, so he finally said to her, "I'll be there in a second."

"I tell you what. You go finish her off, put her to sleep, and then call me back, okay."

He didn't offer a response. Just held the phone. I held it too. Didn't say a word.

"Later." He finally said.

Now he sounded like he wanted to talk. Some men are so predictable and transparent.

Maybe I'll give men up and become a nun or something. Then, I won't be stressed the hell out every day.

I lay across my bed thinking and reminiscing. I called my kids who were enjoying themselves so much that they really didn't have time to talk to me, so I told them I'd call them the next day. Nobody wanted to be bothered with me today. That thought really hurt.

Then my mind fell on my work obligations. I was to host an acquaintance party at my home for the mortgage brokers that were coming in for the conference to be held in the city next month. Not only that, I was to host the event. I'd been working on everything for some time, but lately I hadn't done a thing. So one thing was for sure, next week has to be all about work. My conference definitely has to be the best. So no men or drama allowed.

I wrote, planned, and made notes to make some calls tomorrow. When I'd done as much as I could do considering it being a Sunday evening, I got up, showered, dressed and left to go mingle with somebody; anybody. I felt like letting my hair blow in the wind.

I set out to go pick up Mia. I wasn't sure she was ready to talk to me, but I went anyway.

I'd gotten rid of my convertible so we switched my Rover for her Benz. We didn't speak a word of our prior conversation. It was old news as far as we were concerned.

Mia and I ended up at the comedy club. The Sunday evening show was very entertaining. We laughed until our sides hurt. Unexpectedly, we met the club's owners. Two very handsome brothas, Chris and his younger brother Chad. Chris was thirty-five and Chad was thirty-three.

Mia and I noticed Chad staring at her throughout the show. During the show he approached our table, introduced himself and asked if we were comfortable. He worked the room greeting guests while Mia and I kept our eyes on his very tall, like 6'7" tall and very handsome self.

When the show was over, he came back to our table and began small talk with Mia. He asked if I was married and thought his brother would like to meet me, then left to retrieve his brother from the office inside the club.

Chad's brother Chris was just as handsome as Chad. He was as tall as and as fine as his brother, wore one diamond in his ear, while Chad wore two. Their height and build made them look as if they could be athletes. Chris was nice, but another man in my life was exactly what I did not need. But I went with the flow for the evening. We all ended up exchanging numbers. The guys escorted us to our car when the night was over promising to stay in touch.

7

Later that night, my home phone awakened me from a deep sleep. I looked over at the clock next to my bed.

Now who could be calling me at two o'clock in the morning? I thought.

Calls in the wee hours of the morning always made my nerves bad so I reached over and grabbed the phone without looking at the caller ID box.

"Hello." I said with a sound of urgency.

"Hey boo."

Nobody calls me boo like Todd. I thought.

"What's wrong?"

"Nothing. Open the door."

"For what?" Agitation in my voice.

"I'm outside."

"Where are you coming from this time of morning?"

"Just open the door please."

"Look, I'm not in the mood for sex."

"Krisha, I didn't say anything about sex. Just please let me in."

I dragged out of bed and cursed all the way to the door. I looked out my peephole then opened the door to Todd with a big stupid grin across his face. I could immediately tell he'd been drinking. He stepped in and pulled me into his arms. Gave me a peck on the lips. I undid his hands from around my waist and slipped out of his arms, then walked off toward the living room. He closed the door, locked it, and trailed behind.

"Todd, I'm telling ya', you aint about to come up tonight so you can go on home."

He grabbed me again stopping my stride.

"I'm straight boo, besides, you wore me out." He grinned.

I laughed a little. That made me change my tone.

"I just left you less than 24 hours ago. Why do you wanna see me already?"

"I wanna hold you. I told you, I need you."

I ignored that. He should have needed me months ago. I turned to go back up to my bedroom; proceeded up the stairs.

"Damn!" Todd screamed.

I stopped in my tracks and turned around to see him still standing at the bottom of the stairs in the living room.

"What?" I asked with attitude.

Shaking his head and eyeing my body through the thin nightshirt. "I was a damn fool to leave all of that."

"You already know that, so either come on up to go to sleep or leave."

I turned back around and proceeded up the stairs to my bedroom with a walking headache in tow.

"What you got on under that?" He said while walking up the stairs.

"You know I sleep in the nude or no underwear."

Catching up to me and lifting the hem of the shirt to take a peek.

I swatted at his hand.

"Aww girl you gonna make this hard for me."

"Just get in there and go to sleep please." I rolled my eyes. I really wasn't for him this morning. *Why did I open the door?* I chastised. "I gotta go to work in the morning so no drama."

Once we reached my bedroom, he took hold of me from behind and tightly hugged my neck. Planted kisses to the back of my neck while his love jones hard against my behind.

"C'mon now I'm tired. You said you didn't want to do anything." I whined.

"I didn't but I just can't resist you. You do things to me I can't explain."

"Why do you always..." I gave a deep sigh. "Nothing." There was so much I could have said behind that. I just assumed not even go there. It didn't matter anyway. It was already determined that his ass had a sex demon. So I left it alone.

Instead I said, "I'm sorry, but if you don't plan on sleeping you have to go Todd."

Still kissing my neck.

"Why are you being so cold?"

"It's after two in the morning and I need my rest...and where the hell are you coming from this late anyway?"

"Out."

"Doing what on a Sunday night?"

With his nose buried in my neck, "Umm, you smell good." Obviously changing the subject.

"Whateva bastard. Go to sleep or get out!"

He made me go there. I broke his grip and got into the bed.

He was still up to the bullshit that I didn't have time for. I wonder what all that crap was that he put in my ear on the cruise. It is what it is. A bunch of crap.

He sighed deeply. "I went out to Shady's with Trent and time got away from me Krisha." He calmed down and got serious.

"You don't owe me an explanation. Just go to sleep."

"Yes, I do. If I'm coming into your house this time of morning disturbing you, I do. I just needed to hold you that's all."

He put on that puppy dog face that I loved so much.

"Riiiight? Guess you didn't come up on anybody else tonight huh?"

"I told you, I want you back and I'm gonna do everything possible to get you. I don't care about nobody else."

He undressed. Put on his birthday suit and climbed into bed behind me snuggling into my body. Todd was the spoon and I was the sugar that filled it. I gotta admit it felt good to sleep in a man's strong arms. But Todd was foul, and had to go.

"I love you baby." Todd rose up and kissed my cheek. His kisses trailed from my cheek to my neck.

"Todd, I'm serious. Stop or you gotta leave." I protested softly.

"Okay, I'll try."

He laid his head down on the pillow and within thirty seconds he was snoring in my ear.

That let me know, all required is to say no and mean it. Real men will respect that. It's called *will power* ladies, *will power.* I had some at that time. I was proud of myself.

I awakened at 7:00 am to find that Todd had gone. He left $2,000 in cash and a note asking me to wire $1,000 to his sister for the kids and to buy me something nice with the rest. He was being overly generous now days. A few months ago he'd turned into a dead bead dad, not providing for or seeing his kids. Guess he must have his business together with his baby momma or he was trying really hard to impress me. Whatever. He already knows money aint the way to get me. I could never be bought. Aint enough money in the world.

8

I hadn't heard from Craig since Todd and I had been back at home.

Today while having lunch with a city official, I saw Craig having lunch with a cute Caucasian girl. He spotted me across the room and blew me a kiss. I offered a sophisticated wave. I knew this would prompt a phone call later, so I would wait.

All week, I was in and out of meetings, planning for the upcoming conference and also handling my company's business. Since Cheryl was at the new office, I had to take on her duties, in addition to my own. I was so swamped with work that the month went by so fast.

My event had turned out to be a huge success. The kids were back in school. Things were back to normal for me.

I hadn't spoken with Ryan for a month. He never called me back, so I let it ride. I cared for him but I was never one to run behind a man. I was a fool for only one man, *my husband.* If Ryan wanted me, he knew how to find me.

As for Craig, he started calling like crazy. I was dodging him like bullets. We'd hooked up on a few occasions for the usual tension breaker, but I turned down everything else he offered from trips, diamonds, walks in the park, dinner, and commitment. I just wasn't interested. I felt if I took things from him I'd feel obligated, and I wasn't having that. I didn't want to be obligated to anything or anyone else at this point.

Then there was Chris. I'd had dinner and several phone conversations with him. I learned that he was an ex-New Orleans Rocket. His brother still played on the team. Mia had come to know Chad quite well. Their relationship was definitely on a very different level than Chris' and me. I guess Mia wasn't as screwed up in the head as I was. She knew what she wanted, I didn't.

Todd was more agitating than anybody though. He called daily at least five times and was often at my house for the kids, or so he said. He sent gifts, offered trips, left messages, but something in me just wouldn't allow myself to go there with him either.

I had not shared my body with him since the cruise and I didn't intend to. He just didn't get it. Wouldn't leave me alone.

Kyra and I had gotten a little closer; just a little. Or maybe I should say, I tolerated her just a little. Which was far more than she deserved. We'd all gone out together last Saturday night just like old times. The only problem was that the trust was gone. I cared about her, way down in my soul. But our relationship would never be the same as before. But it was cool just hanging out. I practically ignored the fact that she was there. She was still the same Kyra when it came to partying. But that bitch could go to hell for all I cared.

9

On Friday Kyra, Mia, and myself went out on a girl's excursion. One that Miss "Make a Mends" Mia had thrown together.

We were sharing a table at one of our favorite restaurants when my cell phone started singing, "My Boo" by Usher. It was Craig. Not really my boo, but my little sidekick of pleasure. I figured this would be a cool ring tone for him. He claimed to be just leaving his office and wanted to take me to dinner. I told him we were already out, so he asked if he could stop by to see me. I agreed. Fifteen minutes later in walked Mr. Luscious. To say he'd been working all day, he still looked fresh in the slacks and sports jacket he was sporting. This was one sharp brotha. *Boy I sure can pick 'em.* I thought.

Craig spotted us immediately and started walking over to our table. When he reached the table, I stood to greet him with a light hug and kiss.

"Have a seat." I offered.

I introduced everybody.

"I didn't come to rain on you ladies parade. I just came to see this pretty lil lady." Caressing my shoulder.

"Would you like something to eat or drink? You're more than welcome to stay."

"Maybe I'll have one drink then I'll go."

"You haven't eaten Craig. You can't drink on any empty stomach."

Kissing the back of my hand, "Thanks for the concern, bae, but I'll be fine."

We all shared drinks, conversation, and laughter. Then Craig decided it was time for him to go.

"It's been nice ladies but I gotta run." He dug into his wallet and pulled out his Platinum Visa then handed it to me. Tonight's on me ladies. You can bring it by later." Pointing at the credit card.

So that was the deal. Men always got game going on.

"Okay, Thanks." Everyone said his or her thank yous and goodbyes.

I got up and walked Craig to the front of the restaurant. We embraced for a brief goodbye and a quick kiss.

"You really want me to bring it to you later?" I asked in a soft seductive tone.

"In the worst way." He whispered. He slipped a house key off his key chain and gave it to me.

"Have fun and let yourself in."

Craig planted a quick kiss on my lips then turned to make an exit.

Yes indeed. Why can't I make up my mind when it comes to men? Craig would make any woman happy. Any woman in her right mind would turn flips to have him. Any woman but me.

I strolled back to the table with a smile glued to my face.

"Krisha you didn't tell me he was a cutie." Mia said as I sat down.

"I don't have to tell you everything."

"You are one twisted chick. How could you be confused about a man like that?"

"Looks aren't everything Mia."

"Bullshit. You gotta be attracted to 'em also."

"Chill out girl…that's just a special friend. You know me."

"Yeah, I know trick."

We both laughed. Kyra smiled not knowing exactly what Mia and I were talking about.

We ended up having a great evening at Craig's expense.

My boys were with Todd for the weekend so I went to Craig's around 11:30 p.m. He was sleeping but as soon as I stepped into his bedroom it was on. I'd never heard my named called so much in one night. The evening had started off good and ended magnificently.

10

The following weekend, I rolled over in my bed wondering why I felt like the bottom was falling out of my stomach. My head was spinning out of control and I felt dog-tired. This was the second day I'd been in bed, so I knew I had to get up and do something.

I called Mia to come help me because I was exhausted and I was sure the kids had wrecked my house downstairs. Of all times, Carmen was out of town for the weekend. So, I had to do things on my own. And I simply could not.

Malik and TJ came running up the stairs. I heard their little feet hitting each step hard and fast. Walking was just out of the question for those two.

"Mom, do you need anything?" My little man TJ asked.

Malik had made his way over to the bed and laid a big wet kiss on my forehead.

"You don't look good Mom." Malik said looking into my eyes.

"I know baby. I feel even worse."

They both stood next to the bed staring at me.

"What wrong mom?" TJ asked.

"I don't know baby. I just feel really sick…could you guys start the shower for mommy." I said finally pulling myself up into sitting position in the bed.

"Sure mom. Want me to get you something to wear?" TJ asked as Malik went to turn the shower on.

"Yeah, baby that'll be great."

"Mommy, I'll take your sheets off the bed while you're in the shower."

I couldn't believe my ears. My babies were being so responsible and mature. I'd always taught them to be considerate and helpful. Guess they were really listening after all.

Malik pulled an old light blue, velour jogging suit out of the closet for me to put on. Which was a perfect choice. It was comfortable and just what I needed to relax in. I definitely wasn't going anywhere near outside.

When I got out of the shower, they'd changed my sheets, made the bed and straightened my bedroom to the best of their little abilities. It was definitely the gesture that meant so much.

As I headed downstairs, the doorbell rang.

"Get the door please." I threw out to either one of them. That immediately meant a foot race to the door.

Mia had walked in before I reached the bottom of the stairs.

She looked over at me coming toward her.

"Damn! What's wrong with you? Your head looks a hot mess."

"Good morning to you too."

"Good morning but you look horrible."

"Thanks. I know. I feel like crap." I plopped down on my couch.

"You wanna go to the doctor."

"No, I'll make an appointment to see my doctor next week."

Looking around downstairs Mia said, "Krisha what's suppose to be the problem? It looks quite nice down here."

"I guess the boys must have cleaned the house for me. I haven't been down here since yesterday."

I couldn't believe they'd actually picked up behind themselves. They were seven and nine now, so I guess it was time for them to start showing some responsibility around the house. I was so proud of them.

"Hey guys I brought you some boiled crabs. They're in the kitchen."

"Thanks, Tee Mia." They both jumped up and ran to the kitchen.

"Sit down on the floor Krish. Let me do something with your head."

"I need to go to the beautician on Wednesday."

"Well let me just give you some braids for now. That's better than scaring people to death."

"Real funny Mia."

"What's ailing you anyway?"

"I think I ate some bad seafood for lunch on Thursday. I didn't start feeling like this until Thursday night."

"Today is Saturday and you're still sick from Thursday? If you're still feeling bad, you need to go to the doctor Krish."

"I will."

I sat on the floor as Mia combed my hair. Preparing me for the braids she was so dieing to give me.

"So you still haven't heard from Ryan?"

"No, Mia. We've been done a long time ago. I'm not waiting to hear from him."

"I think you guys need to talk that's all. He seems like a cool guy. Besides, everything I've heard about him was all good."

"I guess the sources were all men, right?"

"Yes, but that doesn't mean anything. Derric would tell me if he wasn't shit, knowing that you're involved with him."

"Derric doesn't know what goes on in Baltimore."

"Yeah, you got a point there."

"All men aren't the same Krish. Everybody's not that snake in the grass ex-husband of yours."

"I know that Mia."

"Are you still doing him?"

"No!"

"You lying whore."

"I promise I'm not. I haven't been with him since he took me on that cruise two months ago. He's slept here a few nights, but I haven't done anything with him."

I know I sounded defensive but that was the truth.

"Why do you even allow him to sleep here again?"

"Mia, you wouldn't understand. He has kids here."

"So what? He wasn't sleeping here before. His ass was glad to be out of here, especially when he had Kyra. His black ass just don't need to sleep here Krish." She said sternly.

Silence.

"You let a man hang on too long. Cut your losses and move on." Mia said.

"I'm cool Mia. Don't worry about me."

"How can I not? You're living dangerously these days messing with the minds of these men. A man can be crazier than a woman. You know a jealous man will blow your damn brains out."

"I don't know anybody who would be capable of that."

"Are you crazy girl? That simple ass ex-husband of yours is more messed up than you think. That's a Dr. Jekyll and Mr. Hyde type brotha."

"Todd aint crazy."

"Hel-looo. Were you not here when he broke into your house with a gun and beat your ass all the way to Miami, or did you forget? Do you not remember that episode?"

"Yeah, I remember. He did not beat me all the way to Miami Mia. He just wanted me to go with him."

"And did he not wild out in the process? Don't make excuses for his actions Krish. You can't force people by gunpoint to go somewhere with you. It's against the law. Okay?" Mia said sarcastically.

I sat there and got my sermon. It was a long time coming. Took her almost two months to bring it up. But, I always knew she would. In her own time and in her own way. I listened.

Mia gave me seven long braids going to the back of my head. I looked like a tomboy, but I guess with jewelry and lip gloss I'd be okay.

My phone started to ring. I couldn't get up off the couch fast enough, so I yelled for one of the boys to get it.

After a few seconds, Malik came running into the family room where Mia and I were sitting.

"Mom, Daddy wants to know if we can go bowling with him tonight and to the football game tomorrow."

"Yeah sure baby."

"Yes!" He screamed in excitement pumping his arm in the air. He ran back into the kitchen with the phone.

Seconds later they both came running through the family room on their way up the stairs.

"He said he'd be here in an hour. We gotta pack."

"Malik who does the Thunder play tomorrow?" Mia asked for no reason.

"The Braves. So we get to see Mr. Ryan." He threw out as he raced up the stairs.

I looked at Mia. She smiled at me.

"Call him."

"I couldn't. You know how I am."

"Seems to me you spend too much time on the shit you shouldn't and don't put enough into things you should."

"Mia don't start again." I found enough strength to pull myself up trying to excuse myself from the conversation. I headed for the kitchen.

"You want something to eat or drink?" I offered.

"No thanks. I'm good."

As soon as I stepped into the kitchen, my stomach started doing back flips.

"TJ and Malik!" I screamed to the top of my lungs. "Get down here and take these crabs outside!"

They'd left a mess all over my kitchen table. The smell was horrible and it wasn't agreeing with my head or stomach. I was about to lose the little breakfast I'd eaten. I walked back into the family room and took to the couch holding my stomach. My head hurt so badly.

"Krish what is it?" Mia asked.

"That smell is making me sick." I uttered.

I heard Malik and TJ run down the stairs and into the kitchen.

"Let me get you something." Mia said as she exited into the kitchen behind the boys.

She came back with a wet towel and a can Sprite.

She folded the towel then laid it on my forehead as I sipped the drink.

"Mia I feel so bad. What kind of crabs are those?"

"Krish, the crab smell isn't that bad. No more than usual. Your stomach is just sensitive for some reason…just stay lying down for a while. I'll go help the boys so they can get their things together before Todd comes."

Guess I dozed off for a few because Todd was now standing over me when I opened my eyes.

He kissed my cheek.

"I could stay and take care of you if you'd like."

"Thanks Todd, but no thanks. I'll be okay."

"Are you sure?"

"Yeah. Thanks for taking the boys though."

"No problem. They're mine. I can keep them all week if you need me to, or until you feel better."

"I'll be okay."

"We'll call to check on you."

My sons both came to give me a hug and kiss goodbye.

"Be good guys. Mommy will miss you."

"Hope you feel better Mom. Love you." They both shouted as they eagerly made their way out the door behind their dad.

When they left Mia plopped down on the sofa next to me.

"Feeling better?"

"A little. It was just that smell."

"You know what I think?"

"What?"

"You're pregnant heffa!" She yelled.

"I don't think so."

"Think? If you gotta "not think so", your ass is pregnant."

"I take my pills Mia."

"Tell that to someone who don't know you Krish. You know I know how you are with taking those birth control pills."

"I can't be pregnant Mia."

"Oh yes honey you can. All the sex you been issuing out. I'm not surprised. All I wanna know is, who's the daddy?"

"That is so insulting Mia." I rolled my eyes.

"Well, at one time in your life I wouldn't have had to ask, but things are different now."

"I know, it's not insulting that you asked, it's insulting for me not to know."

"What! Are you serious?"

"If I am pregnant, I couldn't even call it. One thing is for sure, I couldn't be pregnant for the only man I'd rather be the father."

"Who is that?"

"Ryan of course…if I am, its either Craig's or Todd's."

"Krish! Oh my God, Todd? Didn't you make them strap up?"

"Yeah every time, but one broke with Craig then one broke with Todd within only days of each other."

"C'mon girl, you're kidding right?" Mia asked looking at me like I'd lost my mind.

"I don't think I'm pregnant, but if I am, there is no way I can have a baby."

"Why not?"

"I don't want another child."

"You wanted a man all up in you so why can't you have a baby."

"Mia!"

Her words were so harsh.

"Well. You know I'm gonna be real with you."

Silence.

After a minute or two, Mia broke the silence.

"Let's just cross our fingers."

She intertwined my fingers with hers then helped me sit up on the couch.

It hadn't dawned on me that I might be pregnant. I'd forgotten all about those two incidents with all that had been going on. And here I am talking about the crabs. I pray my simple behind aint pregnant.

Mia comforted me by draping her arm around my neck. She didn't say anything else about it.

After about thirty minutes of me dozing and thinking, Mia watching TV and talking on her cell, she suggested taking a ride.

"I need some fresh air. Whatcha say sis?"

"Cool." I said as I pulled myself up from the couch.

11

We drove to a few hot spots in the city for a few hours before I got up enough nerve to call Ryan. I knew he had to be in Louisiana today if he was playing here tomorrow. He was too close to me and I at least had to try.

I dialed his cell phone number but to my surprise, it was no longer in service.

Oh well he knows how to find me if he wanted me. I thought. So I let it ride.

After a couple hours of sightseeing and wasting gas, it began to get late. We went to Kyra's but she wasn't home. So we swung over by Shar's house. I stayed in the car while Mia went inside and Marcus came out to talk to me. His company was good but I wanted to be alone.

Shar stood in the doorway of her apartment and looked out at me sitting inside the car. I threw my hand up for a quick wave hello. Instead of greeting me she screamed from the doorway, "Miss Rich Bitch, you too much to come in my house now? You aint all that hoe."

I glared at her through the windshield of the car. She turned to go back inside then slammed the door.

Was she serious? I thought. I wasn't about to stoop to her level if she was. She knew as well as anybody that if I responded to that it wasn't going to be anything nice, up in her house at that. Drama. Nothing changes around the hood.

I dismissed Shar and continued to chat with Marcus for about fifteen minutes. He had to go play cards so I sat in the car pondering if I should go inside and cuss Shar out. But before I could decide, Mia came out of the house.

"Sorry 'bout that girl. I told Shar to shut her drunken butt up."

"She was drunk?"

"Yeah."

"Oh, because I was sure she didn't want to go there with me."

Before we could leave, Shar came running outside calling Mia's name. Mia put the car in park.

"We're having a party next Saturday night at Club 21 for Hakeem's birthday. Why don't you roll through?"

She didn't invite me so that told me she meant what she'd said earlier.

"Fo' sho. Is my girl invited?" Mia asked.

"Look no disrespect to you, but hell no! And don't bring that bitch back around here either."

Just like that. Like I wasn't even sittin' there.

Shut up Krisha. Just shut up. Don't do it. I tried to convince myself.

After a couple of deep breaths, I listened to myself. I held my tongue and let Mia handle her cousin.

"What's up with that cousin? You got beef with my sister?"

"Please girl you know that hoe aint yo' sister and yes I got beef with the bitch and so do a lot of hoes."

I shook my head. Again I ignored the bitches and hoes. That was just the way they talked around here whether harm was meant or not.

"Give my girl some respect. What's the problem with her?"

"She knows what the problem is."

I finally spoke because she was getting on my nerves.

I wasn't going to stoop to her level but I had to check her before she starts thinking I'm soft.

"Shar you know damn well you don't wanna see me. So stop actin' a fool and tell me what you're talking about?"

"She's a rat. She knows what the deal is." Talking to Mia. Still ignoring me.

"What?" Mia said. "Shar please, go on with that."

I was shocked. I didn't expect her to say something like that. Now, I felt like a sittin' duck. Everyone knows what happens to rats on this side of town.

"She knows what's up? She was around here all that time checking shit out. Then she took it back to that prosecuting mothafucka she sleeping with."

Damn, that stabbed me in the heart. *Was she talking about Craig? How did she know about Craig and me?*

Mia got out of the car as if she was about to get with her blood for me.

"You can't be talking about Krisha. Where'd you get that from?" Mia dug while looking Shar straight in the eyes.

"Let her speak for herself Mia. She aint saying nothing."

"No. Tell me what you know." Mia screamed.

"Alright I'll break it down for you."

"She was screwing Craig; the dude from across the way that's the assistant District Attorney now. She came around here long enough to get information to take down Lil Lo, and Git Money. Then they say they got information on C-Bo, my baby daddy cause of her."

"Where'd you get Krisha's name from?"

"I know it was her. She the only other person that started coming around that didn't used to be around here. Then I find out she's banging Craig."

"Did someone around here say her name?"

"I'm saying her name to you. I didn't tell nobody I thought it was her. I don't like her ass, but I don't want to see her hurt. Besides, that skank friend of yalls said it was her."

"What friend?" I said quickly.

"That bitch that took your husband."

"Kyra?" Mia said.

"Yeah!"

"Why would Kyra say something like that?"

"Cause she aint no good. You two must have a serious liking for the same type men."

"Why do you say that Shar?"

"Because she's creeping with Mr. D.A. too. You didn't know?"

My mouth flew open. I was stunned. I looked at Mia in disbelief. Hey, but why not believe? She'd done it to me before. I knew I should always be in good grace with these petty hoes over here. They keep all of the gossip going and know everybody's business.

"How do you know this Shar?"

"I talk to her. She started coming over here with T-Lo."

"So how you know it wasn't her who leaked on them?" Mia asked.

"The bust had already gone down before she started coming around. Just so happened I remembered her from being with you guys and she started talking about Miss Bitch over there."

I heard Shar and her insults but I didn't care. I was still stuck on Kyra and Craig. Why does she keep coming behind me?

"What did she say?" Mia asked.

"She talked about how she took her husband. How she thought she was above everybody. She said a whole lot of nothing that kept conversations going."

I shook my head in disbelief.

Shar continued. "After I told her we all used to kick it not too long ago, she said Krisha was probably the one who snitched. Then about a month ago, she started screwing Mr. D.A. too. She said he told her that Krisha was the one who sold them out."

"That's a lie! Besides Craig would never share any confidential information like that." I rang out. "Shar I know you didn't believe that."

"It all added up."

"Look Shar, we may have had our differences in the past, but lets face it, we've been cool for a good while. You know I wouldn't do anything like that. I stood right here in your yard and took blows for you and your drama. And after they rammed my car, I took that whole incident home and didn't mention it to nobody. And you let an outsider come in here and fill your head up. You know better than that."

"Yeah Shar, I can't believe you'd believe that snake bitch Kyra. She ain't even down. We went on runs with you and everything back in the day. Why would you think Krisha would change like that?"

"Money changes people." She said with her head hung low.

"Shar do me a favor. Please, please." Mia asked putting her hands together as in prayer.

"What?"

"Please do not mention that to anybody else. That is a lie and Krish could be seriously hurt behind it. Please, I beg you cousin. This is my sister, don't ever say that again."

While Mia stood there and begged Shar for silence, I knew that nine times out of ten Shar was not gonna keep quiet. She lived for the bull. I just prayed that for once she'd let the gossip go.

I looked up at Shar with pleading eyes.

"Shar I don't know who set them up, but it wasn't me. But, if it's the last thing I do, I'm gonna kill Kyra's ass. So if what you said is not true please let me know now. Because that bitch is dead."

"I told you what it is." Shar said.

"C'mon Krisha, don't get carried away. Calm down."

"Can't let it slide Mia. She got something for me...I don't know why. I never did anything to her."

"She'll get handled but don't go talkin' murdering her ass."

"Don't you understand Mia? If Shar had mentioned that to anybody, I'd probably already be dead with nobody knowing why. Why would she do this to me?"

"She wants to be you."

"But why? I have more problems than anybody. I loved that girl and she wants me dead! She fucked my husband but she wants *me* dead. I've done everything for her and her child and she wants me dead! Why?" I screamed.

"She didn't say she wanted you dead." Shar said softly.

"What do you think saying something like that was gonna get me…a trip to Cancun? I *will* get her Mia. I gotta get her. And don't you stop me this time."

"Krisha calm down. You already know you can beat her ass. You did that before. So what's that gonna prove?"

"Nothing. But it'll make me feel better."

"Look, I'm sorry Krisha for coming at you like that, but I was mad. I didn't know this chick had issues with you like that. I understand now the reason she talked about you every single time we talked."

"A hater." Mia said. "This time I'm cuttin' her off too. She don't want me to get in her ass too."

"Watch out cousin. She rolls with Cut Throat and Monique now. You know they all like to butcher bitches first and ask questions later."

I looked at Mia, she looked at me, both surprised at Shar's words.

"Kyra's really trippin' now. When she started doing all that?"

Those were some of the most ratchet chicks in the hood. The association was so unbalanced and unbelievable.

"I told you her man is T-Lo. So she goes hard now. She's always over here. But she tippin' out with Craig though."

"Why would she tell you about Craig?"

"We girls. You know how I do it." Shar said followed by a wink.

"Yeah. You swear her to secrecy then tell all her business."

"Damn right! You know me cousin."

"Girl you are a trip." Mia laughed. I wasn't in the mood.

"Shar on the real, keep this conversation between us okay." Mia said.

"I will boo."

"I'm sorry Krisha." She came around and gave me a hug. "I shoulda known not to believe that trick."

I wiped my face and hugged her back.

"Thanks Shar. Good lookin' out."

Shar turned to walk away. She stopped suddenly then turned around to face us again.

"Cuz, you got a bill on you til I get my child support check next week?"

"Yeah. Are you gonna keep your mouth shut?"

"Hell yeah. I know you'd go down with her and I don't want nothing to happen to you, or her."

"In that case, here take this too." I handed her another bill.

She hurriedly took the bill from my hand.

"Cool. For that, a little extra information." She leaned in closer to the car.

"Go ahead." Mia urged.

"She with yo' man right now."

I laughed. "Which one?"

"The D.A. She rolled through about two hours ago. Said they had a date. He picked her up from Monique's house."

"Thanks Shar." I said.

Mia hopped in the car and we drove off.

As Mia drove, my mind went into full thought mode. That explains why I hadn't heard from him today. The more I thought about it. I was beginning to believe the things Todd had said about her. *But why did she hate me?* Craig wasn't officially my man, but to my friends, he was. I guess Kyra wasn't really my friend, so he was fair game.

"Krisha when he came to the restaurant that night I had a feeling that was a bad idea. I just wanted to give her some credit. I figured she'd made a mistake and learned from it."

"You'd think she would have after all she went through."

"Mia can I share something with you about Todd without you gettin' in my ass?"

"Sure."

"I believe he really truly love me and regrets that Kyra episode."

"I never doubted his love for you Krish. He just doesn't want to be faithful anymore. And he is very disrespectful in what he does. I believe you'll always be number one with him. And what brings you to say that anyway."

"He told me that he and Kyra fought because she wasn't a good friend to me. He said she slept with his friend and hurt me, so he had no respect for her anymore and he didn't believe the baby was his."

"Yeah, but *he* slept with *her*. He hurt you too. And that's no excuse for putting his hands on a woman."

"That's what I said too. But he swears she means me no good. I asked him to tell me about how they hooked up. He said I didn't want to know, so I dropped it."

"I never saw jealousy on her part; but I did detect a little animosity lately. She seems uptight when your name is mentioned. She tries not to show it, but I be watching her ass."

"She hates me that's why. I believe she came on to Todd. I don't think it's like she said."

"I don't know about that Krisha. He's no good too."

"That freak bitch probably made him an offer he couldn't refuse. He would never just leave me for her. She did some serious shit to him to get him then it played out. That's the way the game is played right? Shit gets old."

"Don't worry about them Krish, its old news. Think on what's before you now."

"What time is it?"

"8:45." Mia answered.

I took out my cell phone to call Craig. I looked at Mia and told her to be quiet. The phone rang four times before he picked up.

"Hey boo." He chimed.

"Hey baby, what's up?" I said.

"Nothing, what's good with you."

"Trying to see you."

"Tonight?"

"Yes, is that a problem?"

"Well, I kinda had other plans tonight."

"You're not cheatin' on me are you?" I teased.

"Naw baby it aint even like that. I'm just in the middle of a business dinner with an old client."

"Okay, well I know that's not gonna last all night. My kids are gone, so you can come over?"

"You know what happened the last time I did that."

"I understand. Then I'll come to you."

"How about I call you later when I'm done?"

"Sure but don't take too long. I need to see you tonight."

"Okay momma. I'll see what I can make happen."

"I'll be waitin'." I threw out before hanging up.

Mia looked over at me as I disconnected.

"You think he'll call back."

"He'll call. It may be six hours from now but he will. I don't care if he does or not I just wanted to see if Shar's information was accurate."

"You think she's with him?"

"Oh yeah, somebody is. He's never once turned me down before. He'll turn a million flips to get to me if he had to. Then after the incident with Todd he still wanted me. Tonight something's not right." I sighed heavily. "You know what Mia. Take me to Baskin-Robbins then let's go home. I don't care about them. At least he's out of my hair now. She thinks she's doing something to hurt me, but I don't care. Matter-of-fact they make a cute couple."

"This shouldn't be about him anyway. This is about her and the crap she's telling Shar and Lord knows who else. And all the hatin' she's doing."

"Let a hater hate. That's what they do best. She'll see me soon enough. I got other things to be worried about right now. But when I see her, I'm bringing it to her."

"She definitely needs to be checked but come on now lil sis. We're professional adults."

"Unn huh." I mumbled. I wasn't trynna hear that.

When we arrived back at my house, I was still trying to finish the two scoops of butter pecan ice cream on the original cone I'd picked up. The ice cream was really the only thing that I'd eaten in it's entirely all day.

"Will you stay over with me tonight?" I asked Mia.

"Heffa, I gotta go home." She screamed.

"And do what?"

"Sleep in my own bed."

"Please Mia. I need some company. I don't wanna be in this big house by myself."

"What if ole' boy calls?"

"So what, I'm not going anywhere with him...Please." I begged.

"Girl you get on my nerves sometimes. Nothin' but a big ass baby!"

I smiled. She got out of the car like I knew she would.

12

I made a dreaded appointment with my gynecologist for Tuesday of the upcoming week. I was still feeling a little weak but the nausea had subsided. The first thing I wanted the doctor to do was take a pregnancy test. But I needed someone by my side to go through all of this. I was sure I'd pass out if the results were positive.

It seems Monday came and went faster than normal and Tuesday was knocking at my door. I called Mia to come ride this thing out with me.

If I were pregnant, this would be the first time that the pregnancy wasn't an exciting event and that I had no father by my side. To me, this demeaned my character. When I looked in the mirror, I saw a stranger. I'd allowed my misfortunes and trials to transform me into someone I was not proud to be. The hurt and betrayal of one man still plagued my life. Not admitting it to myself was my self-destruction. It was time I shaped myself up and this doctor's appointment would be my first step.

"Come on Krisha, you've gotta pull yourself together."

I don't remember walking out of the doctor's office. The only words I remembered hearing were "congratulations Mrs. Taylor". But I was sitting inside my truck with Mia under the wheel crying like a newborn baby.

"What am I gonna do?"

"You're gonna do exactly what you did the first two times."

"I can't Mia, I just can't."

"Krisha calm down. Don't worry about it right now."

"I can't help it Mia. How could I be so stupid?"

"Baby it'll be okay."

"I'm the stupidest woman I know. I can't do this again."

I tried to get myself together. I wiped my eyes and blew my nose as Mia drove me home. The tears fell quickly.

"Why do you feel like you can't do this?"

"Mia I don't even have a steady partner. I don't know the baby's father. How's this gonna look for "Ms. Citizen of the year"?

"People are gonna talk regardless of what you do."

"I know and I don't really care about that, but I'm over thirty years old. I don't wanna go back to changing diapers. I love kids but I'm just not ready for that again."

"Well Krisha I just don't know what else to say except I'll be there for you and you already know that."

"I'm sorry to put all this on you Mia. I'm so glad to have you. I wouldn't make it without you."

"Of course you wouldn't, I already know." She said with a smile.

"Can you please take me home so I can cry alone?"

"I'll take you home, but crying won't help."

"I know I just need to sleep."

"Whatever you say sis."

The very next day I was sick again. I couldn't eat. I couldn't smell anything without emptying my stomach. I was exhausted and sleepy. All I could do was lay in my bed and sleep.

The next day I decided to have Todd take the boys so I could get away for a while. Cheryl was back from the Monroe office so I had no worries about my business. I decided to take two weeks to myself to get my mind right. I didn't want to fly or go far due to the nausea and constant vomiting. I thought I should stay close to my doctor since I had never experienced this type sickness the first two times. I made reservations for a cabin out on the Tickfaw River and decided to stay there at least a week, if not two.

I called Mia to advise her of my plans.

"Okay Krisha that's a good idea. You need to rest, but if you need me call and you know I'll be there."

"Thanks Mia. One day I'm gonna be there for you just like you've always been for me."

"You have been. What are you talking about? Look, go relax and think things over so you can stop feeling sorry for yourself."

"I will. I promise."

"Did the doctor say how far along you are?"

"No, I'm going back in a few hours before I leave to get blood work done and an ultrasound so I can find out. I know I'm in the first trimester, with all this sickness, besides I already know I'm at least two months. I remember the exact dates to both incidents."

"Krisha when you have this baby, please consider getting a tubal ligation, IUD, or something. I'm sick of you and those damn birth control pills. That's how you got pregnant both times before; not taking those pills right."

"Mia, who said I was having this baby."

"I just assumed…Well, hey, it's your life. I'll be there with you no matter what. Just let me know what you decide."

"You know I will. I love you."

"Love you too girl. Take care and call me."

All my plans were set. I showered, dressed and threw my bags into the truck so I could make it over to my doctor's office by 1:00 pm. I was definitely calmer today than I had been yesterday. I was ready to get everything over with so I could go to sleep.

I weighed in at 130 pounds, but I knew that wasn't gonna be for long. I took all blood tests in less than five minutes and was ready to see the ultrasound technician. A nurse escorted me over to the tech's station where she led me into a small fairly dim room and instructed me to lie back on the table and pull my pants down to my thighs. The technician was a middle aged white lady who was much too jittery for me today.

Looking down at my chart, she said, "Mrs. Taylor I see this is your third child. What's the sex of your other children?" She was really friendly. Wore an absolutely beautiful smile.

"I have two boys." I answered.

"Two boys. That's great. Now let's see if you're having that little girl this time."

"Will you be able to tell the sex of the baby so soon?"

"I'll definitely try. The doctor's report is guessing that you're about fourteen weeks based on the information you gave him. He ordered the test to further verify that."

"He didn't mention that to me yesterday."

"They normally let us verify the age of the fetus before they inform the mother."

"Okay, but I'm almost certain that fourteen weeks is incorrect."

"Okay, we'll see in just a few Mrs. Taylor. Now this is gonna be a little cold." She squeezed a good amount of clear gel from a tube onto my stomach and began to move the little hand held device that was hooked to the monitor in the gel across my stomach.

She moved the device for a couple of minutes before speaking. I pondered her expression to see if I could read her mind.

"Is there anything wrong?" I asked.

"I'm trying to find the heartbeat. Sometimes it takes a minute. After hearing swishing sounds for seemingly forever, the sound of the rapid paced thumping of a heartbeat came through the monitor.

"There he is. Settled right here in this lower right corner." The baby was almost on my side. I didn't feel a thing. She moved my stomach around so the baby could reposition.

"I'm trying to get a better look." She typed on the keyboard and printed pictures.

She held the small sonogram picture of the fetus in front of my face.

"Can you see the head right here?" She asked as she pointed to a mass on the paper. "And those are the eyes. This is the spine." She pointed out and traced with her finger. "These are the hands, legs, and feet. Everything seems to be growing just fine and the heartbeat is strong."

I smiled but remained speechless.

She continued, "From what I can see Mrs. Taylor, looks like you have that little girl."

My heart almost crumbled. Did I hear her correctly? Did she say the fetus growing inside of me is a female, a little girl? Exactly what I've always wanted. I prayed the first two times for girls, but God blessed me with boys. Now, I have a precious baby girl growing inside of me and I didn't even have to pray for her.

"Are you okay Mrs. Taylor?" The tech asked concerned. I had drifted off.

I smiled. "Yes thank you. I'm fine."

"I'm all done here. Here you go." Handing me a framed picture of the fetus. "You may get dressed if there aren't any questions."

"Thanks." I said.

"You can expect your little bundle of joy just in time for the New Year." She chimed.

"The New Year? Are you sure?"

"Yes, from the growth of the fetus. You should be around sixteen weeks."

Sixteen weeks! I screamed in my head. No indeed, she must be mistaken.

"I'm not suggesting you don't know your job, but are you sure? I thought I'd be around eight or nine weeks."

"Oh no honey. This fetus is way over eight weeks. I can tell that at first glance. Your doctor said fourteen weeks, but looks like around sixteen. I'm pretty sure."

My head was in a whirlwind. Looking down at the picture of the baby. Prior pregnancies told me that that *was* a pretty big fetus to be eight weeks. Now I don't know what to think.

Who is the father of my child?

I needed the rest of the five months to figure that one out.

When I got into my car, I cried all the way to my destination. I slept and cried in my sleep once I got there. I showered and cried some more. I had no appetite so I didn't eat, just cried. I watched TV until midnight and went to bed again.

I'd forgotten to turn my cell back on after leaving the doctor's office, so I know I'd missed a thousand calls. I didn't care. I didn't want to talk to anyone anyway. I cried in my sleep and tossed and turned all night.

I awakened around 6:00 am and prayed. I managed to eat an apple and keep it down. I went into deep meditation to try to find my way out of the mess I'd made. My mind had been so mixed up lately until I hadn't allowed myself to really think about the chain of events.

On my third day at the lake, I decided that I had to face my adversities. I decided I'd try to stop beating myself up and learn to deal with the situation like the woman I am. I told myself that it was okay to make mistakes; God didn't expect man to be perfect. I decided to finally call Mia after three days to tell her where I was in my dilemma.

Every since the ultrasound tech gave me my expected due date and advised me of the age of my growing baby, I knew that this thing had turned into much more than I expected to deal with. I stressed over not knowing whether Todd or Craig fathered the child. Knowing the both of them claimed to love me and wanted to be with me was consolation for my broken heart, bruised ego, and disappointed soul. I at least would have one of the men by my side to take care of his child. I knew both were capable of and would readily accept that responsibility.

But what I knew in my heart was that those two men had not a chance in this child's life. Everything about this child was none other than Ryan Mathers. The situation turned from what I thought was bad to what I knew was worst. Now I had to deal with the fact that a man who no longer wanted to be with me, who is no Todd or Craig in that they would break down the highest barrier to jump hurdles on top of a burning house if I asked, a man who can turn his back and carry on with his life and not give me another thought, a man who can probably have any woman on this earth, so little ole' me ain't shit, was the contributor to the DNA of the fetus that lay inside my flat belly. With this in mind, I cried. I cried because that revelation made me that much lonelier. More confused. That much more stupid. It made my situation that much harder to deal with. *How can I face him now?* I asked myself. I definitely didn't want a relationship because of a child. And I sure didn't want anybody's pity.

I called my sister and my best friend. Poured my heart out to her. Being herself, she wanted to come be with me. She wanted to take care of me. She wanted to rescue me. Though I needed her emotionally, I knew I had to deal with this on my own. But I just didn't know how. I had to let my heart lead me and give my mind a rest.

I spent a whole week at the cabin in deep thought. The peace and serenity that surrounded me at the lake wouldn't let me leave. I reserved my cabin for another week. Regardless of whether I stayed its entirety or not, I needed to be there.

I finally decided to listen to the twenty messages that were left on my cell phone after being in solitude seven days.

Craig, Todd, and Chris several times and then somebody named Jay then Blake. I think Jay is the guy at my health club. I don't even know how he got my number. I didn't recall who Blake was. If they both knew like me, they'd run like hell to get away from me. Of all the calls, still no Ryan. Not that I was expecting him.

Later in the evening, I called to talk to Mia.

"Krisha, I think you should call him."

"Mia, I tried before I left home remember?"

"That was before all this."

"His cell number was changed."

"You have other numbers for him."

"I only have his home number and he's probably on the road."

"He should be back and you know it Krisha. Stop stalling."

"Mia this is not easy." I whined.

"Can I ask you something?"

"Yes."

"Are you sure the baby is his?"

"Yeah. I am now."

"What makes you sure?"

"Mia!"

"Krisha I'm asking for your own good. You know the situation. You don't want to tell a man he's fathered your child when he hasn't. You'll definitely be thrown in that hoe category then. Now how do you know for sure?" She said sternly.

"Because a few months ago, Ryan and I had unprotected sex once."

"Intentionally?"

"No, we were just caught up in the moment. We'd already had protected sex once and you know, things got intense again and he just kinda eased his way inside. He was trying to pick me up off him when he unexpectedly started to umm...you know. At the time, I didn't think much had gotten inside me, so I figured I was good. I'd totally forgot about that incident because we've had protected sex every time before and after that."

"You're kidding right?"

"No. What?"

"You thought you weren't gonna get pregnant because just a little bit got in, dummy?"

"Well, I was sporadically taking my pills too, so I figured they were working."

"Krisha, I just don't know 'bout you sometimes. You're thinking like a teenager. That man's sex game can't be that good to have had you all messed up in the head."

"Girlllllll, you don't even know." I blushed.

We giggled.

"Stop it. That's why your hot behind is in this mess now."

"I know. Honestly. Mia, I don't know what's wrong. My sex drive was already pretty good, but after I got over Todd, I felt a big relief and things jumped up to the highest gear. Almost out of control...and with Ryan aint no turning him down. He got the kinda loving you just wanna..."

Cutting me off, Mia screamed, "Hey! Too much information."

We laughed. Felt good to laugh again.

"Sorry I got carried away."

"Talk to the man. He should know he's going to be a father in five months."

I thought about those last words.

"In five months, my life will take a drastic change. Unbelievable."

"So that means you *are* gonna keep the baby?"

"Yes. This is my flesh and blood regardless of who the father is or the situation I'm in. I loved it all when I was doing it, so I shouldn't have any regrets. And I don't need a man for me to handle my business. I'm a businesswoman. Besides my precious baby is a girl."

That made me smile.

"Really?...Thanks girlfriend."

"Thanks for what?"

"For deciding to let my little niece live."

"I don't think I could have gone through with an abortion anyway."

"Go on and call Ryan. If you can't get his number, I probably can. Call if you need me."

"Thanks sis. Love you."

"Love you too. Bye."

13

After talking to Mia again, her encouraging me to call Ryan put the thought all up inside my head. This was so not me. Hounding or continuously calling a man was not in my nature. However, considering the situation, I thought I'd give it another try. I needed to talk to Ryan. He did deserve to know. I just hope he didn't think I was running game. Because he should know damn well I don't play that weak bitch shit when it comes to handling my business. Now when it came to love and relationships, I was one weak bitch.

I dialed the number I once knew as Ryan's home phone number. The phone only rang once before a soft female voice answered.
"Hi, is Ryan in?" I said nervously.
"No honey he's not. But I can take a message for him."
"Thank you. Please ask him to call Krisha when you speak with him."
"Yes, I can do that Krisha."
"Thank you."
"Bye." She said.
I didn't know how to call that one, so I assumed I'd wait for his call. If he didn't call this time, I'd just have to live with that.

For the first time since being at the lake, I got into my car and went out. I found the city and did a little shopping. I actually felt pretty good today. No nausea, no headache, no exhaustion. My stomach was even growling for food.
I shopped until I almost dropped. Even shopped for the baby. I couldn't help it. I was finally able to buy those cute little girl clothes. I still wasn't pleased about being pregnant under the circumstances and starting all over again. But I couldn't do anything about it, so I might as well get glad.
After shopping a couple hours, I grabbed a meal to go from Applebee's and headed back to my cabin.
On the way back, my cell rang. I picked it up and answered while driving.
"Hello." I said.

"Krisha?" A deep and sexy masculine voice sang into the receiver.
My heart stopped instantly.

"Ryan?"

"How are you?"

"I'm okay, and you?"

"I'm good."

There was an awkward moment of silence so I took the opportunity to swallow really hard.

"So, I got a message to call you."

"Yes, we need to talk."

"Okay shoot."

"I don't know if we should speak over the phone. Can I see you?"

"That wouldn't be a good idea."

"I'd just rather see your face when I'm speaking to you."

"Look Krisha, it's been months. Why would you want to see me now?"

"Why didn't you call me back the last time we spoke?"

"I decided to just let things be as they were."

"You made that decision without me?"

"You'd already made your decision when you stayed out all night with dude."

"I need an opportunity to explain some things to you. Can you at least give me that?"

"It doesn't matter."

"It does to me."

"No, it doesn't. Things have changed."

"I'm sure they have. But we just need to talk."

"There's nothing more to talk about."

"Ryan just…"

Cutting me off.

"I'm engaged Krisha. I don't have anything else to say to you."
Silence.

Did he say what I thought he said? Naw couldn't have. I thought.

Just to be sure, I asked, "Engaged?"

"Yes."

"Engaged to do what?"

"To be married."

"You're kidding right."

"I can't say that I am."

"Yes you are." Was all I could think of saying.

"I'm getting married in six months."

"Six months? To who?"

"You wouldn't know."

"Were you already involved with her when you met me?"

"No, I wasn't. I met her days after you pulled your little stunt."

"Then you got with her because you thought I intentionally hurt you?"

"I found someone who loves and appreciates me and who wants what I want; a family and happiness."

"That was too quick Ryan....*I* love you."

"You decided that before or after you slept with dude numerous times at your house then left with him."

"That's not what happened."

"It doesn't matter."

"Do you love her?"

"Krisha just…"

"No! Answer me. Do you love her?"

I was getting emotional. My voice trembled.

"I wouldn't be marrying her if I didn't."

"That's not good enough. Something tells me you don't."

"I'm good Krisha."

I let a pause secure the line. Wasn't sure what to say next.

"Was that her that answered earlier?" I mumbled.

"Yes."

"I didn't know. I wouldn't have called."

"She knows the situation."

Awkward silence hung in the air again.

"Well…It's good to know you're doing good." He said.

"I didn't say all that. But hey, why worry about me?"

"Krisha stop. I loved you."

"Loved?…Who are you kidding Ryan? You still love me. You know you don't love her. So why are you marrying her?"

"Look, we've been through that."

"Tell me you don't love me anymore."

"Krisha please…"

I cut him off.

"No tell me Ryan. Tell me you don't love me and I'll hang up right now."

I began to choke up. My words burned my throat.

"It doesn't matter now." He said sternly through what sounded like clinched teeth.

"Don't do this. She's not the woman you want."

"I've made my decision. I'm sorry if you can't accept it, but you don't need to call me again. It'll only create problems."

I couldn't believe what I was hearing, but I still had to know something.

"Was she the one with you when I spoke with you last?"

"Why? Krisha, just stop please." He raised his voice.

"I just want to know."

"No."

"Thanks for being honest. I guess there's nothing else for me to say."

I quickly hung up the phone in tears.

I'd made it back to the cabin five minutes before disconnecting but sat inside my car and talked on the phone to Ryan.

After disconnecting, I sat unmoved staring into the sky as tears took refuge under my chin. I sat a few more minutes contemplating whether to get out of the car and go inside or punch the accelerator and smash into the front of the cabin.

Love hurts.

Bad wasn't even a descriptive word that could be used in my love game. It went far beyond that three letter word. I'd realized that I did love Ryan a couple months ago but when I finally realized it, it was little too late. Now nothing mattered at all. He didn't love me anymore. And it was all my fault. I had played myself.

I was hurt, so I cried. I cried hard. I thought I was all cried out, but I managed to find more tears. The pregnancy didn't make it any better either. I had a few other storage places for tears once my ducts were dry. I was a big bag of emotions.

My life. I thought.

I just couldn't seem to find the calm I needed to live my life free of stress and drama. In the midst of bawling my eyes out, my cell rang again.

I really wasn't in the mood for anybody at the moment so I thought about just ignoring it.

Before I could change my mind I picked up my cell to give a weak hello while trying to disguise my trembling voice from the sniffling and wiping of tears.

No one replied. Silence was on the other end.

"Yes." I managed to say a little better.

"I do love you." A familiar voice uttered softly.

I burst into tears again. The sound of his voice did a number on my heart.

I closed my eyes tight in an attempt to calm myself. Tried my best to stop the tears. Wanted to let my heart talk.

"Please don't do this Ryan. Come be with me."

"I can't."

"Please." I begged.

"Krisha, I can't do that."

"How could you just turn away from me like that?"

"I didn't just turn away. I've thought about you everyday. I was hurt too."

"All you had to do was call me. I waited to hear from you."

"I couldn't."

"You're marrying someone you don't love. That's wrong." I cried.

"I need to go; just wanted you to know."

"Wait! I'm in cabin #4 on the Tickfaw. I'll be here all week."

"I told you I can't come."

"Just in case. I love you Ryan."

"Bye."

He hung up.

Why was it so easy to admit that I loved Ryan now? When he asked for my love a long time ago I couldn't give it to him. Now it seems the tables have turned, the shoe is on the other foot, what goes around comes around, karma is a bitch; all that shit.

Why did I have to experience the chain of events to know I loved him? Well, I'd promised myself that I'd never beat myself up over a man again. So, I dried my eyes, unloaded some of the packages from my truck and went inside the cabin to try on some of the things I'd bought. After playing fashion show, I showered and curled up on the sofa to finish reading "She Aint the One" by Carl Weber and Mary B. Morrison. Now this was drama, just like I liked it. As long as it wasn't starring yours truly, it was all good.

14

After two more days of relaxation and deep meditation, I began to work from the cabin. I'd gotten some calls from my staff who needed my input on a few things. So from there I had to place calls to banks, mortgage lenders, and clients. I figured I might as well go on home since my work had resumed.

Tomorrow I would cut my week short by four days and go home to face my life as it is. Today, I decided to take my last evening stroll along the lake before going back inside to pack for my early morning trip home.

As I strolled along the lake, I imagined my life with Ryan and our child. Then I imagined my life as it is now, without him, raising his child alone. He'd made his decision and I was not one to interfere. Ryan was getting married and he was no longer interested in being in my life. Guess he found someone who could really love him; who could offer him the life he dreamt of. Someone who was open to receive all he had to offer.

During our short relationship, I could not. Instead of trusting him, I compared him to Todd. I let the hurt and burden that weighed on my heart due to Todd's infidelities affect my ability to love and trust him and share a meaningful relationship with him. I allowed myself to believe that I had to play a man before he played me. It was good when I was young. Back then I was carefree and didn't give a damn about nothing. Nor was I intimate and giving of my soul, which meant I hadn't much to lose. In my adult life, I'd lost. I'd lost a lot more than the things that were easily evident. My inner self was what was tearing me apart.

I'd been with Todd for so long that I didn't really realize getting a man was still easy, juggling two or three was kind of fun but dealing with the consequences that were going to arise from it all, wasn't worth it. And yes there are always consequences. My actions to the challenges I faced with men over the last few months have been ridiculously irresponsible and uncharacteristic of myself.

In summation, everybody who knows me already knows my problem with the number one man, Todd Taylor. Why I keep allowing him back into my heart and my bed, I can't even call it, but I think clearly evident. One day I plan to rid myself of Todd Taylor for good. I hope I already have, but who knows. That man is a part of me. It's gonna take more than time.

And though Craig confessed his love and desire to be with me constantly, his feelings obviously weren't strong enough to keep him from allowing my so-called friend into his bed. He too went there; even though he knew every detail of my situation with Kyra and Todd. Guess he wanted to see what she had to make a man leave a woman like me.

One thing for sure is, a woman should never think her body or beauty alone will keep a man on lock forever. One day he sees nothing but you, and then the next day he sees everything but you. As the saying goes, you find a man with the prettiest woman in the world, you'll find a man tired of screwing her.

Longevity in a relationship means offering him more than good sex and a cute face. It has to be about you, and what's inside your heart. I can't hate on Craig for being a curious brotha though. He has a little game too. He'd just better stop calling my damn phone.

I promised myself that my next relationship will be of a different caliber and on a much different level. Absolutely no sex before marriage. If I waited all those months after my divorce, I can wait even longer. I hope.

I shoveled all thoughts to the back pockets of my mind and headed back along the lake to my cabin. As I got closer, it appeared that someone was sitting on the bench outside my door. As I approached, I could see a bent body with head in hands.

I could never forget that head and frame.

"Ryan?" I said softly as I approached.

He raised his head in response.

"Hey Krisha." He spoke while standing.

I ran to him throwing my arms around his neck.

"You came to me baby." I whispered with a glowing smile.

He hugged me tightly. "I'm gonna be in so much trouble for this."

His lips found mine. Kissed me softly. I hugged him tighter. Melted in his arms.

I pulled away to look into his eyes.

"I'm glad you're here." I said stroking his face.

"I need to explain."

"Shhh. We'll talk." I shushed him and continued to kiss his soft lips.

My tongue took matters into its own hands and found his. Our tongues danced.

Pulling away, he said with a smile, "Come on, let's go inside."

"Oh yeah…okay." I smiled and took his hand in mine. Led him into the cabin.

Looking around, Ryan said, "This is really nice."

"I love it up here. It's so peaceful."

"You were right. We do need to talk face to face."

Positioning myself in his arms again, I said, "I missed you so much." I kissed his face.

Looking deep into my eyes while stroking the sides of my face with both hands. "It's so good to see you. You're still the most beautiful woman I've ever laid eyes on."

I bashfully pulled away.

"Are you hungry?"

"Yeah, I really am."

"Good. Let's go into town for an early dinner."

"I'd like that."

Ryan suggested driving. We chose a small seafood restaurant and had a nice cozy dinner. I wanted to treat him, but he wouldn't allow it. Said a woman like me should be taken care of at all times and that I'd never have to spend a dime when I was with him. I didn't fuss. I'm generous but I aint crazy. I know how to let a man be a man.

When we arrived back to the cabin, it was still early. We both showered, separately, and then went outside to watch the sunset. I spread a blanket on the ground and sat between Ryan's legs with my back to his chest.

"Ryan I'm sorry it took me so long to realize that I loved you. It was just my past that had me apprehensive. I wanted to be sure."

"You know I always understood that."

Leaning back in his arms, I said, "What's the problem with us?"

"You and your actions. You really hurt me Krisha. I felt like a fool waiting for you in your house only to find condoms in your bathroom. Can you imagine how humiliated I was? The fact that I'm here right now tells you that you meant the world to me and still do."

"I'm sorry Ryan. I can be honest with you and tell you the whole situation. I wanted to tell you weeks ago but you never called me back. Why?"

"Pride, anger. Why didn't *you* call back?"

"Pride, anger. That little situation I walked into in Baltimore wasn't one to just excuse you know."

"Now you didn't give me a chance to explain either. That's why I was at your house in the first place."

"Looks like neither of us gave each other a chance. We refused to communicate."

After swatting a million mosquitoes in less than fifteen minutes, I suggested going inside.

We retreated to the cabin where we both settled on the couch.

"I realize that I really love you with all my heart."

"I love you too Krisha but things are different now."

"How can things be so different so soon?"

"I'm with someone else now."

"Is this what you came all this way to say? You already said that over the phone. I told you before I didn't care about nobody else. I can get past that. I just want you."

"But I don't know if I could just forget what you did."

"What are you talking about? Not coming home that night? I can explain…"

"No, not just that. When I was waiting at your house a female called looking for you. She said she called to confront you about being with some dude. Said her man had spent the night with you. She told me all about your relationship with him. She said they were still seeing each other and you were sleeping with him.

"What? Are you serious?"

I turned to look at him.

"She said she was hoping he was still there to catch him."

"So you went along with that?"

"Krisha, I live away. I don't know what goes on here with you. When someone tells you something like that and it all seems true, what else was I to do? Besides I didn't expect that, I was at your house."

"You talk to me that's what you do. And who was this woman anyway?"

Now this was working my nerves. Female friends always spell trouble. That was one reason why I had very few.

"Desiree or something."

"I don't know a Desiree."

"Well she sure knows you."

"A couple weeks after I got back. She emailed me these."

He threw five pictures on the coffee table. I nervously picked them up. After looking them over, I could have cried. I wanted to scream. I wanted to hide. I wanted to get my hands on this Desiree.

The pictures were of Craig and I. We were at a restaurant all up in each other's faces. Then we were kissing. Another photo showed me in his arms and another getting out of his car. They were all dated at least three months ago.

On top of that he said, "Then I got these." He gave me six more pictures of Todd and me. Others were of Todd and me, and our children.

Someone had taken a lot of time out of their day to upload and scan these pictures and send them to Ryan. I must be really important to somebody. I thought.

"Looks like you've been really busy lately baby."

Aw hell. I was at a loss for words. I thought for a minute. Now what was I gonna say. I had to think fast. Choose my words carefully.

"Who is this Desiree that you just gave your contact information to like that?"

"What does that matter?"

"These pictures don't mean anything."

"Looks pretty clear to me."

I threw the pictures down and turned to face him.

"Somebody is trying to get at you and ruin our relationship."

"I don't think anybody but you did that."

"No I did not. Can you be honest with me Ryan?"

"I always have been."

"When I came to see you last, were you sleeping with that girl who was in your bedroom?"

He looked wide-eyed without responding. Instead he hung his head.

"It's time we get things out in the open. You come here with photos accusing me, but I think you have some things going on with you that you're not admitting to."

"Let me tell you then since you so desperately want to know." He stood up and began pacing. "She used to be my girl. But I only invited her over when I wanted her over. So there were no real strings attached. She meant nothing to me. That's why I don't know why she was tripping. I was trying to tell you that."

"So that makes it all better. Women don't see it like that regardless of what you could have said. Okay, now I want you to take me and put me in your situation. It was the same with him." Picking up Craig's picture. "Just filling a void…the only difference is I wasn't telling you that I loved you everyday. I believed you loved me and I was coming to realize that I loved you, but I wanted to be sure before I said it. But you were saying you loved me then lying down with her."

"The distance is hard. I was trying to get adjusted to it. That's why I begged you to come see me so much Krisha. Sex doesn't make a relationship and I can definitely abstain if I know I have your heart but sometimes it's hard. I started fooling around with her again, just to relieve a little frustration. I was gonna leave her alone when I was sure of how you felt for me. I had planned to make sure you were there with me every week until I could come to you. But she pulled that stunt that day. And that reminded me why I left her alone in the first place. She knew about you and our relationship. She just wanted to trip."

"You'd just slept with the girl and you thought she was gonna up and run because I came. She didn't give a darn about me. She had no reason to."

"Yeah, but she claimed she understood and it wasn't a problem."

"That was just to be with you Ryan."

"Women should stick to the agreements made. She's the one who started catching feelings again."

"Are you telling me you're one of those heartless men?"

"I'm saying I stated what the deal was. She agreed. Then she decided to change her mind without informing me."

We stared at each other.

After a few seconds, he finally looked away. Fiddled with his thumbs.

Now I'm thinking this is unbelievable. You mean I've encountered three of these type male whores in my lifetime. Boy could I pick 'em or what?

"While I'm confessing..." He rubbed his head as he paced. Avoiding eye contact with me. "umm...She *is* the one I'm marrying."

Silence. I searched his face to make sure he wasn't joking.

"Ryan, no. You just said she's not the kind of woman you want."

He plopped down on the couch next to me. Sat there with his head down. Watching his hands as if they were gonna help him out.

"Why baby? Why would you? How could you?" I searched his face for an answer. Tears fell.

He looked at me with embarrassment in his eyes; a questionable request for forgiveness.

"She's carrying my child." Was barely audible.

"What? Please tell me you didn't say what I thought I heard?"

He remained quiet while watching the floor.

"Tell me that's not true." I muffled as I put my face down in my hands.

I shook my head feverishly.

"I didn't intend for things to be like this. That's why I wanted to tell you in person."

"What kind of relationship do you have with her that you're having unprotected sex? You never went there with me, but you claimed to love me so much."

"I don't know Krisha."

"You don't know. Oh my God!" I screamed.

I shook my head in disbelief. Stared him down.

"She planned this pregnancy. And you were stupid enough to play right into it. She trapped you. She knew you wouldn't turn your back on your child."

"I'm just as much at fault as she is."

"Yeah you're right. And you're naïve. See this is where the age difference comes in. It's called experience with life. You are oblivious to the things scandalous women will do. I bet she got pregnant after she saw me. After I came there."

He didn't have a response.

"How far along is she?" I inquired.

"Six weeks."

"See what I'm saying Ryan. I knew it."

I jumped up off the sofa.

We'd forgotten all about the pictures and the drama with me. I was shedding tears and he wanted to. He came behind me and wrapped his arms around me from behind.

"I messed up." He whispered. "I'm sorry."

"Just leave me alone."

I didn't care to hear that. I am so tired of hearing I'm sorry that I could scream.

I went into the bedroom and dove into the bed. I cried alone for minutes before I realized crying wasn't helping anything. *This is his mess. What am I crying for?* I asked myself. I undressed and climbed under the covers. Covering head and all. I didn't want to breathe.

I didn't know where Ryan was and I didn't care. He could leave all if I cared. My situation was still screwed up. The way I saw it now, it didn't matter if I told him I was pregnant or not. It wasn't gonna change anything. He was getting married to be with his family. I couldn't offer what she could.

In my mind, I couldn't erase the fact that they would be a lovely family. It would be the first marriage for both with their first child. I, on the other hand, came with baggage. Two kids and scarring from my first marriage. I knew what I had to do; I would raise my baby alone. My child would have a mother, two brothers, and an aunt who loves her very much. I wouldn't dare interfere with Ryan's happiness.

I heard the door to the bedroom open, but remained still under the covers.

Ryan sat on the edge of the bed next to me. Placed a strong hand on my back; began massaging me through the comforter. Neither of us said anything. He slid in the bed next to me. Then pulled my body over to his, picking me up so that he could spoon me from behind. He enclosed me in a tight hug. Snuggled the side of his face against my head. Strong arms around my waist. Masculinity along my backside.

He whispered in my ear, "I love you Krisha."

I've heard that before, but that still didn't change a thing. Why couldn't he just drop her and take care of his child if he loved me so much?

I already knew the answer.

Ryan was a private and reserved person with strong family values. He would never bring attention to his life for the media to get hold of. And this conniving woman would most likely bring baby momma drama. *I knew I shoulda whipped her ass the day I had the chance*. I thought.

He began to speak softly in my ear, ending what seemed like an hour of silence. "I forgive you for whatever happened. I understand."

I didn't say a word.

He let his lips graze the side of my head.

"I know the other guy is your ex, so that could have been misconstrued. But why didn't you come home when you knew I'd flown so far to see you?"

I hesitated before speaking. "He took me against my will."

Rising up to look me in the face, "Who?"

"My ex."

"Serious?"

"Yes."

"For how long?"

"A week. That's why you didn't hear back from me. He took my phone. I couldn't call you."

"Did he hurt you?"

"Not really."

"Krisha, I'm so sorry." He pulled me close. Embrace grew tighter. "I'm sorry I didn't listen." Kisses to the side of my face. "I shoulda talked to you. I've been upset all this time for no real reason. I shoulda been there for you." Kisses on my neck. "I don't know why I let things go this far. I love you so much Krisha."

I thought I felt tears on my neck. Maybe not. He was so loving and understanding. Had a forgiving heart. I loved him.

I relished in the soft touches of his lips on my neck while he whispered apologies in my ear. Felt him growing hard behind me. His mouth was telling me that he was marrying someone else. But his actions told me it was all about me. I wanted him. I needed him. I know it probably wouldn't be the wisest decision to act on my desires but I'd been walking down that road lately anyway, so it was already familiar with me.

Hands massaged my waist, down my leg, back to my chest. Traveled under my tank and found my breasts. Big, strong hands warmed me up. Immediately found the switch that turned me on. Lightly caressing my breasts. Then down to my now still relatively flat, soon to be large stomach.

"You're so sexy." He whispered. "You're breasts seem bigger." He whispered as his hand moved down over my hip and down the side of my leg. "I like that."

Ryan raised the back of my white tank and placed tender kisses on my back. Made his way back up to my earlobe.

"Can I feel you?" He breathed heavily in my ear.

It had been so long since I was with him. Every touch was like heaven. I was melting. Fingers heavy yet touches so light. So pleasing. Smoothly gliding over my skin. Made love to my inner ear with his tongue. Burning sensation inside.

My boy shorts were being tugged off as strong hands raised one leg up, stroking my middle to utter satisfaction. Hands roaming my breasts, stomach, down to my thighs while teeth grazed my delicate skin. The warmth of his talented mouth and soft tongue tantalizing my shoulder and lower neck sent me over the edge. He loved every inch of my body; back and front before uniting with me body and soul.

I was there. Standing on that mountaintop, arms spread wide, and as free as a bird. I didn't have to think, I didn't have to stress; I never had to wonder. I just had to be there to enjoy it all. My mind wasn't mine, yet I sought no end.

He was so good. Felt so right. When in essence this night would leave me nonetheless brokenhearted, I felt it in my spirit. I stayed up on that mountaintop half the night. Never wanting to come down. I wanted to hold on to Ryan forever; but how often is it that we get what we really want.

15

Ryan left the next morning, as did I.

I talked to Mia the entire drive home. After discussing things with her, we determined that Kyra had to be the mysterious Desiree.

We guessed that the night at dinner when Craig came to see me Kyra took those pictures with her cell phone. Mia made me remember how she briefly talked to somebody and then fiddled with her phone. The other pictures only meant that she'd been spying on me. I didn't understand the thing about me fooling around with her man. I didn't know she had a man before Shar informed me. And I sure as hell didn't want C-Lo with his ugly, hustling ass.

My nausea had subsided so I was full of energy and actually glad to be back at home.

I went to see Mia at work then on to my office. I stayed there the remainder of the day before picking up my kids from Todd's house.

To keep simplicity in my life, I worked in my office the remainder of the week and kept a low profile. I longed to speak with Ryan so badly, but it was what it was, so I left it alone. I'd have to learn to live with the situation.

Craig called on Friday night to invite me out to some kind of high profile affair he was to attend next week. Wanted me to be his trophy I guess. I decided to rid my life of the BS and let it be just what it was.

I cursed him out.

Just had to get it off my chest.

"Excuse me?" He said after getting an ear full.

I knew that would get his attention.

"How could you do that Craig?"

"What are you talking about?" He was trying to play me.

"Look Craig you're holding up my line for nothing. Tell you what, lose my number okay."

"Wait, wait, Krisha. What are you talking about?"

"Craig please stop okay. You know I'm smarter than that. I just thought you were too."

When he didn't say anything I knew I had him.

"Ya know I really thought our little friendship was more than a piece of tired ass."

"Krisha. C'mon baby. It was nothing. It's not like we were committed or anything. I don't want that tramp."

"Why not? So *you* Mr. DA, you get down with tramps?" I said sarcastically. "So what does that make you?"

"She could never compare to you baby. C'mon you can't blame me for being a man."

"Oh I know she can't compare to me. And yes I can blame you. I thought you were a respectable man with some decency. Don't ever call me again. You two deserve each other."

I hung up with a smile.

I called Carmen to work for me. She readily agreed. I was feeling pretty good, so Mia and I headed over to Shar's to get some information.

When we got there, the usual was going on and the house was packed. After going in for a couple seconds, Mia and I went back outside to sit in the car. We called Shar outside to holla at us because the girls in her house were mugging something terrible. Plus Kyra was up in there, and I had to find out some things before I got in her ass.

When we got outside, Shar said, "What are yall doing here?"

"To ask you something, why?"

"Some of them chicks in there got it in for you girl. You shouldn't be here." She said directed at me.

"I thought all was good Shar?" Mia asked.

"Yeah, with me, but ole' girl been running her mouth. I called you three times yesterday Mia to tell you what was up."

"I haven't checked my messages."

"Well, you guys might wanna bounce."

"You know I aint running from nobody." Mia said.

"Shar, do you know somebody named Desiree?"

"Yeah, she's inside. That's Cut Throat's real name."

"Do you know something about Kyra and my ex-husband?"

"Hell yeah, she's still fooling around with him too. She says you're with him too. I know they been plotting some shit with that ball player too. But I aint found out what that is yet."

"Thanks Shar. I think I already know." I said.

"Good lookin' out cousin. We gonna run. We'll catch up with her later." Mia said.

"Alright see yall later." Shar walked back to the house as we pulled away.

"So Todd's still seeing her."

"I told you that jackass wasn't about nothing. Dismiss him for good."

"I don't understand why she's doing this to me. Every man that claims to love me she's trying to get with them."

"Jealous and unhappy."

"I never would have thought. What was all that, I love you stuff on your bathroom floor?"

"I don't know. Now it's not helping that she's over there with those haters. She is so weak-minded."

"I'll see her real soon but first I gotta see my ex-husband. Drop me over there."

"I will not."

"Why not? I'll be okay."

"No and hell no. And don't ask me again."

"Mia you make me sick."

"So, die hoe!"

I rolled my eyes.

"Let's go back to your place then, I'll call him."

She rolled her eyes.

Once we were at Mia's, I dialed Todd's number.

He answered on the second ring as if he was expecting someone.

"Did I interrupt something?" I asked.

"No indeed. Your call is always welcomed boo. What's up?"

"What's up with you and Kyra?"

"That's ole' news Krisha. Why are you asking me that?"

"Remember when I asked you how you got with her?"

"Yes."

"I'm ready to hear the answer."

"Where is this all coming from?"

"I'll tell you soon enough. Now tell me please and be honest."

"Huhh." He sighed. "I don't know what to say."

"Tell me how it started."

"You're gonna hate me."

"No more than I have in the past."

"Are you sure you wanna know?"

"Come on Todd."

"Well when your mother died she stayed over at the house to help take care of you..."

"Yes."

"Well, the first night she stayed, I came home late and she was downstairs. She asked me to come see what was wrong with the TV and DVD player in the guest room. She was trying to get them to work. She went into the bathroom while I messed around with the TV. Then I noticed she had two drinks on the nightstand. She came out of the bathroom as naked as the day she was born. I was shocked speechless. So I stood there looking at her not knowing what to do. She just walked over to me, unzipped my pants and started...I just couldn't...she wouldn't stop."

I looked over at Mia who was on the other phone listening. She had her hand over her mouth.

"So you mean to tell me you let that..." I cut it short, had to take a deep breath. "You were with her right up under my nose in *my* house?"

"If I would have yelled or caused a scene you or the kids would have heard me. I told you that you didn't want to know."

"Just be honest with me okay. I gotta deal with you regardless." I shook my head in disbelief. "So how did the *relationship* start?"

"I don't know Krisha. I told you I just got caught up. I know it wasn't right. But that girl does some shit no man can refuse."

"So you kept seeing her after that?"

"Sporadically. She would come to my office and do her thang every now and then."

"Whatever Todd."

"If I could take it all back, I would. I was just a very weak man at the time."

"So it was all about the sex with her?"

"Of course. I was never interested in your friend long term."

"Todd you were getting good sex at home. You didn't have to go out to get sex. You did that because you wanted to."

"I admit that. I just got caught up in all the uninhibited shit Kyra does. I was interested in seeing what it was all about."

"And you're still caught up huh?"

"Nope. Why would you say that?"

"You claim to want our family back so badly but you're still letting her freak you."

"She means nothing to me baby. If I knew I could have you back, I would dead that right now. It's just that useless."

"How can you treat her so bad and talk about her so badly but still lay down with her?"

"Did you know your friend likes it both ways?"

"What…you mean women?" I said in amazement.

"Hell yeah. She can satisfy a woman almost better than me."

"Stop it Todd!" I covered my mouth with my free hand.

"I'm serious. She's tried to get me to ask you to join us in bed. But I told her that would never, ever be an option. Matter of fact, I put her out the day she suggested that."

I looked at Mia. We covered our mouths and laughed, but that wasn't funny at all.

"So she allowed other women in your bed?" I egged him on. I was really interested in what he was saying.

"Yeah! Why you think her and Cassie got along so good."

"Oh my g…Todd you one nasty… And you think I want you back? Oooooo I'm so glad we used a condom last time I was with you."

"You know I'm straight girl. I just got caught up with her. I wasn't even screwing around until she came on to me."

"Stop lying!" I said.

"Okay, I'm sorry. I just wasn't doing all that."

"You are no good Todd Taylor. No damn good!"

"I've changed. I stopped all that."

"How have you stopped and you're still carrying on with Kyra?"

"Only when I want a threesome."

I shook my head.

"You're really making me sick."

He laughed a little.

"I told you before that you didn't want to know the truth about me and her. But seriously though, I told you she meant you no good. I've seen a changed Kyra. Not the same girl that was once your friend."

"You probably had a lot to do with that. And if you thought that and you love me then why even go there?"

"Sometimes it's hard to think with the right head."

"And I'm convinced that you are truly a deranged man."

I had to laugh a little. The crap that came out of his mouth was ridiculously funny. Impossible that this was my college sweetheart.

"Why are you asking all of this anyway?"

"She has some beef with me and I want to know what it's all about. I've never really done anything to her. Other than get in dat ass when she deserved it."

"She wants to be you. She wants what you have. I recognized that long after it was too late for us to get back together. It took me a minute to recognize that she had a motive in mind. She used me to get at you because her ass is envious of you. So I started treating her like the hoe she is. She messed up my family."

"Be for real Todd. You were the only one responsible for that. She was just an accomplice."

"Yeah I know. But more importantly I believe she's in love with you."

"Don't make me lose my lunch. And how can she be in love with me and hate me at the same time?"

"Why else would she want a piece of you?"

"Stop playing."

"I'm serious. I know her like you and Mia never have."

"Oh my God! Stop! I'm sick right now."

He was laughing hard.

"All jokes aside though. I seriously think that might be the problem. She is obsessed with you and your life. She wants it all. She thought she had it when she thought she had me, but all she got was screwed in every way imaginable. I let her ride in your leftovers but you never saw her in my shit did you? And I gave her a little change to live because I had to keep her healthy and satisfied to get what I wanted. But you gotta know it wasn't much. You don't see that she's come up. She still doesn't have shit to show for all her hard work."

"You're wrong in so many ways. I'm not cosigning but right now, I aint mad at ya. But Kyra knows my life aint a bed of roses. I don't understand why she would want that?"

"Ever heard of a hater Krisha?"

"Yeah I just never thought my best friend would be one of them."

"Scandalous hoes don't care about friendship. She's desperate."

"Well that scandalous hoe is in the hood making noise."

"I'll deal with her."

"No Todd. My life could depend on it. Please don't mention this conversation."

"I won't. But if your life depends on it, I need to do something. I can't sit by and wait until something happens to you."

"I'll be okay. Just let me handle it."

"I'm here if you need me love."

"Thanks."

I hung up the phone, and then Mia hung up. I'd wanted to shed a tear but quickly shook it off. For some reason, hearing his revelations was like we were saying goodbye forever, and saying good-bye is always hard for me.

Why oh why did he have to mess up like he did? I wish things had been different for us. That man was my life. I used to love the hell out of him. Hopefully, he'll finally move on with his life and let me do the same. I thought in silence while staring at nothing.

"Are you okay girl?" Mia asked taking baby steps over to where I was sitting. I'm sure she didn't know how to exactly approach me. Wasn't sure of my reaction to what Todd had told me.

"I'm good."

"I see what you were saying; he does loves you. What he did will eat his ass up forever."

"Yeah you may be right." I stared blankly at the wall.

"The more I think about what Todd said; I think he may be right."

"What?"

"I believe the freak whore may wanna taste of you. That's why she's ridding all the men from your life. She wants you to herself."

"Well she damn sure can't have me. Besides why would she want to bring harm to me if that's the case?"

"Don't know. But I will find out. I'll take you home and I'll go back over to Shar's. That's the only way for me to find out anything."

"You know if I weren't pregnant there's no way you'd get rid of me."

"I know. You just take care of my niece. Let me take care of our little friend."

We chilled for another hour at Mia's. She swung me by Baskin-Robbins, which was beginning to become a daily routine. Then I went home.

I brought ice cream for everybody. My kids, Carmen and I sat up and watched a movie and ate ice cream until we all fell asleep in front of the TV.

16

When my phone began chiming at 3:15 am, my heart immediately began racing. I snatched up the receiver.

"Hello." I rushed to say.

"This is Shar."

"What's wrong Shar? What happened?" I screamed.

She'd never called my house before so I knew something was definitely wrong.

"Krisha, go...go to..." I could barely understand her. There was so much noise in the background.

I was already up and had thrown on a pair of jeans. I could feel it in my gut, this wasn't good.

So I asked, "Where is she?"

"Hospital." She managed to get out.

"What happened? Which hospital?" I was screaming now. So loud that Carmen came running into the room.

Shar was hysterical. I couldn't understand anything she was saying. Then she stopped speaking. "Shar? Shar are you there?"

"Krish, they took her to Pike's." A masculine voice that sounded like Hakeem said.

"What happened?"

"Shit went down. She got caught up."

"She's alive right?" I asked as Carmen stood there wide-eyed holding her stomach.

"I don't know...I mean yeah, I think so. She was stabbed and cut up pretty bad."

"Thanks." I hung up. I was dressed and heading for the door.

I informed Carmen of what I knew on my way down the stairs. Carmen was shaken. I felt bad leaving her with the kids at this point. But what else was I to do.

I was at Pike Hospital within ten minutes.

When I made it inside, Shar and Hakeem were in the waiting room with other project cats. There was a truck load of hood rats and others from around the way all standing outside the hospital.

"Now what in the world happened?" I thought. The whole hood was at the hospital.

I ran to Shar and hugged her.

"They won't let us go in there." She said through tears.

I went to the desk in emergency to find out what was going on with Mia myself.

"Excuse me. Can you please tell me the status of Mia Davis who was just brought in?"

"Are you a relative?"

"Yes, I'm her sister."

"Let me go get an updated report. I'll be right back."

She came back exactly five minutes later.

"Are you Mrs. Taylor?"

"Yes."

"She was asking for you. The doctors are asking that you make decisions on her behalf."

"Yes, but what is it? What's happening?"

"Well, she sustained two stab wounds and several cuts mostly to the top half of her body. One wound was inches from her heart and one right in the stomach. They're gonna have to do emergency surgery to stop the bleeding. The doctors will be out to speak with you in a second and to get you to sign some consents."

I called Shar and Hakeem over. The doctor came out and further explained what the nurse had already said. She had lost a lot of blood and her blood pressure was dropping so they needed to move fast. I signed the consent forms and waited in the lobby. The nurse advised that it could take a couple hours before the doctor came back out. It didn't matter to me. I wasn't going anywhere. I would be sitting right there until next year if I had to. I called Carmen while I waited.

Hakeem was furiously pacing the floor. He was steamed and wanted to get back to the hood to settle some debts.

While waiting, Shar and I were finally able to stop crying long enough to talk. Different people came up to us telling us their version of what went on. Turned out Mia walked in on some shit getting started. Then when she approached Kyra, she and Cut Throat jumped her.

As the story goes, Mia was handling them both until three of Cut Throat's girls jumped in to save their butts. Hakeem said he arrived as all five of them were on Mia.

"Cuz was still handling 'em the best she could." Hakeem said pacing back and forth. "I forgot dem bitches were bitches and started throwing dey asses all across the street. It don't make me no difference when you fucking with my peoples."

"C and some more brothas started poppin' dem too; one by fuckin' one. Then dey boys jumped in it, including C-Lo; den it was on. Everybody was bustin'. The whole block was lit." Hakeem said.

"I drove up when all the smoke was clearing." Shar said.

"How'd she get here?" I asked Hakeem.

"Me and C brought her. Wasn't no ambulance gon come over there this time of the morning. We'd probably still be waiting on dem mothafuckas."

That's when I looked at Hakeem. His shirt and pants was soiled with blood.

"She was bleeding so damn bad, man. She was going in and out, and shit, but she kept asking for you Krisha."

Hakeem was trying his best to hold those tears. A G like him wasn't supposed to cry. He was both sad and furious.

Still pacing, "Imma fuckem' up, real time. I didn't see that shit going down outside til dem hoes had jumped her. C-Lo and nem stood around and let all that shit pop off. They let 'em jump her."

Though I was upset too, I decided to be the voice of reason. "Hakeem don't make matters worse. Let's just pray for Mia."

"Imma pray for her. But Imma bury me some mothafuckas too. Real talk."

"Where's C?" I asked.

"The doctors seeing him too. He was cut too."

"Oh goodness." I put my face down into my hands. This is too much. And all because of me and my shit. "Where's Cut Throat and her friends?"

"Probably at the General or somewhere cause I tried to kill them bitches. I know Cut Throat in somebody's hospital."

"What about Kyra?"

"Her ass ended up running when the real street brawl started. She let her woman and her man finish her battle."

"Her woman?" I looked up at Hakeem with a perturbed look.

"Yeah, Cut Throat her woman. That's why she jumped in it so fast."

"No shit Hakeem?"

"C-Lo tricking both of them. They all on tape Krish, where you been at girl?"

"Minding my own damn business Hakeem."

Shar chimed in, "I got something for Kyra's ass though."

"Her man fucked up too. He probably got broke ribs and all." Hakeem added.

"Thank God you weren't hurt Hakeem. And I hope C will be alright." I said.

"He'll be okay. He just caught that big ass butcher's knife in the arm when he was grabbing at Mia. Shit, C a soldier, don't worry 'bout him."

That bitch ass Kyra. I wish I could get at her sorry ass. I thought.

I sat there a minute. I got a thought and jumped up.

"Hakeem call me if the doctor comes back out. I'll be right back."

I put my cell number in his phone.

"Come go with me Shar." She jumped up to follow. We rushed out of the hospital.

"What you 'bout to do girl?" I heard Hakeem call out.

17

The hurt and anger for my friend wouldn't let me keep still. I could be losing a friend because of my drama-filled life of men and promiscuity. She was in the hospital because of me and silly drama. It definitely had to end. But I had to get a little revenge of my own before I closed the childish crap that plagued me at the moment. It was all so senseless and had no part in my life whatsoever.

I knew Kyra's scary behind would run back to where it was safe; her apartment way on the other side of the river. She probably high tailed it out of the hood quick fast and in a hurry. She knew she couldn't handle the heat that goes on over there.

I needed a favor, so I decided to take Todd up on his offer to call if I needed something. I needed Kyra and I knew who could get her to come out of hiding.

Groggily, Todd answered the phone on the first ring.

I explained to him what I wanted him to do. I left the hospital en route to Todd's.

Shar and I made it to Todd's and parked behind his house.

We were in the guest bedroom when we heard Kyra arrive. Todd had coaxed Kyra over to his house at 4:30 am. I really couldn't believe that she actually came. The girl was undoubtedly unbelievable.

Todd played her first. He started asking her what was going on as I'd told him what had happened earlier.

She began explaining her version of story. Todd assured her he'd make her feel better as he had planned to cater to her. He told her to go shower, then they went to the bedroom where he laid her naked body on the bed and massaged her back. Told her he wanted to relieve her of her troubles.

Shar understood her role so she waited outside the bedroom door. Todd rolled her over on her back to massage her front. She closed her eyes to enjoy his strong hands on her skin. I stepped into the bedroom and slid out of my jeans. I wore a black thong and a white Old Navy tank top. Pulled the tank over my head.

"I have a surprise for you." He told Kyra. "Something you've been waiting for a long time."

"What is it baby?"

"Open your eyes." He said.

She opened her eyes to look right into mine. She jumped.

Fear consumed her beautiful but troubled face.

I spoke first.

"I heard you wanted something from me."

She didn't say anything; just stared at me.

"I tell you what, if I join you two in bed, would you leave all the drama behind and stop putting my name out there like that."

"I didn't mean for it to go down like that tonight."

"I'm talking about me and you. Mia will be alright." I said piercing her eyes with mine. "Do you want me? Is that why you're trying to make my life miserable? Steal my husband, having sex with my man, sending my friend pictures, calling me a snitch. Is that the reason for all that? Tell me what's going on."

Silence.

"Well all you had to do was say so."

I could tell that comment calmed her a bit, so she finally spoke.

"I always told you I loved you Krisha."

She had sat up in the middle of the bed. Todd sat on the edge. I moved over to the head of the bed, climbed into the middle and rested my back against the headboard. With my body above hers, I sat with my chin resting on my knees.

"You really meant that huh…then why do you keep trying to ruin me?"

"I told you I missed you and I loved you at Mia's that night, but after that night, you acted like I didn't even exist. You wouldn't even come see Mia because I was there."

"I was cool Kyra. We all got back together, went out and everything. But you were still plotting against me."

"You changed Krisha. You got all uppity and shit."

"No I didn't. I was still ridin' for you; always have."

"That's not the way I saw it."

"What did you really expect after having my husband?"

"I apologized for that Krisha. I thought you'd gotten over that."

"That wasn't something you just get over overnight Kyra. That was a 'slit a bitch throat' move. But I handled it the best way I knew how. You didn't exactly make it easy you know."

"If I have to say I'm sorry until the day I die, I will."

"Look, it's whatever you want right now, if you just leave the BS alone after tonight, enough people have already been hurt.

"You never know. You just might feel towards me what I feel for you."

"I might huh? I hear you're good."

"I aim to please."

Gave my lips a nervous lick.

"I see why Craig and Todd are crazy about you. Your body is beautiful. Is it as good as it looks?" She said.

"I think you already know that. And for the record, this one will always be mine." I looked over at Todd. "I've got something on this man nobody can take off; so back off him, okay." I said seductively motioning toward Todd.

"To hell with these no good men. I can really love you the way you want to be loved Krisha. I know you inside and out."

"Go ahead and show her how bad you want her." Todd urged.

He stood up then moved toward the top of the bed giving us total access.

I spread my legs while looking her eye to eye. She looked uneasy and unsure.

"Don't get scared now boo."

"Oh! I aint scared."

"Do we have a deal?"

"Yeah we have a deal but when I get through with you, you'll be running after me."

"Put up or shut up." I said.

She crawled toward my open legs. Reached out to touch me.

"No, no hands."

She nodded.

"Tell me what you want me to do." I said softly.

"Wider."

I did that.

She moved in closer to my body.

"You're amazingly beautiful." She panted before moving up to kiss my cheek.

I smiled.

She placed a kiss on my chin.

The scent from her body was invigorating. She smelled of fresh fruit; her body just as beautiful as mine.

As she moved down to find my bare chest with her lips, I let out a loud gasp. The touch of her soft lips sent surges throughout my body.

"I want to love you Krisha. I wanna be your friend again."

I closed my eyes tight. Thought about what she'd just said. Let it roll around in my head.

As I felt her head lowering to my stomach then to my thighs, I opened my eyes to see Shar creep up from her right side.

Then all of a sudden Shar delivered a lick that knocked her clean off the bed. Striking her one time in the jaw with brass knuckles.

Before she knew what had happened Shar was over on the other side of the bed putting a good ass whipping on her.

Todd threw me my jeans as I threw on my tank. I hopped up and slid them on quicker than the blink of an eye. I put on my shoes as Shar messed her up real good; keeping her down on the floor with her feet.

I knew if she was able to get up, it was gonna be a fight between her and Shar; Shar just simply wouldn't be one of my original tag team members. So I'd told her to keep her feet on her. I just didn't think she couldn't handle Kyra. Matter of fact, I knew she couldn't.

Once I was dressed, I told Shar to chill. I needed her there because of my pregnancy. I didn't want Kyra to get me down and get to my stomach. I had to tell Shar I was pregnant and instruct her of what to do if I came up short. I wasn't about to wrestle her ass anyway. Blows to her face and upper body is what she was gonna get.

Todd left the room. It was clear he didn't give one care about Kyra. She hopped up off the floor and stared me down.

"You bitch! You need this hood rat to help you." She spat.

"You know I don't need help." I said calmly.

"You are so bougie. That's why I can't stand your ass!"

"And you're one twisted sista."

"Fuck you Krish. Yo weak ass. Every man you get I can take from you." She spat.

"I didn't know we were competing for one. Especially since you were once such a dear friend of mine. I didn't think I had to watch my man around my girl. But that just goes to show you can't trust nobody. And furthermore if I gotta do what you do to get 'em and keep 'em, I don't need 'em. And bitch this aint about no fuckin' man, that's old news! This is about my sister."

She got nervous. Started out toward the door. "Look, I don't have time for this. I already whipped one bitch tonight." She threw out.

With that said, Shar ran up behind her and punched her again in the back of the head. She stumbled forward, maintained her balance, turned around and rushed at Shar. I stopped her in her tracks.

I came up on her nose in one quick half second move of the fist.

She quickly covered her nose with her palm.

"You bitch!" She yelled. "You're always hittin' me in my damn nose!"

She tried to run out of the room holding her nose, but I grabbed her by the back of her hair and pulled her rail thin behind back in.

"Where you going Ms. Bad Azz? Ms. Whipped One Bitch Tonight. Why don't you go for two?"

"Just let my hair go. I'll show you something."

I did just that.

She turned around and rushed at me. I held her back pretty good. If I wasn't pregnant, I was going to jail and didn't care one bit.

Then Shar got in. We whipped her ass for I know a good five minutes straight. I was dog tired and breathing heavily. I stopped hitting her. Watched Shar stomp her.

"Come on Shar let's go check on Mia."

Shar stopped kicking Kyra but continued talking noise.

Kyra lay on the floor beaten, bruised, bloody, and barely moving.

"If I ever hear my name in the streets again behind you, I'm gonna really mess you up. Mia talked me out of doing major damage to yo' tired behind and you had the audacity to jump her. How the hell you gon' jump Mia? That girl gave you and your child a place to stay when you didn't have a damn thing. Took care of your triflin' ass. Consider me out your life forever."

"If you only knew bitch. And if it's the last thing I do, Imma get yo' pretty ass for this. You better believe that."

"No. Not pretty. Beautiful."

I laughed.

"Bitch!" Kyra threw out as I exited the door.

I looked back at her on the floor holding her nose and stomach and kinda felt sorry for her. My heart really wasn't into brawling tonight; guess I acted on impulse. It served no purpose whatsoever. I could have easily taken her life tonight and be regretting it for the rest of mine. That's just how angry I was.

As I left Todd's place, I left behind my relationship with Kyra and all the drama that she presented to my life. I was over her and the so-call friendship that we once had. I had to move on.

On our way back to the hospital, Shar began laughing to herself.

I looked over at her strangely. "What?" I asked.

"I saw you watching that door. Your eyes were as big as an asshole when her head went down between your legs."

"Damn right. I was gonna hurt you bad if you would have let her go there."

I had to laugh myself. I felt a little better. I got to the bottom of what she had for me. But that still didn't help Mia's condition. It really was an episode in my life I'd like to quickly forget.

My cell rang while we were riding back to the hospital. It was Hakeem.

"Dey asking for you."

"We're on our way."

18

The doctor informed me that the surgery had gone well but Mia would still be in ICU in stable condition. Her blood pressure kept dropping and she hadn't awakened. She also informed me of the risks involved with the surgery that she'd undergone. The doctor added that Mia was a very lucky woman. One more inch to the right and the blade would have caught her heart.

"Can we see her now?" I asked.

"Yes. She'll be on the second floor in ICU, but only one person is allowed in at a time during normal visiting hours. However, I'll let you all go back one at a time when we get her settled into the room. Hopefully she won't stay in there too long. Give her about two days and everything should be stabilized. She's a strong woman."

"Yes she is." I thought.

We waited an hour before we were allowed to visit Mia in ICU. Hakeem went in first. When Shar went in she came right back in tears.

"She looks so helpless Krisha. She couldn't even hear me. It hurts to see her like that."

"I know Shar, but the doctor says she'll be fine after a while."

Drying her cheeks with a Kleenex, she said, "That's why I kept my mouth closed. I knew she would go down for you."

"I love that girl Shar. I wouldn't make it without her. But I sure as hell didn't want her to take a knife for me."

"Let's hope Ms. Kyra has learned her lesson. She knows she can never come near my spot again."

"I know her and I don't think you'll see her in the hood too often now. She tries to play the bad girl role, but she don't know hood life. She can't handle it."

"You better go on in there before they call it quits."

"Yeah I better." Go on home and get some sleep. I'll be here."

"Yeah I need to go take Hakeem home, but if you need me or if anything changes call me immediately."

"You know I will." I gave Shar a sincere hug.

I moved slowly toward the intensive care unit. Through the double doors and around the nurse's station to Mia's room. My friend lay hooked up to all kinds of monitors and IVs. I couldn't help but shed tears at first sight. She didn't deserve this. She didn't need to be here. I stroked her face and kissed her forehead. "I love you girl." I whispered. "Hurry and get up out of here. We got some baby shopping to do."

I stood by Mia's bedside and held her hand until the nurse asked that I leave. Visiting hours were again at 8:00 am, and I would sit right there and wait. I'd wait for the visiting times after that to come around also. For the next two weeks, I sat and waited and prayed. Mia didn't come around after two days. She came around on day four in a lot of pain. She had set up infection in one of the stab wounds and fell extremely ill. This prolonged her stay. She and I stayed in the hospital exactly twelve days. After her release, she stayed with me for three weeks. I wanted to make sure she wasn't moving around too much because those wounds had to heal properly. Mia had cuts on her arms, hands, in her chest, and a couple on her leg. She said she dealt with the razor cuts but there wasn't anything she could do when somebody threw Cut Throat that big ass butcher's knife.

And as for Cut Throat, word is no one has heard from her or C-Lo since that night of the big fight. Either they ran off together without Kyra or Hakeem followed through with his promise. I'd rather believer the first scenario.

I'd been so consumed with Mia until I didn't realize a month had already gone by. I was twenty-one weeks pregnant and just beginning to show. I looked so funny. I was still able to wear my regular clothes, but I knew that wouldn't be for long.

I decided to tell the boys that they were having a little sister. They were so excited. I told them I wanted to name her after Aunt Mia, so Malik suggested we name her Tamia. We all agree. Mia liked that too.

19

I opened the front door to my house today to find a small package. Looking at the return address, I immediately knew who the package was from. Just didn't know what he could possibly be sending *me*.

Eager to see what was inside, I tore into it. When I opened the box, I found an envelope sitting on top of the wrapping. There were three tickets and a note.

Hey Love,

Hope you're doing well. If you can, please bring my boys to the game in Houston next week. I'll really feel good knowing you guys are there. I can fly you in. Just let me know so I can make the necessary arrangements. If you don't want to come, I'll understand. Just tell the boys to watch for me this Sunday. The game will also be televised. Tell them I'm gonna score a touchdown for each of them. Hope they enjoy the jerseys. Wear them in Houston.

Love Always,
Ryan

I hadn't heard from him since he left the cabin more than a month ago. Now he wants me to come to a damn game. I don't think so, besides, I can't leave Mia.

I gave my boys the jerseys. He even had one for me in there. They wore the jerseys Sunday while watching the game on TV.

I gave those tickets away to a friend of mine who ran a teen counseling center for boys. Said he'd take two of his most deserving teens to the game. I felt better about that than I would have ever felt going to that game.

As for Ryan, he did exactly what he'd said in the letter. He scored two touchdowns for my boys. In the interview after the game Ryan stated that both touchdowns were for his boys, TJ and Malik.

They both went wild. "Did you hear that mommy? Did you hear Mr. Ryan say our names?"

"Yeah, baby, I heard him." I was excited for them.

No sooner than I said that. My phone rang.

"Was that lil boy talking about my sons?"

"Why don't you call him and ask him?"

"Don't be smart."

"What's the problem with that?"

"If he wants some sons, tell his ass to go get him some. Those are my kids. And besides, I thought you didn't see him anymore."

"Bye Todd."

"Hold up."

"No bye, you all up in mine."

I hung up.

I could see if he wanted something. He just wanted to aggravate me about Ryan and I didn't need that. Ryan had already worked a nerve by pulling his little stunt just up and out the blue.

Todd called right back. I answered like doing so was killing me.

"Make him remember they're my sons."

"Todd get a life okay."

"I'm trying to have one with you."

"Been there done that remember? Now bye."

"Hey wait a minute..."

"What!" I screamed.

My patience was so short these days.

"The boys told me they're gonna have a sister in four months."

I calmed down a little. "I figured they would tell you."

"Krisha is the baby mine?"

"No Todd."

"Just checking. I remember that condom breaking."

"No you're off the hook."

"I wouldn't mind."

"Why? You have two girls already."

"Didn't I tell you? I have only one daughter. I took a paternity test last month for Cassie's child. She's not mine."

"After all this time huh?"

"Yeah, she just didn't look like me or any of my children. She didn't have the eyes or anything. The eyes are indication that you are a Taylor. I always dreamed of what our baby girl would look like. I wanted us to create another little you."

"Stop Todd. You're going there." I softly scolded.

"Okay. I'm sorry, but it's true. But hey, if you need anything call me. I'll baby sit lil' momma too."

I laughed. But I knew he meant that. He was a sweetheart at heart.

"Thanks boo." I said softly.

20

The next three months zoomed by. It was already February, my last month of pregnancy. My due date was a week later, on the 20th, and I was ready.

The baby's nursery was decorated in pink and lime green. Mia had healed well and was back to her old self, thank God. I really needed her.

As for my baby daddy, he called one time since he sent that package, but unfortunately I didn't answer my cell when I saw it was him. He left a message saying he wanted to talk. I thought it would be easier for me to have no contact with him at all. I didn't want to hurt myself knowing he had no intentions of being with me.

As my due date neared, I wondered how in the world I would pull the whole thing off. It was easy hiding the pregnancy from him, but to hide a child for the rest of the child's life was unfair. TJ and Malik shared every chance they got with their father. My baby girl would only have me. I contemplated calling him several times to get it out in the open, but I would rule it out every time. Mia did not agree with my decision, but she didn't push me or tell me what to do. I respected that.

One thing that was a deciding factor for me was that Ryan's team had just won the Super Bowl and he was MVP. He looked so happy on television while living his dream. One that we'd discussed several times.

At the end of the big game, he was greeted by his new fiancé'. Then at every interview, Ryan showed up with her on his arm. Every time I turned on the TV, there he was and she wasn't far behind. I got so tired of looking at them together. And she sure didn't look pregnant to me. I had to admit, she was pretty and they did make a cute couple, but I know I would have looked better on his arm than her.

Anyway, I accepted that he was happy with his life. He'd chosen the way he wanted to go. I couldn't allow that to hinder me.

I loved so hard before that it almost ruined me, and to this date I am still feeling consequences from that relationship. But, I found strength within myself to persevere. So, I let Ryan be. He was young. He had to live and learn just like I did. Ryan was about to be that much wealthier, that much more popular, he was getting married and having a baby. I couldn't mess with that. Besides, if he wanted me he would have called and said so within five months. I guess he came out to the cabin to hit it for the last time and hadn't looked back since. I guess it wasn't enough to make him stay.

I still love him though. But he'll never know. Everything I feel for him and Todd will forever be hidden in my heart.

I thought I'd stop thinking so much and clean out one of my kitchen cabinets to make room for the baby bottles and formula. I was taking the dishes out and stacking them on the counter when cramps hit my lower stomach soon after I started. I took to the sofa to rest for a few minutes to see if they'd go away. Thank goodness they subsided as I rested. So I finished the cabinet, showered and changed then stretched out across my bed to watch a little TV and ended up falling asleep. That little work had worn me out.

Later that night, I was startled awake by severe cramps in my lower abdomen. My water hadn't broken but I knew then I was going into labor a week early. I tried to ride it out for about twenty minutes. The contractions came and went every ten minutes. I called Mia, and Todd to get the boys after school. I retrieved my already packed bag from my closet and sat on the couch and waited for Mia. As I waited the contractions intensified. They were about five minutes apart, and hurt like hell. When Mia pulled up, I was already waiting in the garage.

I gave birth two hours later at 12:32 pm on February 13 to a seven pounds, 2 ounces baby girl. One day before Valentine's Day, but she was my sweetheart. I named her Tamia Simone Taylor. She was so tiny and perfect. So precious. The daughter I always wanted. The only thing I didn't agree with was her last name. On everything I owned my name was Taylor, so I had to give my baby that name too; though she hadn't a bit of Todd's blood in her body. I did list Ryan as the father on her birth certificate, but couldn't give her his last name. He wasn't there to sign for her.

Todd brought the boys by after school. When he looked at the baby's name card on the bassinette, he quickly looked at me.

He leaned in close to me and whispered, "Are you sure she isn't mine?"

"I'm positive." I smiled then explained the last name thing.

He was cool with that. Kept saying he wished she were his. For a moment, I wished that too.

21

My baby was six weeks old already and I was released from the doctor's care and able to go about my daily routine. The past six weeks were definitely a life adjustment for me. My second son was now seven years old and here I was changing diapers again. There would be no more going out on weekends and hanging out for a while now. I was so thankful for having Mia and Carmen to aid me in my new adjustment. When I had my sons, I had the help of their father, my mother, and Mia. They all made motherhood seem easy for me. But I was afraid that things wouldn't be the same this time around. I no longer had my mother nor did my child have her father. We both had Mia and I knew she was going to do everything in her powers to help me with the baby.

From the day we came home, Mia wanted to take the baby as hers. I believe that Mia's stabbing incident and the birth of my daughter had changed her in many ways. She stopped fighting her feelings for Derric and decided to be with him exclusively; I think. She had slowed her roll and even talked about having her own child. Derric loved Mia to the fullest and has been by her side the entire time throughout her ordeal. Although Chad was tied up with his team most of the time, he spent every moment he could catering to Mia. He was just as supportive as Derric. I thanked God everyday that Chad's busy schedule didn't allow him and Derric to bump heads. However, I guess Mia had things more together than me. But, again its Mia I'm talking about, so only God knows how this boat will sail.

I've been thinking hard on talking to Ryan about the baby, but I just refuse to feel like some groupie who got knocked up and seeks after the man for support. From the looks of it that's exactly what it seems to be. Lord knows I don't need his money. At this point, I just want his child to know him.

Last week I picked up the phone and hurriedly dialed Ryan's cell number before I lost the nerve to talk to him. And once again, the number was no longer in service. I'm not sure if the change of the numbers was to keep me and others away or just me. Still I say if he wanted me, he knew where to find me. All my contact information was the same.

In the meantime, I was still conversing with Chris, who was well informed as to the fact that I'd just had a baby. He didn't mind, so he said.

He had one son by an ex-girlfriend. Chris had never been married and desired to be a family man, so he said. Little did he know I was not about to have another baby for nobody. I don't care who I marry again or who I'm with, they'd better already have kids and love mine as if they were their own. I was no baby-making machine. I loved my bunch, but they were a handful. My baby girl made me realize just how much of a handful they were.

What was shocking was that all my kids looked exactly like their fathers. It was as if my DNA wasn't working properly or something. Little Tamia was the spitting image of Ryan. They had the same smooth honey skin. The same sparkling light brown eyes, the same soft wavy hair texture, the exact same deep dimples in both cheeks, and the same little pointy nose. My boys were pretty boys just like their daddy. With those big loveable eyes.

When I first saw Tamia it was evident who her father was. Usually, it's hard to detect the resemblance of family members in newborns and you can't judge by skin color because African-American babies skin tone changes so much. But with Tamia, it was rather easy. Looks nothing like me. Maybe she'll have my personality, my brain, my temper or some other characteristic that makes me who I am. But, for right now the only resemblance I see is of Ryan.

22

"Krisha, would you like me to stay any longer?"

"No, Mia you can go ahead. I know you have a date tonight. Thanks for watching the kids while I was at the gym. I really needed that workout. Gotta get this body back 100%."

"No thanks needed girl. These are my babies. And as far as your body is concerned you look great. If I didn't know, couldn't tell you just had a baby."

"Yeah but look at this." I patted the extra meat on my stomach.

"You know some of that will leave. And the rest you can get with sit-ups girl. Stop trippin'."

"Guess I am huh? Anyway, I need to go over to the mall later on. Gotta get something to wear tomorrow night."

"Why didn't you say something, I can stay."

"Mia it's almost 4:00 pm. You need to go. I can take the kids with me. We'll probably have dinner while we're out."

"Are you sure?"

"Positive. I need to do a little bonding anyway."

I was just getting over post-partum depression so going out with my crew would be therapeutic for me.

"Where are you going tomorrow anyway?"

"To a dinner party that an ex-teammate of Chris' is hosting at Chateau Rouge."

"Sounds like that's gonna be nice and elegant. A lot of ballas up in there."

"Yeah well I'm not interested in anymore ballas."

"Well pass 'em over to me then."

"Girl please. You better keep the man you got. Nobody else is gonna put up with what you put that man through."

"Oh you mean Derric?" I looked at her. We laughed.

"Yes Derric silly."

"I'm just playin' girl. I love me some Derric. But I think I'm falling in love with Chad."

"Are you serious?"

"Yeah girlfriend I really am. I've never felt this way before for a man. Not even with Trent or Derric. It's so different."

"You'd better decide because I don't want you to get as messed up as me when it comes to men."

"Naw boo. Don't think it'll come to that. I'm just weighing my options right now. I gotta see where this is going with Chad before I let Derric go."

"If you're considering letting Derric go, then you must be really feeling Chad."

"I think what makes our relationship even more special is that we've never been intimate. He's not pressuring me for sex at all. I think we enjoy other things about each other and have never really focused on our bodies. But for right now I need to focus on Derric. He's really been there for me."

"You're right. You have to recognize when someone has been by your side. But I'm just curious. I know you better than I know myself, and you mean to tell me you've never thought about getting down with Chad?"

"And you're right, you do know me. Hell yeah I've thought about it, but I've never mentioned it or acted upon it. There's no spending the night with each other yet so there's not too much temptation. But I just don't want that kind of relationship with him right now. Derric is enough for me to deal with."

"I understand completely. Maybe if I would have thought like that I wouldn't have gone through the things I went through with men."

"No regrets Sis."

"Yeah right. No regrets." I dragged.

"I'm gonna go now girlie. I'll call you later."

"No matter how late, call me anyway."

"Why?"

"I'll be bored. I'm not used to this on a Friday night anymore. You know how we used to do it."

"Okay. Promise."

When Mia left I asked Malik and TJ to listen for the baby while I showered. I dressed the baby and myself and we all headed out to do a little shopping.

My sons dreaded going shopping. They only wanted to go if I was going to a toy store, or if they could go to the game room. I promised them I'd take them to the Pizza Jump if they came along. They loved that place. They could play games, jump in the space walk, play on other inflatables, and also have pizza for dinner. I enjoyed the Pizza Jump also because it got them out of my hair for a while. They were cool with that.

I'd found the tightest ensemble at a boutique outside the mall all within two hours. Record time for me. I even picked up some things for the kids. Though all of them had enough already, I always found myself in the children's sections buying something else.

I must say Tamia was surprisingly very good while I shopped. She slept the entire time. TJ and Malik had gone to the game room after fifteen minutes of waiting on me when we first arrived at the mall. So I swung by there to get them on my way out.

TJ came running out screaming, "Mom, Mom guess who I just saw."

"Who baby?"

"Mr. Ryan."

"Who?" I asked again to make sure I'd heard him correctly.

"Your friend, Mr. Ryan."

"Where did you see him baby?"

"He saw us in here and he came in to say hello."

"Where is he now?"

"He left. He said to tell you hello."

"Are you sure it was Mr. Ryan?"

"Yes Mom. Ask Malik."

Before I could summons Malik over, he walked up yelling. "Mom, Mr. Ryan said hello."

"Okay guys lets go." I said.

I had to get out of there and fast. My desire was not to see Ryan Mathers today.

"Mom, can we get a cookie?"

"Baby we're about to go eat."

"C'mon Mom just one won't hurt."

"No TJ, now come on."

I was pushing that stroller so fast through the mall. Trying to make it to the exit door when Malik said, "Wait Mom I left my phone on that game."

Great, just great. I thought.

"What?" You brought that cell phone with you?"

"Yes and I left it by that game."

"Malik, I told you to leave that phone in the car."

"Daddy told me to always take it with me."

"Do you see your daddy here? When I tell you to do something, you do it okay?" I said sternly and aggravated.

"Yes mam."

My nerves were bad. For one, I don't know why the hell Todd would buy a nine year old a cell phone in the first place. Now we had to go all the way back through the mall.

"TJ go back with Malik to get the phone. I'll sit right here."

I sat down on a bench to gather my nerves. My heart was racing from trying to get out of there. You would have thought Jason was chasing me the way I was moving.

The baby started crying so I went in the bag to get her pacifier. While I was digging around in the sack with my head down, my kids ran back up to me.

"Got it Mommy." Malik chimed. I'm sure they ran full speed through that mall as fast as they returned. I can only imagine the people they'd trampled over.

"Good baby." I said with my focus on Tamia.

"Look what else we got." TJ said.

"What baby?"

I looked up and almost passed out. I immediately began trembling. The most handsome, but shocked face stared down at me. It was Mr. Ryan in the flesh.

He managed to take his eyes off the baby stroller long enough to say, "Hello Krisha."

"Hi." Was all I could muster.

T.J. took over the conversation.

"Mr. Ryan, this is my baby sister." He happily chimed. Then took Ryan by the hand and led him over to the stroller.

Ryan looked from my face to the baby's face, about three times before speaking to T.J.

"She's beautiful man". He uttered with his eyes glued to Tamia.

"Thanks Mr. Ryan." T.J. said acting like a proud big brother.

"Her name is Tamia." Added Malik.

"That's a beautiful name man."

I got up to gather the baby's sack and my purse.

"How've you been Krisha?" He said turning his attention toward me.

"Good." I answered with my back to him.

"When did you…..?"

"Come on guys tell Mr. Ryan goodbye." I said to my sons cutting him off. "Nice seeing you Ryan." I threw over my shoulder as I walked away.

"Krisha, wait." I heard from behind.

I hurriedly walked away not even looking back. I wasn't ready for this. I didn't know when and if I'd ever be ready, but today wasn't the day.

After the fiasco at the mall, we went to eat pizza. The boys played more games, jumped around and wore themselves out.

On the drive home, Todd called Malik's cell to chat. Malik found out that Todd was going to north Louisiana tomorrow to a friend's house and begged to go with him. Todd asked me to drop them by his house on the way home. He could never say no to them, which was good because I gladly obliged. I still wasn't used to being out with three kids. I was tired as hell.

I walked into my house to a ringing phone. I couldn't get to the phone in the kitchen before it stopped ringing, but then the ringing was replaced with the chiming of my cell phone.

"Hello, Hello." I said. I could barely hear the caller due to the baby screaming in my ear.

"Hey Krisha." I finally heard the caller say.

"Hi."

"Did I catch you at a bad time?"

"Ryan?"

"Yes."

"Well, yes, you did sort of catch me at a bad time."

"I'm sorry. Well, call me back when you're free. The number should be on your caller I.D."

"Okay, bye." I said.

I went on about my business. I'd been doing fine without him. No need in changing the script now.

I bathed my child, fed her, and then put her down for bed. I showered, dressed for bed, and pulled out a book to read. I never got through the first page before the phone rang.

It was Chris, so I talked to him for about fifteen minutes, and then started watching reruns of the Jamie Foxx Show. It was 10:30 p.m. and I was restless.

My phone rang again. *Probably Mia*, I thought.

"Hello." I answered.

"Are you dissing me or something?" A loud male voice pierced my eardrum.

"Excuse me." I countered.

"I can't get a call back?"

"I was busy".

"Sure you were."

"Is there something I can help you with?" I asked with attitude.

"Yes, as a matter-of-fact there is."

"Shoot."

"Why didn't you tell me?"

"Tell you what?"

"Don't play stupid Krisha."

"What are you talking about?"

"Why didn't you tell me you were pregnant?"

"Why would I?"

"Why wouldn't you?"

"Because you had no place in my life, so I didn't have to tell you anything."

"Yes you did. I should have known."

"Would it have made a difference?"

"Hell, yes!" He yelled.

"Why and how Ryan? You made your decision months ago. You kicked me to the curb."

"Stop it Krisha. You know it wasn't like that."

"That's how I saw it. That's how it felt."

"We weren't even really together then."

"Together enough for you to hit it and move on. You know what...forget it Ryan. I don't have time for this."

"You're tripping." He spat.

"No, you're tripping. Why are you calling me so concerned about my business after seven months of not hearing from you? You couldn't call to say Merry Christmas or anything?"

"I thought it was best."

"It's best if you get off my phone and leave me the hell alone." I yelled.

"That might be best because you're really on some crazy shit tonight." He replied noticeably irritated.

I met Mr. Click.

I couldn't believe he'd really hung up the phone in my face. But it was all good though, because I was about to hang up in his.

I was so vexed until I had to go to the kitchen to get me a drink of cold water.

After quenching my thirst, I moved back up the stairs, checked on Tamia then commenced to watching Jamie Foxx act a fool. About twenty minutes later, my phone rang again.

"Hello." I said wondering why everyone wasn't asleep at this hour.

"Open the damn door!"

"Who da hell you hollering at? You don't run nothing here." I snapped.

"You wanna bet? As long as my daughter is up in there I do."

Silence.

For some reason, I was speechless. I was trying to think of what to say next while skipping two steps at a time to get to the bottom of the stairs.

I held the phone in silence.

He calmed down and softly said, "Just open the door Krisha, please. I wanna see her."

"Nothing belongs to you in here!"

I slammed the phone down.

I peeked out of the kitchen window to find his truck sitting in my driveway. I didn't see him in it, so my guess was that he had gotten in through the side door of the garage and was at my kitchen door. *I gotta remember to lock that door.* I thought.

My home phone continued to ring, but I didn't bother answering. For a second, I thought about how stupid and childish the scenario really was.

Just let it be. Something told me. *It's his child too, so stop acting a fool.*

I went to the kitchen and opened the door. Ryan stood there and eyed me as if he could beat my ass blue. I stared him right back. Before I knew it, he'd taken me into a tight embrace. I didn't reciprocate. Just stood frozen.

"You could have told me." He whispered as he held me close. "I would have been there."

I didn't say anything. Wanted to hear what he had to say.

"She's mine isn't she? I'm sorry baby." He apologized in my ear.

I showed no emotion whatsoever. I guess he really thought he could just walk back into my life with a tear and an apology and I'd accept him.

When he finally released me, I looked into his eyes and got emotional too. He looked too pitiful. And I was a sucker for a sad face. Especially on a man who I loved.

"I love you. I want you. I want our baby." He cried.

His lips found mine. I pulled away.

"Come in Ryan". I stepped back and offered him entrance into my home.

He held my hand as I led him into the family room. Sat next to me on the sofa.

Turning to look at me, he said, "Why didn't you tell me?" He cupped my face in his large hands and kissed my lips.

"I couldn't."

"Why not?"

"I didn't want to ruin your family. Besides, you'd already made it clear you were gonna be with her."

"It's been seven long, hard months. I've regretted saying that every single day."

"I just couldn't find it in me to tell you after you dumped me. I know it wasn't right, but I was hurt. We made love that night and I thought maybe our relationship could survive, but it seems like you ran farther away."

"Baby, believe me, I ran because if I didn't, I wouldn't have been able to be there for my child with her. But if I would have known you, the woman who I've always loved, was carrying my child, there's no way in hell I would have left you. I always wanted you. It's always been about you Krisha. I just wanted to do the right thing."

"You wanted to marry her because of a child. I didn't want that pity Ryan."

"It's different with you Krisha. It's not pity. Forgive me but I'm still learning baby. I just wanted to give my child what was needed."

"So what do you want with me Ryan?"

"I want you to understand me."

"What is it to understand? You're a married man now."

"I'm not married nor am I marrying her."

"You're not married?"

"No, I found out she wasn't pregnant. And I realized I really didn't love or respect her enough to even try to pretend."

"Are you serious?"

"She tried to fake a miscarriage after there was no sign of pregnancy after a while, but I found out. Her little trick backfired."

"I told you that was game from the start."

"Yes you did and I should have listened. I know I'm the biggest fool".

I hugged him and kissed his lips.

"Just another lesson learned."

"I called you about a month ago to mend things between us, but I could never reach you and you never returned my calls. I figured you'd moved on."

"No, not quite."

"Not quite, what you mean by that?" He let my hand go. "You can just tell dude to get to steppin'."

He was fishing and I knew it.

"Wait a minute. You can't just come up in here and..."

"You must be gon' give me my baby out of here then." He stared me down. "Girl, stop tripping. You know you want me."

Ryan playfully pulled me onto his lap and kissed my neck.

"You ain't all that." I pushed his head playfully.

We laughed.

"Can I see her?" He lifted me up from his lap and got up from the couch.

"She's sleeping upstairs. And tell me how did you know she was yours?"

"The moment I looked at her I knew. I see myself all in her. I'll tell my mom to show you my baby pictures and you'll see."

"She *is* your spitting image. I can't deny that." I smiled.

I led Ryan up the stairs to the baby's nursery. Ryan and I stood over the crib looking down on our beautiful sleeping angel.

"I can't believe how much she looks like me. This is my child. My first and only child. You could have never kept her from me."

"I don't think I would have. I was just the circumstances."

"I want to take you guys to meet my family. My mother has got to see her."

"Okay." I agreed.

"Let's go tomorrow. Is that okay?"

"Well, I kinda have plans for tomorrow evening."

"That's okay, we can go the next day." He suggested.

"I'd like that."

"Can I be nosey and ask what kind of plans you have for tomorrow?"

I breathed a heavy sigh. "Honestly Ryan... I have a date."

He stared at me then turned his head to look at the baby.

"Okay, good, well, I'll be waiting up for you."

"No, you don't need to wait up."

"Does that mean you'll be out all night?" He questioned with a stern look.

"Ryan, please."

"I'll stay here with the kids." He offered.

"The boys will be gone and Carmen will be here."

"No, I'll keep my baby. We need to bond." He said quickly. "Just bring her over to me before you leave or I'll come get her."

He had pulled a funky attitude out of the blue. He kissed the baby, turned and stormed down the stairs. I was so sure he would come back in until I heard his truck leaving the driveway. Well, I'll be damned. Brothaman had just returned to the scene and wanted to lay claim up in my house. The baby yes, me, hell no. He was really trippin'.

Mia called an hour later. She and Derric had just gotten in. I ran my evening down, as usual. Mia was so happy that Ryan finally knew he had a child.

She and I chatted until Derric came up with something else for them to do so she dismissed me quickly.

23

I went to the gym and the beautician Saturday morning in preparation for my date with Chris. He was to pick me up at 6:30 p.m., so I had plenty time to get ready.

I hadn't spoken to Ryan since the night before but around 3:00 p.m., I took the baby to his condo as he'd asked.

When I arrived, there were two other guys sitting in his living room watching television and chatting it up with Ryan. He introduced us and after eyeing me up and down on the slick, both guys excused themselves and left.

"Are you sure you wanna do this?" I asked.

"Yes. She's my child isn't she?"

I ignored that. Did he want me to say *no?* I didn't have time for his attitude; I needed to leave.

"Okay, well, here she is." I handed him the baby in the carrier. Sat her sack down on his coffee table. I gave him her feeding instructions and told him to call if he needed me.

He followed me to the door.

"Who are you going out with?" He quizzed.

"A friend."

"Does that friend have a name?"

"I'll call you Ryan." I walked out and closed the door.

Chris and I had a very good time. He was a perfect gentleman all night. His friends were outstanding and I even befriended the host's wife. We planned on getting together really soon.

When I arrived home around 11:00 a.m., I called Ryan to let him know I was on my way to get the baby. When I got there, the baby was sleeping, but Ryan was wide-awake. Probably had been waiting on me all night like he'd said.

"Hey." I said as I stepped into his house.

"Come on in." He closed the door behind me then plopped down on his couch.

"Did she do okay?" I stood looking at him.

"Yeah, she was great. She knows I'm her daddy."

"Good, I'm glad you had this time to share with her, but let me get her things so you can go to bed."

"Krisha sit down." He said sternly without blinking.

"Look, it's already late."

"Please. Sit down." He pleaded.

I hesitantly took a seat on the chair across from him. "Okay Ryan. What's up?"

"I don't want you seeing him anymore." He said boldly. Just threw it out there.

"Is that what the attitude was for?"

"Call it what you want, but I poured out my heart to you last night. I thought you understood where I was coming from."

"So you wanted me to drop everything and instantly change my life because you showed up at my door after almost eight months?"

"I wanted you to understand me."

"I wanted you to love me, but did I get that? I wanted you to understand *me*, but did I get that? I wanted you to stay with me, but did I get that? There are a lot of things we want Ryan that we just simply cannot have."

"I'm here now. I wanna give you all those things."

"After you found ole' girl out; you'd probably still be with her if she hadn't lied, right?"

He didn't answer.

"Just as I thought." I said getting up from the chair.

"I thought you'd moved on." He said softly.

"Well, I had. Now you're telling me to dump him for you. You are unbelievable."

The room went silent.

Then I spoke.

"There's no way in hell you would have dropped her just by me asking. If I recall correctly, I did; you didn't."

"Krisha, I'd just gotten back here the night before I ran into you in the mall. I was gonna try to reach you. I had to build up the nerve."

"Yeah right and I'm a naïve believe anything you hear young head. Somehow you got me twisted."

"I was. Honestly. I found out she lied about a month and a half ago. I tried to reach you. I left a message, but you never called."

"You looked pretty happy all over the television."

"I wasn't really happy and that's when I thought she was pregnant. That should have been you the entire time."

"Look, I'm going to be completely honest with you, so you listen good. I'm a thirty two year old divorced woman with three kids. One ex-husband and one baby daddy. I got my own and I don't want for anything. My ex does pretty well and takes good care of his children and my baby daddy is doing pretty good his damn self. I'm pretty sure me and my baby will be taken care of if need be. You feel me. But you know what, I'm just happy with who I am and what *I* have. Me, what's mine, Krisha's. I don't need you or any other man's ends because mine stretch pretty far by they damn self. And I sure don't need the drama from your groupie hoes, wanna be baby mommas, and the other triflin' company you keep. Because guess what homeboy? Been there and done that; all that. Whatever your 27-year-old high-strung ass brings, I done did that too. So what I'm saying is you can go on with the game and the bullshit because I don't need nothing and nobody but peace of mind and my children."

Ryan looked at me like I was crazy.

"Girl, you really are ghetto."

"I can be if I need to be. Call it how you see it, but you already know what's up." I folded my arms and looked at him like, *What?*

He laughed lightly. "You are a trip…but I like that."

Ryan got up from the sofa, moved over to the chair to take my hand. He then pulled me up to meet him. Kissed me hard.

I tried wiggling out of his grip but it was too tight. He kept my head steady as his lips pressed against mine.

"Okay you can beat me up. When you get all that anger out of your system, your fine ass is mine. Deal?"

With that said he hit me in the face with a pillow from the couch. And then it was on.

We tore up the living room pillow fighting. I got some good licks in with the pillows. He thought I was playing but those were for real.

After we finished tearing up everything, we made love on top of all the junk we had thrown onto the floor.

I hadn't had sex since the last time Ryan and I had made love up in the cabin. I was weak under his touch. Every finger that touched my skin produced a tear. I loved him with all my heart. With every movement the love intensified.

Through it all, Tamia stayed asleep which made things even better. We made a pallet on the floor in the bedroom to be near the baby. We had to keep fixing it back due to creatively exploratory sex. Loving with Ryan was better than good. It was right on time.

24

"Where do we go from here?" I asked two days later as we awakened in each other's arms. We'd been holed up at Ryan's place for two days. Needless to say, we never made it to meet Ryan's family that day.

"Where do we go?"

"Good question. I've been thinking about that myself."

"Well?"

"Well, first I wanna start in Jamaica."

"That's not what I meant silly."

He laughed.

"I know. But I would like to get away with you. Take you wherever you want to go."

"I went there a few months ago and I don't wanna be reminded of that trip."

"You didn't go with me. It'll be our new beginning."

"If you truly want it to be our new beginning then let's go somewhere else."

"Okay, then I'd love to take you to Hawaii."

"Perfect. I'd love that."

"Hawaii it is. We'll leave day after tomorrow."

"Whoa, wait a minute. We can't go just like that. We need to make arrangements."

"My travel agent will handle that. Don't worry your pretty little head baby."

"Remember I have three children. I can't just go like that."

"I'll pay Carmen to take care of all three until we get back. No problem."

"I'll have to talk to Todd first. He may take the boys for me. I need to speak with him first before I leave them with someone else for an extended period of time."

"Okay do what you gotta do then. We can leave the baby with my family."

"Ryan, we can't do that. They haven't even met her yet."

"The already know about her. My family loves children. My mom and grandmother will be glad to have her. They probably won't let us take her back after they see her today."

"Ryan, why didn't you ever allow me to meet your family before?"

"Things happened so fast. Our relationship was sporadic it seems. I wasn't in one place for too long. Besides, I don't bring every woman I meet to my mother. I have to be sure I have the right one."

"So you didn't think I was the right one?"

"No baby. I always knew you were right for me. There's just a time for everything."

"How many other women have you taken to meet your mother?"

"Where is all this coming from Krisha?"

"Just asking boo."

"Only one."

"Ms. It I guess?"

"No actually, there was a female I met at the beginning of my career. I wanted to marry her. I thought we were really in love. At least, I thought she was."

"So you were, she wasn't?"

"That's kinda how it went."

"What happened?"

"I realized I was in love with her physical appearance. Her inner self was horrible. It took me a while to see that and get tired of it. She was only interested in what she thought she could get from me. A bona fide gold digger and undercover wild child. When I was away she was at play."

"How old were the two of you?"

"She was 19; I was 23."

"And you thought she was ready for marriage? All that girl saw was diamonds and dollar signs."

"Yeah well, I've ran into quite a few like that but little do they know they gets nothin' from me."

"Now I see the reason behind your position on me not knowing what you did for a living."

"That was then. But I know that's not you. You're a grown woman."

"There are some grown women who would be after your money too. But that aint me. Is that why you like me, because you know I don't need your money? You got a problem with doing things for women?"

"No baby. That's not what I'm saying. There's a big difference you know. You're an independent woman and I like that. Men like women who can hold their own. Men with self-esteem issues go for the needy women. Don't get me wrong; I know a woman likes her man to do things for her too. You're used to a man providing for you. Not that you need him to, but that's what we're supposed to do. And I know you won't settle for anything less. That's exactly what I intend to do. I want to give you the world girl and you don't even know."

He brushed my cheek with his fingertips.

I blushed.

"I always wanted the right woman to share everything I have with. Believe me, what's mine is yours. You're my queen." He gave me a peck on the lips.

"You're being too sweet." I kissed him back.

"I am not sweet." Ryan joked.

"You know what I mean silly."

"I'm gonna have to upgrade you since you're gonna be my boo now."

"I think you might need the upgrade, sucker." I elbowed him.

We laughed.

He then took my hand. Got a bit sentimental.

"Krisha I've been in love with you from day one. I just didn't wanna get myself hurt or disappointed again. You're a hell of a woman to handle girl and I love every bit of it. I want us to be together baby. I don't ever want to be without you again."

"Ryan, I'm sorry it took me so long but I'm glad things happened the way they did. Now we know for sure that this relationship is no mistake. I love you baby."

I reached up and kissed his lips.

"I love you too Krisha Taylor." He kissed me back and caressed my face.

"You know what?" He asked. "I don't like that last name of yours."

"What's wrong with it?"

"I don't like calling you by another man's name. We're gonna have to do something about that."

"I can change it back to my maiden name. I thought about that after I had the baby. But that's my business name and I'd really hate to change it."

"I've been meaning to ask you, it's a damn shame I don't know, but what *is* the baby's last name? Is it Taylor too?" He stared hard.

"Umm, well yeah." I said reluctantly.

He jumped up from the bed.

"Oh, hell no Krisha! Why did you do that if you knew I was her father?"

"She had to take on my last name."

"Did you even list me as her father?"

"Umm...well, yes."

"Yes." He paced while staring at me. "Good. But we're going to change her name today. My child is not living another day with another man's name...I can't believe you did that."

All I could say was, "Okay Ryan. That's what I want too."

"Furthermore, you know what? This shit won't happen like this again. I'll be right there next time my baby is born."

Next time? I thought. *This man is really on that ignant shit. I know now wasn't the time, so I wasn't gonna go there.*

"I wish you would have told me this Krisha." He said as he paced the floor. "My baby got that crazy mothafuckas name. I ought to go kick his ass."

"Ryan, Todd didn't have anything to do with the baby's name. I had to give her my name. You weren't there to sign the birth certificate."

"And whose fault was that?" He spat angrily.

I took a deep breath and chose my words carefully. Things could take a drastic turn depending on what I said next.

"Look baby we can take care of this, just calm down. It's nothing really."

"Yeah nothin' to you, but I'm a man and I can take care of mine. It doesn't feel good to know your only child has another man's name."

"I'm sorry baby." Was all I needed to say. Nothing else would have mattered at that point. I let him rant and rave. I understood exactly how he felt.

In mid-rant, he turned to me sitting upright on the bed and said, "Put some damn clothes on so we can go take care of this right now. Then we're going to see my family. I'm not taking my baby around my family with Taylor on her shit!"

25

On our last night in Hawaii, we took a walk along the beach after dinner. Our week had been a very pleasurable romance filled journey into a new beginning for the both of us. Our relationship had moved to another level and I was all smiles.

After all the months I ran from Ryan's affection, I never knew things could be so perfect with him. I didn't believe anyone could love me like Todd could or give me the life I once share with him. But this week with Ryan further solidified the fact that what Todd and I had was once love but the kind of love that was built on a youthful foundation. My relationship with Ryan was all adult.

Decisions were made with well-informed and experienced minds rather than blinded eyes and opened noses. One would ask, "How could you love one man, but be with others intimately?" I knew in my heart I loved Ryan. Admitting it was another story. I tried to run far away from what he wanted to give me. I knew what he was capable of, but I didn't want to ever be in love with someone and end up crushed again. I didn't think I could give him what he deserved. I had to realize that I simply could not run from life. And life is too short to keep running from the unknown.

I love my boo, and truly believes that he loves me, so I plan to give this relationship all I've got. I'll have to see where it takes me.

"A penny for your thoughts." Ryan chimed.
I grinned. Snapping out of my trance.
"I'd be rich."
We smiled. He took my hand in his.
"I want to thank you."
"What did I do baby?"
"You gave me the most beautiful little girl a man could ever wish for."
"Is she beautiful because she looks like you?" I asked with a smile.
"Well…yeah. But…" We laughed as he pulled me close. "She also has a lot of her mother in her. You are the most beautiful woman I've ever seen; inside and out." He kissed the tip of my nose. "Well, that's when you aint on that hood shit."
I smiled and kissed him.
"I can turn it on and turn it off at the drop of a dime though."

We laughed.

"No, but you're pretty hot yourself Mr. Mathers."

He smiled at me.

"The sky is beautiful. I could stay out here with you all night."

"The week has passed so fast. I wish we didn't have to return home."

"We have three very good reasons to return home tomorrow."

"Yeah, don't I know it."

We continued walking hand in hand along the beach. The night was gorgeous. The temperature was nice. The mood was right.

"There's a nice spot over near those rocks." Ryan pointed.

He led me by the hand as we climbed over the small rocks to a serene little spot located between two larger rocks. The spot was perfect for two lovers. The view of the water and night sky was magnificent. The moon was our friend. Its light gave us just enough to intensify the mood. Made it that much lovelier.

Ryan laid out the blanket and helped me to sit down. He sat behind me and pulled me back into his arms. Arms around my waist. Back of my head against his strong chest.

"Are you comfortable?"

"Your arms feel so good."

He kissed my neck.

"You smell delicious." He whispered in my ear.

"I am delicious."

"Don't I know it."

He kissed my earlobe.

"Please baby, you know the ears, the whispering is my weakness." I moved my head away from his. Tried to escape the pleasure.

"I know." He smiled but continued nibbling at my ear.

"Ryan do you believe in destiny?" I asked seriously; again moving my head away from his advances.

He stopped nibbling to answer. "Yes, I believe in fate."

"I believe that there are some things that cannot be avoided, things that are just meant to be."

"Do you think we were destined to be together?"

"I don't know baby. I do know that I'd prayed for a woman like you. A woman with your qualities, intelligence, personality, your heart, your drive. After seeing how some women present themselves to brothas these days, I knew I could never respect the kind of woman that I often came into contact with. I wanted someone who I could love and trust, share with, experience with, and grow old with. I always promise myself that if I found her I would love and respect her to the fullest and make her my queen. And God has given me what I've prayed for."

"I'm more blessed to have you in my life. I never thought I could love so hard again. I thought it was utterly impossible. At one point, I didn't want to. I wanted to go about relationships like some men did. Moving from one to the next; loving no one. I thought that would make me complete. I fought with my heart over what was true and what was right. I denied the things my mind told me. We were apart and I thought I could live without you and that I didn't need you in my life. I probably could have but that life would have been a lie. I would have never been fulfilled without you."

"Looking back, trying to make a relationship with someone I didn't really love was a terrible call on my part. I wouldn't have been faithful to her."

"How do you know that?"

"I would have found my way back to you."

"What makes you think I would have accepted you being a married man?"

He kissed my earlobe and whispered, "I think you know why."

I grinned. *Yes indeed. I don't do married men, but who knows.* I thought.

"Stop it…you are bad."

"I know, but you like it."

He bit my neck.

We laughed.

"Seriously, we don't need to worry about any of that because baby I want this to last forever. I want you to love me every day of your life because I'll be right there by your side loving you."

Stroking the length of my arm, he kissed my shoulder and said, "You have my heart wide open. No other man alive can say they've loved you the way I do. I wish you could see inside my heart. It has your name and face all over it. All I want is you; all to myself."

"You have me. I aint going nowhere."

"No baby." He whispered while placing soft kisses up and down my neck. He hugged me tighter. Brought me even closer to his warm body.

"You don't understand. You're my heart and soul. There's no way I can survive without us being one. I don't want to. I need you Krisha. I need you in my life forever...I want you to be my wife." He whispered.

My heart skipped two beats. *Did I hear him correctly?* I thought.

Ryan continued. "Will you be my wife?" He whispered.

As I looked up at the stars in the night sky, a sweet calmness covered me. And there was peace. There was truth. There was a sense of hope and I saw a brighter day. A melody danced in my head. I saw a new life. A new way to love. A new way to see. A new beginning a new me. A happy us a lovely we. A promising future for us to see. I saw it all in the night sky.

As Ryan turned my body around to face him, the tears began to fall one by one. I'd cried so much, too much over the last couple years. I was tired of crying. Ready to dry my tears. I held my head down as I stared at the colorless sand.

Ryan tilted my chin up with his finger so I could look into his eyes. Kissed me softly. "Say you'll be my wife." He said while looking into my eyes.

Then surprisingly he opened a little black velvet box that came from behind his back. Inside was a diamond that sparkled with the stars. This diamond was serious. This diamond meant that it was gonna be big and meant it was gonna shine; along with the rest of its friends. It was definitely on point. I was absolutely stunned. Not by the size of the diamond. But by the proposal altogether.

Ryan searched my wet eyes for acceptance. I turned completely around to kneel before him. Arms around his neck. My lips slowly moved toward his. I kissed him with a sincere passion. A yearning that made my heart skip a beat or two. The touches of his soft lips made my heart melt. The softness of his tongue and warmth of his mouth made me want to stay with him for eternity.

The vibe was strong. There was an internal magnet that drew us as one. I couldn't turn back if I wanted to.

"Krisha will you marry me?" He looked into my eyes. Nibbled my chin.

"Yes. Baby yes. I would love to be your wife." I whispered softly.

He pulled me to his steel chest. The kiss became more intense.

"I'll do my best at making you happy."

"You've already made me the happiest woman alive."

Ryan gently picked up my left hand and slid the glistening rock onto my finger. Kissing my hand and ring finger, he said, "Forever baby. This is forever."

Too stunned to speak. I smiled.

Caressing my body while planting soft kisses in my chest. His arms surrounding my waist. Eyes deep into mine. Lips softly on my bare chest, softly touching my breast.

"If this is a dream, don't wake me." I said as I gasped for air to enter my lungs.

"No dream. This is how much I love you." Ryan pulled me into his arms and made magic with his mouth against mine. He laid me back onto the blanket and covered my body with his. Caressed my thighs under the thin white linen skirt I wore as he continued to profess his love for me.

"I wanna make love to you."

My head was spinning. At this point, I felt safe. I felt assured that everything was going to be alright with me. With us.

"C'mon baby lets go."

Ryan kept his pace with the kisses.

"Let's go back to our suite. I have something to show you."

He paused, looked into my eyes and smiled.

"I can't wait to see what that is."

He helped me up and folded the blanket. Before leaving, we stood embracing each other in that spot. The spot where I promised to become Mrs. Ryan Mathers. The spot I'll never forget and will always treasure in my heart. We held each other and looked up into the sky for confirmation. The sky was still as we were surrounded with tranquility. As we watched the star lit night, we saw a shooting star.

"Sweetheart, did you see that?" I asked.

"Yes. That means my wish has been granted. Our relationship is blessed."

We walked hand in hand along the beach to our suite. When we reached our room, we showered together. Ryan left the bathroom to dry off and dress. I remained to dress for my surprise.

When I exited the bathroom, Ryan was seated on the bed. He reached for my hand. "Let's pray together baby."

I looked at him in disbelief. This man never ceases to amaze me. He was definitely a man wise beyond his years. A man with morals. A man filled with a lot of love to give. I prayed, but I never made it a habit or consistent thing to do. Hell, I hadn't even been to church in a couple of years, eventhough I was raised in church every Sunday. Bible study and vacation bible school too.

"I want us to pray together as a family on the regular." He added.

I didn't offer a confirmation. I just knelt with him as he began to pray. My boo prayed a prayer that was soul altering. He prayed for me, the kids, his family, the world, life as it is, our health, our strength and our family. I was moved and brought to tears again. This time I thought about my mother. How she would have been displeased with my actions and behavior after her death. It's almost as if her death was a signal for me to go to acting a fool. I wasn't worried about respecting anyone. I didn't worry about being ashamed of my behavior; having to answer to anyone for my actions. My mother was gone. I didn't have to be the good girl that I'd always portrayed for her. I didn't have to worry about being chastised or dug into for doing wrong. My mother was gone. So I did what the hell I wanted to do.

I acted on impulse a lot. Didn't think, just did the damn thang. Now I'm regretful. I'm ashamed of the person I'd become. With no one to put me back in line, I did it. I had Mia, but hell sometimes we did dirt together.

At over thirty years old, I still need her. Still needed guidance. One thing is for sure, you're never too old to learn. I knew full well no matter where I was raised; I was not raised to act the way I'd been in the last several months before my pregnancy. Always humble and conservative. I'd let hurt and bitterness transform me into someone who was open and daring. Those actions almost cost a dear friend her life.

I thought about all the blessings that had been bestowed upon me, and the number of times I'd said "Thank you Lord" for all he'd done those were not many. At one time I was grateful, and then I became deserving. As if someone owed me something. For my actions, I cannot blame Todd and the things he put me through. I can use that as an excuse to live reckless all the days of my life as long as I had something to hide behind, if I chose to. I cannot blame my poor judgment on the fact that I'd lost my mother who was my strength, my guide, a part of me. She'd always taught me good things. Taught me to be good. Taught me to be a strong black woman and to make wise decisions on my own. "Never let anyone dictate your next step." She'd always say to me. Now thinking about it, that's exactly what I'd been doing. Not being myself. Not living my life. If I'd been the daughter my mother had raised me to be, I probably wouldn't have been pregnant, not knowing the father at the time. It's so easy to get into trouble, but the consequences are hard to swallow.

I realized my relationship with Ryan turned out wonderful in the end, but I know I cannot take any credit for securing such a loving man. God knew I needed him in my life. He's begun guiding me in the right directions already. I needed to be led back to God, as I'd been astray for a long time. He sent Ryan to me in his young age. I would have never really been interested in him for that reason alone. Religion, marriage, respect, humbleness, humility, self-preservation, all aspects of my life that I'd put so far behind me. My motto these days was "its whateva."

When we finished praying, we crawled into bed. Ryan dried my tears with his kisses. Held me in his arms. We caressed each other to sleep. I'd forgotten about the sexy outfit I wore. None of that mattered anymore. Our relationship was on a new level. Being in his arms was good enough.

26

"So when do you want to set the date?" Ryan asked as we shared breakfast at my home.

I hadn't mentioned setting a date. I wanted to see where his mind was with that. It took him three days after proposing to bring it up. I think maybe he was being precautious; didn't want to rush me.

"I don't know what do you think? We'll have to consider your schedule."

"How about next spring, or as soon as the season ends for me? I really don't want to wait almost a whole year. Why don't we just get married in Vegas?"

"Is that what you want? Remember this is your first marriage, so it should be like you want it to be. It should be special to you."

"So are you saying it doesn't have to be special to you because it's your second marriage?"

"It'll definitely be special baby as long as you're there." I said then blew a kiss at him.

"Take it easy mama. I came over here for breakfast, not breakfast, lunch, and dinner." He grinned.

"Since you proposed you haven't touched me. What's up with that?"

"Actually, I haven't touched you since the day before I proposed. Believe me I know. I just wanted our engagement to start out on a different note. I didn't want my decision to be based on sex. I did want to seal the proposal by making love to you, but it took a different turn; which was all good. But I felt if I could hold out after I proposed then I was marrying you for the person you are not for how you whip that thang on me." He grinned.

"Cut it out, okay." I smiled. I went over to where he was sitting across the table from me and straddled his lap.

"You know what Mr. Mathers. I really respect that. That makes me love you even more. I always knew you were special and had a place in my heart. I just didn't know the degree to which that was possible. I know it was never just the physical attraction between us. I cared deeply for you before we even touched. You were just so different, and just being in your life is all I need." I kissed his lips. "But right now after five days with your sexy behind around and all the romance that has been going on between us, I need all this." I grinned seductively as my hands roamed his lower region.

"You're a bad girl Krisha."

"As you told me, 'but you like it don't you?'"

"I love it."

We finished off breakfast pretty good.

We stayed in that chair at the kitchen table and I worked him into a coma. I found very creative ways to use that chair and his sitting position; weakened him in a good way.

After my several performances, we were both two happy and worn out lovers; we slept like champs. It would have been some of the best sleep in the world if the baby hadn't awakened. I love my little baby, but I couldn't start all over and do the pregnancy thing again. I guess Ryan and I need to have that talk.

27

With the help of an event planner, Mia and I planned my engagement party within six weeks. The only thing Ryan wanted to have say in was the music. He said he wanted to make sure his special songs were played. I was cool with that.

Ryan wanted to announce our engagement to the world so he allowed a select number of photographers to cover our celebration. I was nervous about the party because I'd never experienced publicity of this magnitude. I would have much rather it been a low-key engagement and marriage.

My kids ended up telling Todd about my engagement before I had a chance to tell him. He came to my office the next day to ask why I didn't tell him myself. He definitely wasn't happy and has been in a foul mood every since. He even told me that hell would freeze over before he allowed his kids to leave the state if I was planning to move. I ignored Todd and decided I'd cross that bridge when I got to it if need be.

On the day of our engagement party, Ryan sent a car over to get me from the house. When the driver knocked on the door, I looked out at the stretch Escalade and smiled to myself. This man was amazing. He'd already hired a stylist and set me up for a day of pampering today. He'd arranged for his family to take all three of the kids on yesterday so I had an amazing and carefree day today. He was acting as if we were getting married today instead of going to the engagement party. Anyway, I'm sure my night would be even better than my day.

As we settled into the limo, Mia said, "Now I could get used to this."

I gave a half smile.

"Okay girl. What is it?"

"Nothing Mia."

"Do you sometimes forget that I know you better than you know yourself? Tell me what's wrong. You've been quiet for the last couple hours. Are you having second thoughts? Because if you are I'm about to slap you back into reality."

I smiled.

"No, it's not that."

"What is it then?"

"I just wanna be happy Mia. I don't need all this. I just want Ryan and me to have a good life together."

"Krisha, do me a favor."

"Yes."

"Accept what God has blessed you with. Allow someone to do something for you for a change. Let Ryan love you and shower you the best way he knows how. There's nothing wrong with that. This is his lifestyle and he wants to share it with you."

"It's just hard to believe Mia."

"Why is that?"

Silence.

"You deserve everything he's doing for you and more. He knows that. That's why he's doing it. Just sit back and let it happen. You're not asking him for anything. He wants it like this because he loves you."

"I love him so much Mia." I said with a trembling in my voice.

"I know you do." She hugged me. "Don't you dare cry. You're gonna make me cry, then we'll both ruin our makeup."

I managed to hold back the tears.

When we got to Ryan's condo to pick him up, a couple guys were standing outside talking. One guy went to get Ryan.

"I believe I done died and went to heaven." Mia said.

I laughed.

"Who was that?"

"I don't know. I've never met him." I said.

"Yes indeed. I sure would like to get to know him."

"Mia stop now. I thought you were a changed woman." I joked knowing good and well that was a lie.

"I am, but we're celebrating tonight. It's all in fun."

"Uh huh. I guess so." I said smiling but not convinced.

Ryan and two other guys who turned out to be his teammates climbed into the limo.

My man was fine in his suit as were his counterparts. Truth be told they had nothing on my baby. I'd never seen Mia so quiet around men. She didn't say much all the way to the hotel. I think she was trying to figure out which one she wanted to flirt with.

We sipped champagne and engaged in idol chat the entire ride there. When we arrived, I was taken aback at all the cars that surrounded the hotel. The hotel was normally always busy playing host to various events being that it was one of the most prestigious hotels in the city with a grand ballroom.

Our engagement party was invitation only and we'd only invited sixty guests, which were our closest friends and family. So I was sure something else had to be going on tonight.

As soon as the limo stopped, security came up to advise us to follow him around a side entrance as the lobby was filled with reporters, photographers, groupies and on lookers. Everyone wanted a shot at this year's Super Bowl MVP and his fiancé. Not to mention his friends and teammates too.

We pulled around the side of the building and were let in by another security guard. We whisked our way through to the back of the ballroom. Mia and others entered and alerted the coordinator that we'd arrived. We made a grand entrance and were then seated. I was announced by my maiden name per Ryan's request. It had been so long since I'd used Monroe until it sounded so weird. This was something I thought was so minor. Didn't think it would be a big damn deal; to Ryan it was.

Ryan announced our engagement to our guests and also the wedding date but stated it would be in an undisclosed location. I'd decided that I wanted to get married on the beach in Hawaii in the same spot by the rocks where my baby proposed to me. Ryan agreed that we would fly our closest family members and friends, which would not be alot for me, down for the wedding.

Ryan shared candidly with guests about his love for me and how he'd found his soul mate. We shared a toast with our family and friends. I was beaming inside and out. Then the DJ announced that the first two songs were songs chosen by Ryan and were dedicated to me. He loved some Babyface so I already knew at least one song had to be by him.

I was led to the middle of the dance floor. When the music started, I almost cried. The song being played was "Spend My Life with You" by Eric Benet and Tamia. We danced slow and exchanged gazes the entire song.

When the song ended, I wasn't ready to let my baby go. I anxiously awaited the second song. Then I heard one of my favorites of all time come blaring through the speakers. I smiled at him and embraced him tightly when I heard "Sunshine" by Babyface. We kissed and I stayed in his arms the entire song.

At the end of that song, everyone else got their dance on while we greeted and thanked people for attending, posed for photos, and mingled.

As I moved about the room, hand in hand with Ryan, I noticed a familiar face standing a distance away. Eyes glued to the spot where we stood. As we moved closer, I put the face with a name as I recalled it in my long-term memory. We got closer to that side of the room so she began to move toward us.

"Ryan, who invited her?" I looked up at him as we stood in place.

"Who baby?"

He turned to look in the direction of my gaze.

It was Ms. It prancing her way toward us.

"I...I don't know." He stumbled.

I looked at him.

"Someone had to, she's in here."

"It's cool babe." He kissed my cheek. "C'mon." He tried to lead me in the other direction toward other guests, but she caught up to us.

"My, my. You two look so lovely together." She said sarcastically but honestly.

"Thank you." We said in unison.

"Congratulations Krisha."

She leaned in to hug me; gave me one of those fake bitch hugs.

"Thank you." I replied with a smile.

"You have my best wishes Ryan." She hugged him and kissed his cheek.

Sister girl just didn't know me. But this was neither the right time nor place so I let it ride and played along with her.

"Thanks." Ryan said.

"You've got yourself a real good man Krisha. Take care of him for me."

For her? Who does this heffa think she is? I thought.

"I'm taking real good care of him darlin' no need to worry."

Ryan interjected.

"Thanks for coming Diamond." He shot out as he led me away from her.

Then he made an abrupt stop and turned around to her.

"By the way, who invited you here?"

"Oh! I'm sorry, is there a problem? Reggie couldn't make it so I came as Felicia's guest." She said with a smirk.

Later I found out that Reggie was another of Ryan's teammates and Felicia was his girlfriend. I was gonna have to make a mental note to steer clear of Ms. Felicia; sounded like trouble.

"No problem. Enjoy yourself." Ryan told her.

When we walked away, Ryan said, "Now why would Felicia bring her here? Wait until I talk to Reggie. Her ass will soon be history."

"C'mon lets go dance. Forget her. Let her suffer." I said.

If she wants to see us together, let her look. She'll definitely get an eye full. There's no way in hell I would go to an engagement party of a man who was engaged to me just a few months ago. That has got to hurt.

We danced a while with Mia and other friends before we got ready to wind everything up. I didn't see much of Mia all night. She was enjoying the company of Aaron, Ryan's teammate who rode with us in the limo.

When the food, drinks and guests were almost gone, then I decided I was hungry. Caught up in all the excitement of the night, I didn't want to eat; just wasn't hungry then. Now I was starving.

"What do you want to eat baby? I'm sure they can still get you something."

"I don't know. It's a shame. There was so much food here tonight."

"That's okay we aint about to go home anyway. Whatever you want, you can have. Want a steak from Ruth Chris' or something?"

"I want something fun. I think I want a big nasty burger from Ms. Ida's." I wasn't in the mood for 'real' food.

Ms. Ida's was a soul food shack located in the hood that stayed open until 4:00 am basically to cater to all the club goers. She had the biggest burgers and pork chops I'd ever seen.

"Ooooo that sounds good." Ryan said.

"We can share."

Ryan got excited. "Let's go."

We rounded up our crew that came with us, in addition to a couple more of Ryan's friends and their dates. Mia and Aaron were a bit chummy. But I didn't comment. I simply watched my friend get her flirt on like she does so well.

We rode by Ms. Ida's. Ryan ordered food for everyone.

Aaron treated. It was still early, only 10:30 pm, so we set out for New Orleans to see what was on and poppin'.

We had a good time inside the limo drinking, dancing, and clowning around. When we arrived in New Orleans, we hit Bourbon Street and the French Quarters then ended up at a club off Tchoupitoulas. We had a blast.

I was tipsy and my dogs were barking. After all the moving and dancing we were all hungry again. We stopped off at a convenience store off Veterans for junk food before we hit I-10 back home.

A limo at a convenience store in New Orleans at 3:30 am made the few people who were out pay attention. Two young ladies recognized Ryan and Chad and started acting a fool. We sat inside the limo looking and shaking our heads. They had to sign a few autographs and take a few pictures with cell phones after their other girl friends hopped out the SUV. We headed out of the N.O. around 4 am. Talk about exhausted.

We all talked and shared for a minute on the way back then halfway back everyone else was lying over on his or her mate's snoring.

"I'm going home with you. The guys are staying at my place…I'm taking a nap."

"Okay baby."

He laid his head down against my thighs, so I laid my head back to take a quick nap too.

At Ryan's condo he woke up to let the guys in, then stood outside and conversed for a minute before going inside.

However, Aaron got back inside the limo with Mia. So I got out to see what was up with that.

"Where's Aaron going Ryan?"

"With Mia."

I looked at him in disbelief. So he repeated it.

"He said he was going home with Mia."

Mia had had too much to drink and was lying down inside the limo.

"Does she know it?"

"I guess so Krisha. He's cool."

"Let me use your phone."

He dug into his pocket and handed the phone to me. I wanted to know what was up with that.

"Can I go to your truck for a minute?" I asked Ryan.

"My truck? For what?"

"I need a little privacy."

"Okay." He popped the locks on the truck. I went to the passenger side as if I were looking for something then dialed Mia's cell.

"Hello." She said groggily.

"Turn your sound down." I said.

"What?" She said.

"Are you taking Aaron home with you?"

"Yeah."

"Why?"

"Not the reason you think."

"Do you think that's a wise move?"

"I don't know…it's cool. I'm straight."

"Are you sure? I don't know Mia. You don't know him."

"It's cool. I'll talk to you."

"Okay. Call us if you need to."

"Bye."

I got back inside the limo as if I hadn't just spoken with Mia on the cell. We dropped her and Aaron off and returned to my house.

Ryan fell asleep ready to roll across the bed. It was approaching daylight so I showered and dressed for bed. I figured I might as well go the extra mile so that I could sleep comfortably. Staying awake a few more minutes wasn't gonna hurt. I missed my babies something terrible. But I managed to get into bed and sleep as they would; with no worries or concerns.

28

The next couple of months passed so fast and it was time for Ryan to go back to Baltimore. He would be leaving in the next two days.

Ryan climbed back into bed beside me.

"We're staying in this room until tomorrow morning. We're gonna have to order room service or something. But I'm not leaving this room."

We'd been in Belize for a week and we were leaving tomorrow morning. Ryan would go pack and catch a flight back to Baltimore the next day.

"That's okay baby. As long as you keep filling me up, I won't be hungry anyway." I said then smiled.

"You're absolutely too much."

"I just love me some you that's all."

"Why don't you come with me?" He asked.

"To Baltimore?"

"Yeah. Come go with me. You can stay the remainder of the summer."

"That would be lovely, but me and my kids can't live in that apartment with Jace and his women. Did you forget I have children?"

"No I didn't."

"I couldn't impose like that. That's not my style."

"Well. Tell you what. Leave the kids, come with me and we'll start looking for a house to buy. We can buy a house as soon as you want to."

"A house?"

"I never bought one because I didn't want to be in a big house alone. But it's time we start looking anyway."

Silence.

"You do plan to move with me when we get married right?"

"Yes. I guess…I just can't up and go right now."

"What do you mean just up and go? We've been engaged four months now. You should be getting things in order to move."

"Ryan I'm not gonna start withholding anything from you. But I don't want you to get involved."

"Involved with what? What are you talking about?"

"Todd told me he wouldn't let the boys come if I decided to move."

"Aren't you the custodial parent?"

"We share joint custody."

"So does that mean he dictates your life?"

"Of course not." I said.

"Then what do you plan to do about this?"

"Not sure yet."

Sitting up in the bed, he said, "Krisha just when were you gonna do something about it. Were you hoping I wouldn't want you to move with me?"

"Not at all. I'm just confused…I mean I can understand where Todd's coming from. They love him to death and he loves them. Despite his dog ways, we were always a tight family. I wouldn't want him taking them far away from me either."

"Krisha don't be so naïve to think it's all about the kids leaving. I think it may be about you more than them."

"I don't think so."

"I know he still loves you Krisha. And you love him too."

"Honestly Ryan. I'll always love him because he's the father of my children and because we have so much history. But don't confuse that with being *in love*. That I am not. And haven't been for a long time now. I'm in love with you and only you."

"Come here." Ryan pulled me into his arms. "It'll be okay. He'll come around."

"I sure hope so." I snuggled into his chest. "Ryan, how do you know Todd still loves me?"

"Krisha when God made you he broke the mold baby. You are so easy to love. What man wouldn't love you if they had the chance? You're everything a man could dream of. Furthermore, he messed up big time and he knows it. So he's regretting it all right about now. He'll always love you, trust." He kissed my forehead. "But he'd better stay in his place now. He had his chance. You belong to me now." He threw the covers over his head and went under.

"Well say that then!" I screamed while laughing.

29

Call me stupid but, *no*, I did not go with him back to Baltimore. Nor have I seen him in three months. I talk to him every day and I've been searching for houses by Internet and through business associates in Baltimore. I still haven't found anything that really suits me. I did promise Ryan I would come in a couple weeks to check out a house that he found and catch his game.

The wedding would take place in five months. Time was rolling by so fast. I'd decided that today would be the day to talk to Todd about our moving to Maryland. I'd put it off long enough. I needed to make some decisions with my business also; however, I'd been stalling on all of those things. I think the closer the time got to the wedding the more I didn't want to leave. I was a dirty south chick for life, and I never saw myself leaving. But I know my husband would want me with him, so I had to do what I had to do. I arranged to meet Todd at his home immediately after work.

When I arrived at Todd's house he led me to the patio where he poured both of us a drink. I didn't bother asking what it was. I needed whatever it was to calm my nerves. I anticipated Todd opposing my move.

"Todd as you already know there are some things we need to discuss."

"You mentioned it was important. Neither of my shorties are sick huh?"

"No. Nothing like that."

"Thank God. So what is it boo?" Looking deep into my eyes in a stare. "And did I mention how beautiful you look today?"

"Thanks Todd, but let's just keep to the subject okay."

"Sorry. Go on." He poured himself another drink.

Bluntly I said, "Todd, do you realize I'm getting married in five months?"

"Yeah, so." He said with much attitude.

"I need your consent to move our children to Maryland with me."

He looked up from his glass to stare at me in what looked like disbelief.

"Krisha, I told you that you weren't taking my children away from me."

"I'm not taking them away from you. I'm just moving to be with my husband."

"Yeah clear across the country."

"Let's be realistic."

"Realistic my ass. If you wanna go play house with that young buck go ahead. My boys are staying here with me."

"You can see them whenever you'd like to. Just like you do now. But they need to come with me."

"Why do they *need* to come with you? They *need* their father. And have you even asked them if they want to move away from me?"

"They do wanna go Todd."

"Do they realize they'll be many miles away from me? I bet you didn't tell them that did you Krisha?"

"Todd please. Try and understand. I love Ryan and I'm marrying him. I need to be with him; me *and* my children."

"Are you crazy?" He stared me down. "They are my boys. They need to be with their *own* father. Remember they are my children too."

"Duh! I know that. I was there remember?"

He stared at me before taking a sip of his drink. I'm sure that sip was to calm down. If looks could kill I'da been dead minutes ago.

Silence filled the room.

Nervously I proceeded.

"Look Todd. I'll send them to you whenever you want them and whenever they want to come. We'll be here in Louisiana often. I'm keeping my house so we'll be here the entire summers."

"Eventually that'll change. That boy will not raise my children! Not as long as I'm breathing!" He screamed.

"Boy? Does it matter who it is Todd? Or is it just the fact that it's somebody other than you?"

"No it doesn't matter who it is. I don't give a damn who it is. I am willing and capable of raising my own sons. Why can't you understand that? These are my sons Krisha." He stared me down. "And this isn't about you, if that's what you're trying to say."

"Are you sure?"

Silence. He didn't respond. Turned his back and walked away.

Then he spoke with his back turned.

"Look all I ask is that you leave them here with me. I'll take care of them. I'll send them to *you* for holidays and vacations."

"Todd they're my babies." I said at the thought of being without my sons.

"And they're mine too Krisha!" He shouted as he turned to face me.

"You're being ridiculous!" I yelled.

"And you're being selfish!" He screamed.

This had turned into a shouting match. And I hated those. By now I was mad and hurt.

My head began to pound and my eyes hurt badly. I felt tears beating my lids.

Feeling defeated, I lowered my voice.

"What do you expect me to do then Todd? Not get married? Not go live with my husband? Just abandon my kids? What? Please tell me?" I wiped a tear from my cheek.

He'd lowered his voice. Looked at me sincerely. "You really want me to answer that?"

I looked up at him. Tears filling my eyes. I was trying my best to fight them. I hate showing weakness. But they were going to win.

"Yes." I said softly as I searched his eyes for an answer.

"I just told you." He said in a low tone. "You go. Let him take care of his. I'll take care of mine. I'm a man Krisha. A man who loves his sons. I don't want another man raising my children. Showing them things I can very well show them. Teaching them the things that I should be teaching them. I want to be a part of their lives; teach them how to be responsible men. I want to continue to take my kids to little league, I don't need him doing that."

"That's not fair Todd." I wiped my face.

"Fair...Fair...Who are you to talk about fair? You want everything your fucking way Krisha!" He began to rant. "You're just a big, spoiled grown ass woman. Always have been."

He'd gotten loud again. He was just as emotional as me. But he had a defense up. And this is the way he chose to handle things.

"I didn't curse you Todd and I don't appreciate the insults. Please don't go there. I didn't come here for this. Ryan and I will take good ..."

"Fuck that!" He jumped up from his seat. Stood over me. "What don't you understand? He can't do shit for me!"

"Todd..."

"No! Hell no and I will fight you if you try. Now that's final."

I looked at him in disbelief as the tears fell freely. I rarely saw him this upset. But I *had* seen it before. Remembering the night he took me from my house, I got a new found respect for his ass, so I decided to let it go for now. I jumped up from the table and turned to run back to my car. I had to get out of there.

"Krisha wait." He called as he grabbed my arm and spun me around.

By now I was crying crocodile tears. I snatched away from him. He grabbed me again. This time pulling me into his chest and embracing me tightly.

"I'm sorry." He said while wiping my face with his free hand. "Are you really gonna do it? You're really gonna marry him?"

Unable to speak, I nodded my head while my head lay against his chest.

"Don't marry him Krisha. Please."

I raised my head and looked up at Todd.

"Don't do this to me." I dragged.

He snuggled me in closer as his chin rested on top of my head.

"I can't let you go. I love you more than I love my own life."

"No!" I screamed through tears while trying to break free from his grip.

He held me tightly against his hard chest.

"I can't let go baby. I just can't."

"Stop it please!" I screamed while attempting to wiggle out of his arms. Arms too strong. Grip on my waist tight.

"Say you love me. Say you won't marry him. I'm so sorry for everything…"

We'd been here several times before. He just didn't get it.

"Todd no!" I cried. "I love him."

"He could never love you like I do."

"So it *is* about me?" I asked looking up at him.

"I don't wanna lose my kids, nor do I wanna lose you. Knowing you're still here is how I survive. I can't have you, but I can still see your beautiful face. If you marry him and leave me, I can't live anymore."

"Don't say that."

"I've loved you since I was twenty-two years old. I don't want nobody else. I can't live without you in my life."

"You're asking me to not be happy…who's being selfish now?"

I tore away and made a dash for the front door. As soon as I opened the front door, it was closed right back. I thought to myself, *Lord not again. This fool gon' kill me.*

I faced the closed door. My back to him. Forehead against the door. Afraid to turn around.

I begged softly, "Please. Let me go." I meant that in more ways than one.

"Tell me you no longer love me."

"Just leave it alone, please." I cried. "You already told me what I needed to do."

"Tell me you don't love me."

I turned around to look him in his eyes.

I saw fear of him losing his first love. The same fear I once had. I saw uncertainty in his eyes along with hope and anticipation.

"Please don't leave me Krisha." He begged softly.

"You left me a long time ago."

"I've never left you. You've been right here." He took my hand in his and gently laid it upon his chest over his heart. "I've carried you in my heart all this time. I could never leave. You don't know how many nights I've gone to bed with you on my mind only to wake up with you still there; with the regret, the shame of my actions. I wish I could take it all back. I never would have done it baby. I've been to hell and back mentally trying to pretend I was okay with your relationship, but it hurts me to see you with someone else...and to marry him. I can't stand by and let that happen. I love you so much."

Todd cupped my face with his hand. Pressed his lips to mine.

"Don't you think I hurt too? My best friend Todd. I still can't get over that." I said in a whisper.

"I can't take that hurt back. No matter how much I try. I can only make it better. You're my wife. The one and only. You will always be my wife." He kissed me again.

My mind was in disarray. Whirling somewhere around five hundred miles per minute. But I still wasn't coming up with an answer to the confusion I faced. Instead I found myself succumbing.

Todd spoke softly as he kissed my face and lips. He shed tears right along with me. Sympathy tears that I'd seen many times before. I was oblivious to that fact as well as our past. I only saw my heart opening once again for Todd Taylor.

I gave in and kissed him back. His hand caressed my back while the other tenderly touched my neck.

Somehow I found enough good sense to say, "Todd, you'll always be in my heart, but I'm in love with Ryan."

"I know you're confused. I hurt you bad and you can't see past that. I'll never forgive myself for what I did. That's why I'll never marry another woman. If I can't have you, I don't want to live."

"Please stop saying that Todd."

"I mean every word. We're soul mates. We'll always find our way back to each other. You're a part of me. Don't you believe that?"

He held my face in his hands as he spoke. The crocodile tears had started again. He took his time and kissed away the tears.

"I can't take this." I shook my head.

"He's a man just like me. He'll make mistakes too…Just let me make it up to you. I've learned my lesson. Give me another chance. Don't throw our love away Krisha. What we have is forever. I want to grow old with my wife."

Our lips met again. He rocked me from side to side in his arms as we stood in his living room.

"I just need you to be able to trust me."

I cried hard. I wanted that so much. At one time, I would have killed for him to say those words. I always wanted my husband. Never, ever wanted any other man. Now, I just can't go back. I just can't go backwards and open myself up to be hurt again.

I opened my mouth to say those words. Somehow my words had their own agenda.

"I love you Todd." I embraced him. "It still hurts." My embrace grew stronger. "Oh my God! I love you." I cried staring into his eyes.

"I know you do, my love. I'm so sorry. I'm so sorry. Let this be the end of it all." He kissed me harder; held me closer.

"I'm so sorry." He continued to repeat as he kissed me.

The soft touch of his lips on my face stirred me. A spontaneous trail down to my chest in search of my breasts made me forget about our past.

"You don't know how much I adore you." His hands roamed my shivering body. My back against the front door; middle united with his.

He looked down at my body as his hands gripped my waist. Realizing that things had taken a turn, he backed away.

"I'm sorry. I…I didn't mean to disrespect you."

He backed up and went to sit on the sofa.

I dried my eyes and watched him from the door as he sat with his head in his hands.

After a few awkward seconds, I walked over to him and kneeled in front of him. Removed the hands that covered his face to look into his eyes. When he looked down at me, I kissed him. He embraced me. We stayed there for a moment. Marinated in each other.

The intensity in the room took me to another level. I was succumbing to a feeling of closeness and I needed to be with the man that I'd promised to love until death forced us apart.

I moved up from the floor in a manner in which I had no business reliving with my ex-husband; a seductive glide to a standing position.

He raised my skirt to thigh level as I straddled him on the sofa. Blood rushed to that part of him that had allowed me to leave my mind stranded on several occasions. Laid my head against his shoulder for a while. Wanted to feel his heartbeat.

I knew that beat. Mine beat for it. Same rhythm. Same intensity.

"Krisha, I…"

I silenced him by placing my mouth onto his; allowed my lips to stay there. Just to share the same breath.

Todd was an irresistible man. Regardless of the dog he was, I was in control. I knew what I wanted; what I needed to do.

I used the closeness of our bodies, the exchange of life as a mental indication that I would live my life without resentment. I would allow him to live at peace and forgive him for causing the skips of my heartbeat.

In an expression of sincerity and as an indication of forgiveness, I used my lips to show him.

As my lips came in contact with the delicacy of his skin, an overwhelming sense of entitlement filled my mind. I moved down to love his lean neck, lower to taste the sweetness from his chocolate drops. His breathing strengthened as did mine.

I began unbuckling his belt.

"Are you sure Krisha?" He asked.

I didn't even bother answering or looking at him. No, I wasn't sure. But emotions had taken over and I wanted to love him. Just one last time.

I made love to him like it was truly our last time. Every move was well thought out and meant to be. Our lovemaking was so intense; so much passion.

When he cried, I cried.

"I love you girl." I heard him cry out.

My arms around his neck. His around my waist. Bodies moving with the same rhythm. The hurt and memories came once again. I was overwhelmed. Full. I burst out in pain, confusion, and ecstasy.

I collapsed over onto Todd. My breath covering his face as he held me into place.

"You were my life." I whispered. Mumbling against his skin.

"I know." He cried as he held my cheek to his. "I know baby."

Todd took my face into his hand. "I can only ask for your forgiveness and become a different person. And that I've already done. I've been saying "I'm sorry" for months, but it still doesn't take away your pain. Allow me to show you. If you never totally forgive me, I'll never live in peace. Please Krisha." He kissed me softly. "Please."

"I forgive you." I said softly.

We stayed in that position for a while to gather our emotions. There was really nothing else to say. I embraced him some more. Felt him responding to my kisses. Without giving me advance warning, Todd got up from the sofa with my legs and arms still wrapped around his body. He walked to his bedroom where he laid me down and finished undressing me. He went into the bathroom and came back with a wet towel. He wiped my body and cleaned away the fluids that he'd left behind. It was at that moment that I realized I'd made an even bigger mistake.

We hadn't used a condom.

Guess he read my mind because I know I had "the look" written all over my face.

"It's cool. I'm good."

"Are you sure?"

"Yes. I've been tested. Besides I haven't had sex in a few months."

Now I didn't believe that, but I did believe he was clean. He's always taken care of himself and I know he cared for me too much to put me at risk.

After cleaning me real good with the towel, Todd brought the whole package. He had years of experience at loving me; we meshed and that was all it was to it.

Regardless of it all, I was in love with Ryan. I knew I could never really see past the Kyra episode, but I'd always love Todd regardless of who came into my life. He would always be my first love. Who could possibly take his place?

We made love throughout the night and slept until the next morning. I awakened around seven am staring at the ceiling while Todd lay sleeping.

He was so beautiful on the outside with a heart of gold on the inside. Somewhere his judgment got twisted and he became blinded to who I was in his life and what I meant to him. Lost sight of what was truly important in his life. He had definitely made some awful moves in our marriage that cost him my heart and his loving family. I know now that he's regretful for his actions. My heart went out to him, but I can't do anything about the love I feel for Ryan. *Could I try to move past Todd's adversities? Is it possible for me to fall in love with him again?* I asked myself these questions as I watched the world turn by staring at the ceiling.

As I lay in thought, I dug deep into my heart for the truth. In all reality, I *was* still in love with him. I knew that as long as he wanted me, I would accept him. If I stayed away from Todd, I was fine. If he made no advances toward me, I was fine. It could be several months between us, but the minute he expressed love for me, I was gone. The moment he touched me, I was over. Mind, body, soul. Gone. Even if for one night.

I know it couldn't be like this if I were to marry Ryan. I couldn't end up in Todd's arms every time he cried out his love for me. I just had to make a decision. I had to finally end it; I had to move on. The problem was…I couldn't. I still just can't leave him alone.

30

An hour later, I showered threw on my wrinkled skirt and one of Todd's shirts. I was in a very slumber mood. I'd come here and accomplished nothing yesterday except getting into more hot water.

I didn't believe his position had changed concerning our children moving with me, and on top of that my cell rang half the night until I silenced it. I know it was Ryan along with Carmen. Good thing I didn't tell him I was having that talk with Todd. Only Carmen knew where I was.

I kissed Todd goodbye and went to gather my purse from the living room to leave. He had awakened but he didn't say anything. I think he understood my mood. When I got to the front door, I felt him approaching from behind.

"Just let me leave. Please." I said softly.

He reached out and hugged me from behind. Kissed my cheek and whispered "You can never love him like you love me. Stop fooling yourself. I'll always have your heart. Remember that."

I bolted out the door without looking back. I had to free myself from that hold. If I didn't, I'd never be able to move on.

Looking at my cell when I got inside my truck, my suspicions were confirmed. Ryan had called up until 3:00 am. Being that he had to get up at 5:00 am, I know he was mad. He'd stayed up calling me all night.

When I got home, Carmen had sent the boys to school and was feeding the baby. She was definitely my savior. The way I felt this morning, I didn't give a damn about nothing. My other suspicions were confirmed when Carmen advised that Ryan had called there all night.

Now really realizing the consequences of my actions, I started my tears again.

"Carmen." I called out. I dropped down in the chair next to her at the kitchen table. "What am I going to do?"

I laid my head down on the table and poured out nothing but tears. A full heart and a confused mind spelled nothing but disaster.

"I can't be everything to everybody. I'm just tired."

She rubbed my back and assured me all would be fine.

Carmen reminded me of my mother. She'd been in our lives every since Malik was born. She probably knew me better than I knew myself.

She saw a lot but said nothing. Carmen was forty-six years old. Had a grown son that she rarely ever saw. Mainly due to always being at my house helping me hold shit together. She was my family.

"Krisha I need to share some things with you?"

I nodded my head okay.

"I've sat back and watched you grow into a fine woman and a loving mother. I've followed you from house to house and been with you through it all for three reasons. I feel like now is as good a time as any to tell you what those reasons are."

I looked up at her pitifully. Anticipating what she was going to share.

"Reason one is that I love you and those babies. I love you like you are my own. You are a good-hearted woman who has seen some tough times. Hasn't always been treated fairly but you dealt with it like the woman your mother raised you to be. The second reason is that your mother told me to look after you for her. She'd always told me that from the first day I stepped foot in your house. She called me after you left her house that night. She told me she wasn't feeling well. And she made me promise that if anything should ever happen to her that I wouldn't leave you. She asked me to take care of you and those kids for her. She said that in time it would seem that everyone who you loved or who claimed to love you would disappear from your life. I promised her I'd never leave your side, and that I'd take care of her baby when she no longer could. She sheltered you from a lot of things in life. She knew you needed someone. And I'll do that for you Krisha. That's why I'm here. I'll do that for you and your mother."

By now I was sobbing like a wounded dog. Carmen wiped my face with a paper towel.

"It's okay baby. Don't upset yourself too bad now." She whispered. "You have to listen to me. I've got to get this out." She tilted my chin to look at her face.

"The next reason is that I...I'm your blood." I looked up from the table at Carmen who sat with tears streaming down her cheeks. The baby had gone to sleep in the high chair.

"I'm your daddy's sister. I don't know if it's the right time for you or not but I think it's necessary. I believe you're trying to fill a void left by your father. You're looking for a man to love you like your father should have. You don't know who to choose from because it feels so good to know that there are men who truly love you and who'll never leave you. You're looking for the man your father wasn't."

I didn't know what to say, so I listened.

"Let me explain some things you never knew. Your father wanted the world. He didn't want responsibility. He wanted your mother but he didn't know how to be a father. He became addicted to drugs and the environment he lived in. He didn't know how to better himself. All he wanted was what he had been taught and that was to live in the hood and engage in drugs and crime. He tried to live differently for a minute when he met your mother, but he soon fell off again. When you were a toddler, he…" She shed a tear as she shook her head. "He tried to trade you for a hit. Thank God the drug dealer had some decency. He knew and respected your mother, so he whipped your father's ass and brought you home. Your mother despised him from that day on. She had some guys from around the way whip his ass again real good for that. She didn't get the law involved. She handled it like we handled things in the hood. He was in the hospital a week behind that and almost lost his life. My family sided with him and was mad at her for what she did. They wanted to put a hit out on you and her, but your dad said no. He loved her. They figured they'd get rid of you too, because nobody was going to take care of you after she was gone. I was the only one who didn't side with them. Even my mother was down."

"So when your mother got her degree, she moved you out of the hood and away from my family. She even changed your last name to her maiden name. She didn't want you to ever know those type people; the people who wanted to end your life. Because they hated her, they hated you too. I came to see you for a while, but then I got caught up in my own life and stopped. But I always checked on you. I loved my little niece. You were so precious."

"Your mother just didn't ever want you to know. She didn't want you to know that your family, your own flesh in blood wanted nothing to do with you. When she asked me to come help you, she made me promise I wouldn't tell you. She felt like if your father ever came back he should be the one to tell you. My family is one of the most notorious families in the hood. Most of them are dead, in jail, or so cracked out you can't even recognize them."

I was bawling like a baby.

"Carm please tell me this isn't true." I managed to say.

"Believe me baby. I would never lie to you." She stroked my hair. "Don't ruin your happiness because of a man. No man is worth your happiness. Your father and his absence is the reason for your actions with these men whether you see it or not. Todd loved you in the beginning and he still loves you. He made mistakes that he's regretting now, but you also have another man who loves you very much who hasn't taken you to hell and back. You have to use your own judgment. Do you want to continue going backwards or do you want to move forward with your life? You have to move on Krisha but you also must follow your heart. You don't have to hold on and be afraid of letting go because there may not be another to love and care for you like Todd. There will always be someone who loves you. You're a special woman."

"He was the first man who took care of me." I said. "The first man who told me he loved me and meant it. He was everything I wanted a father to be. He was that provider; that nurturer. But he was my husband. I had never felt a man genuinely hold me in his arms before. It's like if I let him go, I'll lose him forever. I can't lose the foundation for who I am today. He made me love myself. I'm afraid to totally let him go."

"Baby, only your father should be as a father to you. Your husband should be just that. Both Ryan and Todd love you Krisha. Look deeper into each relationship and find your answer. The answer is staring you right in the face. You're just too blind to see it right now."

I gave Carmen a warm and loving hug. And cried some more on her shoulder.

"Why now Carmen?"

"Because your mother is probably flipping over in her grave knowing you're going through this. You're thirty something years old; it's time for you to know the truth. I believe it will help your future. Besides, she had planned to tell you one day. Her untimely death didn't allow her to do that. And, there's one more thing baby I'd like to get off my chest."

She left the kitchen and came back with her purse. Carmen unfolded a piece of paper and handed me two photos. The photos were old and brown around the edges. One was of a young girl holding a newborn baby. The young girl resembled Carmen a lot. The other was the same girl holding a baby girl around six months old.

"Who's this Carm?" I asked blowing my nose.

"Me and my baby."

Then she unfolded the piece of paper and slid it to me across the table. It was a birth certificate. I read it and froze.

"Your mother knew it that's why she kept you two close. She was the only other person from the family she let see you and that was because she was no longer a part of my family."

"Carmen I don't understand."

"I was fourteen years old. I couldn't take care of her so I let a lady from the neighborhood who wanted children but couldn't conceive take care of her."

She wiped her face free of tears.

"I didn't have any help. My three brothers and me were products of one-night stands or tricking. My mother turned tricks and hustled for a living. She was a drug addict too. I didn't have anybody. Mrs. Davis around the block was in her forties, could never conceive and desperately wanted a child. She had a good job and stable family and was willing to take care of my baby for me. I allowed her to do that. She let me see her anytime I wanted to. I would bring her to play with you. Then I got caught up out there too for a few years. I had another baby at twenty-one. This one I kept. When I had him, I got myself together and raised my boy. I always did pretty good for myself, but I never could go get my child. Mrs. Davis loved her too much. Though I didn't have anything to do with her upbringing, I could never just completely give her away. I never allowed Mrs. Davis to adopt her. I had to hold on to something. Coincidentally, we both shared the same last name. So there were never any questions asked. Mrs. Davis loved her and gave her a good life; much more than I could give her. I've carried those around in my purse for years. Even when I sold my body and used drugs for breakfast, lunch, and dinner, I held on to the only things I had that reminded me that she was my child."

"She has no idea you're her mother?" I said in disbelief.

"No. Not that I know of. I don't think Mrs. Davis ever told her."

"No she didn't. At least she never told me if she did."

My morning had gotten more complicated. Carmen was my aunt and Mia was my cousin. All of that was very good news but the situation was terrible. How could Mia know this? How would she react? My situation with Todd and Ryan seemed unimportant now. Now I only thought of my girl.

Carmen had definitely helped me this morning in more ways than one. I loved her for all she's ever done for me without my knowing she was my blood. Knowing she's my aunt only makes it more special. However, all these revelations are only unfolding another segment of my life that I know I'm not ready for right now.

Looking down at the pictures, I smiled.

"Carmen?"

"Yes baby."

"I never noticed before, but she does resemble you."

"Yes she does. I've always thought so."

"Look here." Pointing at the photo. "When you were young, she's exactly like you now."

She wiped her tears and smiled.

Looking at the photos, had it not been for the drugs, they would have been identical. But unfortunately, the heavy drug use and street life had altered Carmen's appearance. Gave her a hard core look instead of the softness the photos revealed.

"I love her now as much as I loved her then. It was so hard giving her up."

I hugged her again.

"She'll understand. She has a big heart."

"Krisha I can't tell her now if that's what you're getting at."

"Carmen let's get all this straight and out in the open. We need to be a family. I love both of you."

"Not now Krisha." She stared at me.

"You're right Carm. I'm sorry. Whenever you're ready. I'll be here for you."

"Thanks Krisha."

"Carmen. One more thing…is he still alive?"

She hesitated before saying.

"Yes baby he is."

"Where?"

"Angola."

"Prison?"

"Yes. He never changed his ways."

"Was he ever in California?"

"Hell no. He aint never had enough money to go cross town more less leave the state."

"So you mean to tell me he's right here in the state of Louisiana in jail? I know people are in there who knows me or he should see me in my TV commercials or something."

"Krisha he probably doesn't even know your face baby. I'd be surprised if he remembers your name. The last time he saw you, you were around five years old. Now do you see why your mother protected you from all of that?"

"Yeah, I understand. But I should know him. It's my decision if I want him in my life at this point."

"Yes you're right but as a parent when things happen like they did, all you think about is protecting your child."

"I can understand my mother's reaction." I smiled. "…and thanks Carmen." I hugged her. "I mean Aunt Carmen."

We both smiled.

"You go rest baby. I'm gonna put Tamia down and get this kitchen cleaned."

"Okay wake me if Ryan calls."

"I will." She said clearing the table of dishes. "Oh and might I suggest you be up there thinking of a good lie because you're gonna need it."

"Ooooo don't say that Carm!"

She reminded me that I was in hot water with Ryan.

I jogged up the stairs to the telephone. Called Mia to see if somehow Ryan had called her last night. I had to cover my butt.

"Mia, what's up?"

"Just working."

"Did you talk to Ryan last night?"

"Ryan? No. Why do you ask?"

"Well, it's a long story."

"Long story my ass. You slut. You want me to cover for you."

This girl knows me too well. I thought.

"Please just this one time." I begged while admitting my guilt.

"One time?" She let out a big sigh. "Where were you?"

"It's a long story. I'll explain it when you get off."

"I'm in my office. I have time."

"Mia!"

"Well find you another alibi. Bye!" She spat and meant it.

"Okay, okay, dang!" I screamed. "I went to talk to Todd…"

"Aw shit!" She said cutting me off. "And…"

"No, Mia listen. I went to talk to him about the kids moving with me to Baltimore."

"Uh huh. And you slept with him right?" She said calmly.

"Why do you always have to assume *that* when I'm with Todd?"

"Because I know you. Now, did you?"

"Well, it…"

"Well some shit. You did." She stated matter-of-factly. She breathed a heavy sigh of frustration. "Are you gonna let Todd come between what you have with Ryan?"

"Mia, I told you before you just don't understand."

"You're right. I don't. Tell you what. Maybe we should talk later. I'll stop by when I get off. Cool?"

"Yeah that's straight. But Mia…"

"Yeah, yeah. You know I got you."

"Love you girl." I said sincerely.

"Bye boo."

I called Ryan and left a message. He didn't answer so I assumed he was working.

I lay down and slept half the day away. Carmen awakened me around four to advise me that Ryan was on the phone. I was sleeping so hard I didn't even hear the phone ring. I immediately got nervous.

"Hey baby." I chimed.

"Hi Krisha."

"How are you?"

"Good, considering I didn't get much sleep last night."

"I saw that you'd called when I got to my phone."

"Where were you and why didn't you answer?"

"I was with Mia last night. We went out."

"So why didn't you answer my calls?"

"I'd left my phone in my car."

"Why didn't Carmen know where you were?"

"She knew I was with Mia. She just didn't know where we'd gone baby. I'm sorry. I didn't plan to stay out late, but we had too much to drink, so I crashed at her place."

"On a Thursday night?"

"Yeah you know we do it on Thursdays here."

"That just doesn't sound right."

"What doesn't?" I asked nonchalantly.

"You never leave your phone."

"I have left it before but I went to sleep at Mia's without it that's all Ryan."

"Don't play with me Krisha. Please don't play okay."

"Ryan I'm not playing." I crossed my fingers. *Lord, please forgive me.* I prayed silently.

"I was calling to tell you that I wanted you to stay until at least Tuesday when you come next Friday. And that I was reserving a ticket for Carmen too."

"Okay honey. What you got up?"

"I just wanted to show the guys around and there are also some more houses I wanted you to see. I want everyone to see them to get their opinions. Carmen too."

"Carmen? How do you know she wants to come there?"

"See if you'd been home last night. You'd know. I already got that. Also, I need to start paying her for taking care of the kids. I just realized last night that you've never asked me for anything that I didn't offer. I'm sure there are expenses for the wedding but you haven't mentioned anything."

"Well I have that. Don't worry 'bout me."

"I'm sorry I didn't ask sooner. I need to help you."

"Ryan you don't have to. You paid for the engagement party."

"So what? I told you what's mine is yours. We're in this together. I don't want you to spend another dime. Will you be at work tomorrow?"

"Yes."

"Which office?"

"Downtown."

"Expect a courier in the morning. Make sure you're there."

"I'll be there boo."

"I love you girl."

"Love you too."

I hung up with the biggest smile plastered across my face. *That went really well.* I thought.

I skipped steps to get to the bottom of the stairs. I was screaming like crazy for Carmen.

Carmen came running from the kitchen.

"What is it girl?" From the look on her face, I'd scared the crap out of her.

I had to laugh. I was grinning from ear to ear.

"Why didn't you tell me you were going with us?"

"Girl don't scare me like that." Holding her chest. "That was for him to tell you."

"Thank you, thank you, thank you." I ran to her and kissed her cheek over and over and gave her a big hug.

"Girl calm down. I told you today I wasn't gonna leave you. Not as long as you need me. And right now your behind needs me." She said playfully but stern.

"You're God sent Carm. I love you." I hugged her again.

"Can't help but love you too." She smiled as she hugged me back.

"Let's party!" I screamed. "TJ turn on some music. Let's celebrate!"

DJ TJ put on his favorite song "Walk It Out." We danced around and walked it out until our legs ached. Even Carmen danced and had it going on. After all the years, this was the first time Carmen had let her hair down and really opened up with us. Guess she was glad to get the secrets out and in the open. We felt like a big happy family. Today turned out to be pretty good after all.

31

Ryan sent a car to pick us up from the airport to take us to the hotel when we arrived in his town. He called to say he was in a meeting and we should wait for him at the hotel.

It was late Friday evening and all I wanted to do was rest. Tamia had fussed the entire flight. For some reason, she wouldn't let Carmen touch her. She wanted to cling to me like her life depended on it. I assumed it was due to the flight being her first.

We settled into our hotel rooms. Ryan had reserved a suite for me and him and one for Carmen and the kids. The kids stayed with me while Carmen went to unwind and relax in her room. I spoke with Mia briefly to let her know we'd arrived. After that we all took a bath and changed, then Tamia and I laid down for a quick nap while we waited for her daddy, and the boys played video games.

I was sleeping too good when I felt the worst sting on my butt. I jumped up ready to swing. Ryan fell on the bed on top of me grabbing me in a bear hug and kissing me all over my face.

"Hey beautiful."

"Hey sweetheart. You sneaking up on me huh?"

"I've been here about thirty minutes. I've watched you sleep, kissed the baby and played a couple games with TJ and Malik. You were sleeping hard girl. You tired or you pregnant?"

I kicked him for that comment.

"Yeah right Negro. I'm tired." I rolled over and stretched back out across the bed.

"You can just get up. We gotta go eat. The kids are hungry. Then I want you to meet some people. So get yo' fine butt up." He slapped my butt again.

"Ouch! Ryan that hurts." I whined.

"Sorry then let me kiss it." He kissed the spot he'd hit. "Didn't mean to hurt my baby."

"Move! You're a mess." I laughed as I got up from the bed.

"I missed you."

I went to him slid my arms around his waist. We stood in the middle of the floor and enjoyed each other for a while.

"Umm, I missed you too." His embraced tightened.

"I can't wait until we're together." I caressed his chest and face while he hugged my waist and kissed me as I talked. "I can't wait to be your wife."

"You just don't know how I wish you were here every day. It's hell being away from you."

"I know, but we'll be together soon."

"Let's get going. The quicker we feed them and bring them back the quicker we get to have each other. I need to hold you tonight."

I kissed him before slipping out of his arms to gather up my children for dinner.

32

"Tomorrow morning at 10:00 am we need to meet with the realtor." Ryan said as he held my body close to his. I lay peacefully in his arms on the massive bed.

"Ten o'clock is pretty early."

"C'mon now stop stalling. Ten is not early. I really think you'll like this house. I do want you to see the other two though. Our next appointment is at three o'clock on tomorrow. The other is Monday at one."

"So I'll have to see that one without you right?"

"Yeah babe, sorry. I've already seen all of them. You just need to make the decision. Whatever you want is fine with me. I'll arrange a car to take you or you can try finding them on your own."

"I think I'll drive. I need to get used to getting around here anyway."

"Whatever you want, just let me know."

Ryan looked over at Tamia sleeping in the crib next to the bed.

"She's gotten so big."

"That's because she eats everything." I laughed.

"Do you realize I just missed four months of my baby's life? When I left her she was just a little thing at five months old. Now she's crawling around, eating table food and everything."

"Time just passes so fast it seems."

"You think she knows me."

"Of course she does. You're her father. Babies always remember their parents."

"I missed almost two months of her life after she was born. Now I just missed four months. She's only nine months so she's only known me a good three months."

"Ryan where is all this coming from honey?"

"My father didn't give two cents about me." He said staring at the ceiling. "He came around occasionally but never paid me any attention. Never offered me a hug or a handshake...I...I...just don't see how."

I comforted him by caressing his chest while he opened up to me. This was the first time he'd ever talked about his childhood with his father. I'd asked about his father several times, but he always changed the subject and said he'd rather not talk about him. I knew he'd lost his father to cancer not long ago, but I wasn't sure what their relationship was like.

I respected his take on that because I knew what it was like to hurt from the absence of a father. Many say you don't miss what you never had, but in the case of an absent parent, I disagree.

In that, we have something in common. It was so ironic he got on that subject just as I was about to open up to him also.

"I'll never leave her Krisha. I know my job is the reason I'm not with her, but I feel like I'm abandoning her when I'm gone."

"Ryan don't think like that. You and I both know that's not true. And if you're still playing football when she's older, I'm sure she'll understand. Hey, but by then we'll be together as a family, so you won't have that to worry about."

"I know. It just still bothers me sometimes. It hurts to feel rejected by someone who's supposed to love you when no one else does."

"I feel you, but just remember many people, including myself, love you. So you aren't lacking in that department."

"Do you really love me?" He was so sincere. Still staring at the baby. Never taking his eyes off her.

"Yes Ryan. Never second-guess that."

"Thank you." He turned to kiss my forehead.

"For what?"

"For accepting me into your life. For allowing me to love you and for loving me unconditionally. I know I made some bad decisions, which almost cost me my family and your heart. Thank you for having enough love for me to forgive my faults."

"No one is without fault darling. You've done no less for me." I kissed his neck.

"I have something to share with you."

"Sounds serious." He shifted to look at my face. Pulled me a little closer to him.

I went on to tell him what I knew about Carmen and Mia, my father, and my mother. I showed him the pictures Carmen had brought along, and told him everything Carm had told me about my family. One I never knew existed. When I finished, I was crying a world of tears. Ryan had already set the mood for tears. I found it impossible to hold them back. He held me and rocked me until sleep found its way into my worn body.

The next day we visited both houses that were for sale. I found them to be nice and spacious. The second house was Ryan's main choice. It was very extravagant and bigger than anything I'd ever imagined living in. It was a 17,000 square feet European style home that sat on five acres of property. Ryan loved the things I didn't care about in this house. I couldn't let the indoor basketball court and huge gym be the determining factor for me buying a house.

I kinda leaned more toward the first house I saw because it was smaller and just seemed more like me. This home was only four months old, 10,600 square feet, six bedrooms, seven and a half baths, French Mediterranean style with impeccable landscaping. The home was very lovely, and since Ryan said the final decision was up to me, would most likely be my home.

The next day we all shared a magnificent day out. Carmen and I shopped while the kids hung out with Ryan back at his apartment.

Sheri called to invite me to go out with her since the guys would be in tonight. She said she wanted to attend a friend's party and didn't want to go alone. Ryan assured me that it was okay to go. So I prepared for a night out with my new friend.

I dressed in a pair of sexy, one size too small pants that were a tight fit but accented my hips to perfection. I liked the way they hugged my round bottom and showed off my curves. I wore a top that hung off the shoulder, which added the overall lusciousness my body displayed.

When we arrived, the party was seriously going off. The club was a nice and classy spot. We immediately fell in and started having a good time. Sheri introduced me to the host and a few other friends. I copped a table and sat down with my drink. I sat and sipped as I observed everyone dancing and mingling. Before long I had company approaching my table.

A tall, light skinned brotha with a hell of a smile and nicely dressed pimped over to my table. He seemed to be a professional in whatever he did, but definitely out of my league. I told him I was engaged and showed him my ring. His reply was "a beautiful lady like you shouldn't be tied down to one man. Is there any way I can get you to reconsider?" He asked.

I wanted to say, "Boy stop." But instead I shook my head and smiled.

Must be something about the east coast men. They seemed very open, inviting, persistent, and were up in my face one after the next.

If only this had been a year ago or more, things would have been a little different. I had several offers to dance all night but declined all of them.

I began to miss Ryan as I sat and watched the couples together. It didn't seem fair for me to be so close to him and not be with him. The weekend, so far, consisted of us doing things with the kids or separately. We hadn't had any time with one another, other than falling asleep in each other's arms last night. The more I sat and shook off men, the more I wanted my man. I wanted him next to me. The alcohol had me in the mood for loving him. I was out partying while my man was in. It was beginning to feel more and more ridiculous to me.

Ryan was banking on us being together tomorrow night after the game. He said he didn't want me wearing him out before the game. We were both dealing with four months of celibacy. Well, at least with each other. I'd messed that up a couple weeks ago for myself.

I took out my cell phone to call him but before I could dial, Sheri came over and grabbed my hand pulling me up from the table.

"C'mon girl. Put that phone away. I want you to meet some friends."

I followed her across the room. We approached two very handsome men seated near the rear of the club. They were in a deep conversation at their table.

As we approached, all eyes were on us.

"Krisha these are two very good friends of mine. This is Ken." She directed her hand toward a tall muscular, brown skinned man with a diamond earring in his left ear. He wore a black fitted shirt that showed off his prize chest.

I extended my hand. He took it and held it as he spoke.

"Pleased to meet you Krisha."

"Nice meeting you. Thanks." I said.

"And this is Tyson." Sheri said.

Yes indeed. I thought.

This dude looked good enough to eat. Smooth, silky caramel, just like I like 'em. Pearly whites, bald fade, tall, athletic build, and body cut the hell up. He had unusually long eyelashes and the most sensuous lips I'd ever seen on a man. Lord have mercy! Those features would have been beautiful on a woman, and were just as beautiful on him.

All I could think about was, *why didn't I come to the east coast before getting engaged?*

Brotha wore a fitted shirt, hitting all the muscles on his sexy ass, and chain on his neck with a cross that was iced out. All I could think of was "sexy lil thug" all over his ass.

"Very pleased to meet you beautiful." He said while standing with my hand in his.

The look he gave me was deep. I had to turn away to blush. And that rarely ever happens with me.

"Thank you. It's been a pleasure meeting you both." I said quickly expecting to get away from them ASAP before I got myself into trouble. That little Krisha in the red devil fit sitting on my left shoulder was whispering in my ear.

But Sheri had other plans. She moved over to Ken and began speaking to him exclusively. Which left me in an awkward position, standing there looking at Tyson. I wasn't sure if Sheri was staying or going.

Tyson was still standing.

"Please sit down." He offered.

"No thanks. I guess we're going back to our table." We both looked at Sheri and Ken. Sure didn't look like we were going anywhere. They were all up in each other's grills.

My favorite song of all times was being played. "When We Make Love" by Dru Hill.

The situation was awkward no doubt, but I stood with my drink in hand swaying to the music while Sheri continued having a grand ole' time chatting with ole' boy. They could barely hear each other talking over the music, but they were saying some things that they both were interested in.

"I see you like that song." I heard someone say in my ear. I turned around to Tyson smiling behind me.

"Yes its one of my favorites."

"In that case, would you like to dance?"

"N...N...uhmm." I stumbled on my words. I thought about it a second. Why not? It's a party. Parties are meant to be fun. So that's what I'm gonna do. Have a little fun.

"Yes, I believe I will dance, but only if you promise to keep it clean." I said with a smile.

"I wouldn't have it any other way beautiful." He grinned.

"Thank you."

"My pleasure." He said before taking my hand and leading me to the dance floor.

I knew I should have gotten out of this place earlier.

That song did things to me. Made me remember a few prior occasions.

Tyson's body felt so hard against mine. His hands rested in the small of my back while I placed my arms around his neck trying not to make too much bodily contact. I got lost in the song. Closed my eyes and imagined he was Ryan. I opened my eyes long enough to see Sheri and Ken grooving to the music. Seemed like they were really belly rubbing. I don't know, could be the drinks.

I closed my eyes again and let the music guide me. All I could think about was how I was going to make love to Ryan tomorrow. My nerves were bad. Then I thought about how Tyson's pretty face would look all tied up and twisted while I was putting two weeks of this sex deprived body on him.

The thoughts. Krisha in the red dress was doing it to me. I opened my eyes to snap out of it.

"Your fragrance is nice." Tyson whispered in my ear.

"Thanks. So is yours." I replied.

"Thank you. So you're from Louisiana?"

"Yes."

"Are you married?"

"Engaged."

"Oh I'm sorry."

"For what?"

"I didn't mean to disrespect your engagement."

"How could you? You didn't know. It's cool."

"Can I compliment you?"

"You already did."

He laughed.

"Again please."

"If you'd like."

"You're beautiful." He whispered closer to my ear.

"Thank you."

"You wear it very well."

"Thank you."

The song was over thank goodness. I had to get away from this man and fast. My body was doing things on its own and my mind was taking a detour also. I didn't like that.

"Would you like to dance again?"

"No. I'd better not."

"Okay, can I buy you a drink then?"

Before I answered, I looked around for Sheri. She was still on the dance floor wrapped around ole' boy. Since she was occupied, I figured I'd keep company with her friend a while longer.

"That'll be nice." I gave him a cute smile. He walked me back to his table. Pulled out the chair for me to sit. Then bent to whisper in my ear.

"What are you drinking pretty lady?"

"Whatever you are." I said with a grin.

He smiled.

"You stay put. I'll be right back with your drink."

He left for the bar.

I'd been around men plenty times before and enjoyed flirting every time I had the chance. But I didn't feel comfortable around Tyson for some unknown reason. Not in a bad way. I wasn't getting a negative vibe. The vibe was all positive and the attraction was strong. That was the problem.

"What brings you to Maryland from Louisiana?" He asked as he sat my drink in front of me.

"My fiancé."

"Oh! I see…" Almost as if he'd forgotten I said I was engaged.

"Is he in the same profession as Sheri's husband?"

"Yes. Actually that's how Sheri and I met."

"May I ask his name? I'm sure I know him."

"Ryan Mathers."

He stopped short and put his drink down on the table. Gave me a strange look then a grin.

"What?" I asked.

"Are you serious?"

"Yes, why?"

"You're Ryan Mathers' fiancé?" He asked. Still not convinced. "You sure don't look like her." He grinned. I could tell he immediately thought I was crazy now. Maybe some crazy fan or groupie.

"Oh you think I'm…No that was someone else…long story."

"I understand. Believe me, I know how it goes."

"No you don't. Don't go jumping to conclusions. I'm no groupie."

"I can look at you and tell you're no groupie."

"Now how is that?"

He didn't reply. Took a swallow from his drink while staring straight at me.

"You're eyes tell it all."

I paused as I looked at him questioning his attentiveness. He seemed very interested in my eyes, as he'd been staring directly into them the duration of our conversation. Making me a little uneasy.

"Are you two enjoying yourselves?"

"Uhm..yes. We are. "Tyson said as he tore his eyes away from mine to look at Sheri.

"Are you about ready Krisha? I don't want to keep you out too late?"

"Ready when you are." I stumbled.

This man had made me so nervous. This wasn't real.

"As soon as I come from the ladies room. I'll be ready."

Sheri scooted off toward the ladies room. When I took my eyes off Sheri and turned toward Tyson, his eyes were glued to the side of my face.

"So, Ms. Krisha, when is the big day?"

"February."

"Not much time left being a single woman."

"Not really. I'm ready though."

"Enjoy it while you can."

"What's that's supposed to mean?"

"I know how hard it can be being the wife of a well-known athlete. Especially Ryan Mathers and in this town at that."

"So you think you know?"

"I know I know."

"And how would you know so well?"

"Let's just say...I was once a Ryan Mathers. Minus the Super Bowl MVP." He laughed.

"Really?"

"I had a beautiful wife who was as beautiful and as special as you. But I allowed the popularity and attention from women cloud my judgment and go to my head, in addition to the things I did. Didn't appreciate what I had at home. She was lonely because I was never home. If it wasn't the games it was other things, including other women that kept me away from home. She basically had to raise our daughter alone. It was a time in my life that I'm not proud of.

"So I'm assuming you're divorced?"

"You assume right pretty lady." He said while nodding his head. This time he wasn't looking at me. Eyes were straight down in his glass.

"I'm sorry that things turned out for you like that but that has nothing to do with Ryan and me. Ryan is a totally different type of man."

"I'm sorry, but I wasn't saying that. I was just saying the life of a professional athlete's wife, especially a very popular and highly sought after athlete, can be very challenging."

"Doesn't it depend on who the athlete is?" I said.

"Most definitely. Every man's not the same. Some handle their business like men, while some do things like little boys. If I'd known then what I know now, I would have definitely handled mine differently. But I was a boy then. I did what boys do."

"I'm so sorry."

"Sorry? Nothing to be sorry for. That was over ten years ago. I've grown...Life's a learning experience."

"I totally agree." I said as I sipped my drink.

"So, is that how you know Sheri, through football?"

"Yeah. Her old man and I played together for one season."

"Did you play with Ryan?"

"No, he came on much later. He's much younger than me."

"How old are you, if you don't mind my asking?"

"I'm proud of my age. I think I look pretty good for 35."

We laughed.

I wonder if he knew how good.

"Yes you do. I would have guessed about 28."

"Really? May I ask your age? Or are you one of those women who never tell?"

"No, not me. I'm real. No shame in my game. I'm 32, but I feel 21."

We shared a laugh.

"They say you're only as old as you feel." He said.

"You ready Krish?" Sheri sang as she approached.

"Yes, I believe I am." I said as I pushed away from the table to get up.

Tyson stood up from the chair and extended his hand. I extended mine. He held it as he spoke.

"I enjoyed talking with you Krisha."

"Same here. Thanks for keeping me company."

"My pleasure. I enjoyed every minute of it."

"Thank you." I blushed and turned to prevent eye contact.

"You did say you owned a mortgage company, right?"

"Yes."

"I'm looking to buy a house soon and I know some others who are looking too. Can I have your card so we can contact you?"

"Yes, yes, by all means. I'd appreciate your business." I dug into my purse for my cardholder. I handed him about five cards for his friends. He looked down at my card.

"Nice." He said. Not sure what that meant.

"Good night Tyson." I said.

He didn't reply. Just stared at me as if he didn't want to see me leave. I could feel his eyes on me as I walked away.

When we got into Sheri's car, I remained silent. She broke the silence by saying, "I think Tyson's fond of you."

"What?"

"He likes you."

"Be for real Sheri. He just met me."

"I've never seen him that taken by anyone. Not even his ex-wife."

"Yeah, he mentioned her."

"Come to think of it, she looked a lot like you."

"How do you really know those guys?"

"I'm from here and so is Tyson. We've known each other since high school. It just so happens I met Steve at Howard, married him and he signed with the same team Tyson was on. Steve and Tyson aren't really all that close."

"Why not? They were teammates once."

"Yeah. I don't know. I think they bumped heads with a female once, but you know Steve will never tell me that. Then my friendship with Tyson doesn't make it any better."

"So what about Ken?"

"Ken is a friend of Tyson. I know him through Tyson, not Steve."

"Okay. I see. I was wondering what was up with the dancing and …"

"Listen Krisha. Ken and I are just cool, ya know. Sometimes you need a friend to talk to other than your husband. Especially when your husband is hardly ever there."

"I didn't mean for you to tell me your business."

"No, girl. It's cool. Ken isn't in the league. Never has been. He's always there for me. You're gonna need someone, trust me."

"You sound like Tyson."

"Well, whatever he said, he knows what he's talking about."

"Don't scare me."

"Not trying to scare you. You already know what to expect. Steve and I were married, then he signed, and everything just changed. You're already used to being away from Ryan, I wasn't. My husband was always there."

"But you live right here with him. I don't understand."

"It's the away games that bother me. Then when he's home, its one event after the next. He's never home."

"Oh, I see."

"Don't get the wrong idea. It's not like that for everyone. Some men do their jobs and come home and have a perfectly normal family life. I believe that's who Ryan is. But then some are just caught up in all the bull. Impressed by how many women they can get in one night. And let me tell you, the women will come. They come like flies clinging to fresh shit. Some men let their career ruin what they have at home. That's probably along the line of what Tyson was saying. Am I right?"

"You're exactly right."

"He's a good man. He got married young and made some mistakes early on in his career. But he's over it now, just has learned a whole lot from it all."

"Don't we all." I mumbled.

"Where would you like me to take you?" She asked.

"To the hotel please."

My cell rang as soon as those words left my mouth. It was Ryan's number at his condo.

"Hey baby." I sang into the phone.

"Where are you sweetheart?"

"On my way to the hotel. Why are you at home? I thought you'd be at the hotel waiting for me."

"I had to stay home to get some rest. As long as I'm with you, I know I won't be getting any rest."

"You're right about that. I got it on my mind in the worst way."

"Save it for February."

"What? Hold up. Say that again."

"You heard me."

"Are you serious?"

"Yeah. Our honeymoon will be that much more special."

"If you say so. But can we start once I leave?"

He laughed. I was serious.

"C'mon baby. Help me out here."

"Does oral sex count?"

"Krisha come on. Who's by you while you're talking like that?"

"Just Sheri. She knows what's up. She's *been* married…" I turned to Sheri who was cracking up laughing. "How many years have you been married?" I asked.

"Several."

"She's been married several years. I aint saying nothing new to her ears. She probably enjoys…"

"Krisha cut it out!" Ryan laughed. "Girl you trippin'."
Sheri and I laughed along with him.
"Hell yeah!" Sheri screamed while driving.
We giggled like two schoolgirls.
"Bye baby. I'll see you after the game…I love you."
"Love you too."
I hung up and stuck my phone in my purse.
"Girl you are crazy." Sheri said smiling.
"I'm just real that's all. I like to have fun."
"I knew there was a reason I liked you."
"You're not so bad yourself chick."

33

Back at my office by Wednesday, I gave Cheryl the paperwork to begin on my new home in Maryland. It was a 14,500 square feet, two story European style home with six bedrooms, seven and one-half baths, 4 car garage, mother-in-law suite on a four acre lot just completed three months ago. It was new, beautiful, spacious, and everything I wanted in a home. I was sure that by the end of next week the house would be ours.

I took some time to check dozens of emails inside my office before doing much else. One email in particular stood out. In the subject it read: **Hello Again.** I hurried to click on it to see what was up. The body of the email said: *Can't seem to get you out of my head. Never met anyone like you. Wish I could get to know you better.*

No name. No indication of the sender. Just an address of 21ncountin@hotmail. No clue as to who'd send me an email like this. Wasn't Ryan or Todd's address. Guess it was some who'd seen me somewhere. It had happened several times before. Men calling my office for things other than mortgage information. Whoever it was, I wasn't interested. I went on about my day before picking up diapers for the baby and going home.

"Carmen you didn't have to make dinner. I was going to cook."

"I wanted to. I knew you'd work hard today, being it's your first day back at work this week. I didn't mind."

"Thanks Carm. I wouldn't make it without you."

"Yes you would girl. You are your mother's daughter."

"Sometimes I don't know 'bout me Carmen. I surprise myself." I threw out as I took to the stairs in search of my bedroom.

I showered and relaxed about forty-five minutes before I came down for dinner. Carmen had fed the boys and they were in their rooms. The baby was fed and asleep. I wondered why I couldn't do this like Carmen. Everything done so orderly. If that were me, I would've been still cooking, the baby screaming, and boys running around like crazy. I was still struggling with being a parent of three children. It was harder than I'd imagined. Some days I needed Carmen and that was all it was to it. My mother and Todd spoiled me a little too much. Now Carmen was doing it too. I had to do better.

"Carmen this is for you." I handed her a check.

She looked at it. Then back up at me.

"Krisha I can't accept this."

"We want you to have it."

"Why are you giving me so much money?"

"Ryan wanted you to have it for coming to Baltimore with us last weekend. I feel like you deserve that and much more. So go ahead and enjoy yourself."

"I enjoyed being with you guys and the kids. We're family baby."

"I know Carmen, but if I'm being blessed, there's nothing wrong with blessing someone else."

"Okay well, thanks a lot." She hugged me and kissed my cheek. "You really are just like your mother. A heart of gold."

"You just don't know how much I appreciate you." I hugged her back.

I pondered a while before speaking.

"Carm, I've been thinking about going to see him."

"Who sweetheart?"

"You know...my father."

That sounded so weird coming from me.

"That'll be totally up to you. I love him because he's my brother, but he's not the nicest person on earth. It may not turn out the way you expect."

"Could he still not want me after all those years? I'm a grown woman now. It's not like he has to take care of me."

"Try writing him first Krisha. See if and how he responds. Then go off that."

"I like to look at people when I talk to them."

"I think writing would be best."

"Was he that bad of a person?"

"No, he wasn't a very bad person. He was just himself. He didn't think about the feelings of others. What he wanted to do he did. What he wanted   to   say   he   said. He just didn't give a damn about nobody. Nobody but your mother. She changed him for a while. But when their relationship started deteriorating. He became mad at the world."

"What did he get time for?"

"Three armed robberies and attempted murder."

"Whoa!"

"Yeah, he robbed a bank and two liquor stores. Damn near killed the owner of one of the store with his bare hands. The man gave him the money but tried to push the alarm. He almost beat the man to death."

"Wow. Ruthless, huh?"

"Exactly, but that's the way my mother taught us to be. That's the way she was."

"I guess that's where I get that mean, fightin' streak from."

"Yeah. You and Mia both. Yall behinds used to fight up a storm."

"I know huh. Chicks used to hate on us for no reason."

"Why you kept coming back to hang out in the hood I couldn't understand."

"My girls were there...So you used to see us?"

"Oh yeah. I was all over the streets then. I recall one incident when you and Mia were standing in front of Mr. Bob's Corner store and three girls passed by in this white jeep and called yall some names. Then when they came back through they stopped and three of them got out all up in ya faces."

I looked at her wide eyed and surprised. "Carm, yeah! I remember that. She was tripping over this guy named Gerard that Mia was dating. It was her boyfriend."

"Well do you remember the girl that told them to get back in the jeep because it wasn't going down like that?"

"Yeah. A real skinny girl came from nowhere, took out a switchblade and flashed it, made them back up. You saw that?"

"Who you think that skinny girl was?"

"Nooo! Carm. That wasn't you?"

"I hate to say it but yes, that was me. There was no way I'd let them jump my babies."

"Are you serious? You were so small."

"I was on that shit Krisha. I was young and stupid. I never did let it get me like it gets some people. I took care of my baby. Thank God I had a friend who forced me to get some help."

"I remember that like yesterday. I can't believe that was you. I would have never guessed."

"I always kept an eye on you girls. If yall were good, I was good. But if I was around and it didn't look right, I sent somebody in to help."

"Good looking out Aunt Carm." I gave her a thumb up and a smile. "We were always in something, but you know we rarely needed help." I laughed.

"Yeah. Yall got my momma's blood fo' sho'."

We both laughed.

"Were you like that?"

"Well, I lived in the projects, so I had to handle mine. But I was the only one with a heart. I wanted something out of life."

"What attracted my mother to a man like that? Doesn't seem like her type."

"She was in love...I don't know. He wasn't like that with her. He tried to live up to her standards. He hid the things he and my family did from her for a long time. Besides she wasn't from that part of town. She didn't really know what went on over there until she moved over there with him. He did alot to gain your mother's love. Then after he figured he had her, he unleashed the old Bobby. By then she loved his ass. You know how that can be."

"Yes indeed. Don't I know."

"Well she snapped out of it when the incident with you went down. She was very protective of you every since then."

"I can definitely understand that. I know how love can change the way you think and feel. Can take over your good senses and have you acting a damn fool doing things you never would have dreamt of doing. I can see how my mother got caught up. The same way I did. It's the heart."

"I told you that you had her heart. But that's what made the both of you stronger. For some it's hard to see how a weak heart can make you stronger. But once you let someone get all up in there, either life's trials are gonna kill you or make you better. If you're a strong woman, they can only make you better."

"Sometimes I don't feel strong at all Carm."

"You're not always gonna feel strong baby. But strength lies within. It's there. You've just got to recognize it and utilize it. There's strength in crying if you didn't know. So your behind ought to be the strongest woman in Louisiana."

I had to laugh. "Now you know you wrong for that Carm."

She laughed. "I'm just kidding girlie."

"I know...but it's true." I put on a sad face.

"Seriously though Krisha. I think you should write him first. That'll be best. But don't worry about it okay. I want to see you happy for this wedding. Don't do anything to jeopardize your happiness baby."

"I won't. But I've gotta move on with my life so I need to approach this in one way or another."

I pondered on that last statement. Wasn't sure if I could or not, but I was gonna try. Remembering what Carmen had just said, "strength lies within."

"I love you Aunt Carm." I gave her another hug. "I can't wait to tell the kids."

"I want to tell Mia first."

"I agree. We'll wait until then."

The doorbell rang as soon as we finished our conversation. Carmen went to get the door while I sat there and let the conversation marinate on my brain.

I could hear Mia from the kitchen.

"Hey Carm. How are you?" She sang loudly as usual.

Speak of the devil. I thought.

She approached the family room, where I was sitting on the sofa.

"Hey sis."

"What's up girl?"

"I got a pretty good deal with the caterer today."

"Oh gosh. What did you do?" I laughed.

"Well, you know me."

"Right. That's why I'm scared."

We all laughed.

I could see Carmen watching Mia from the corner of her eye.

Since I knew Carmen's truth, Mia looked more and more like her everyday that I saw her. Had it not been for the street life Carmen once lived I'm sure the resemblance would be more evident.

Underneath, Carmen was a pretty lady. The features were there. She just needed to be jazzed up a bit. The only major difference in the two was that Mia's shade was a little lighter than Carmen. Carmen was a smooth brown skinned lady and Mia was light caramel exactly.

I listened to Mia talk about the caterer and the wedding. She stayed to have dinner with us and I reimbursed her for the deposit she'd left with the caterer. She'd just mentioned leaving when I looked at Carmen to find an unusual look on her face. She looked as if she were gonna break down right then and there. I guess the conversations she and I had earlier weighed heavily on her heart and mind. Then, all of a sudden she burst into tears.

"Carmen are you okay?"

I said as I ran to her side to comfort her.

"Carmen what is it? Mia was at her other side.

Carmen was at a loss for words. She was so choked up she couldn't speak.

"Carmen tell me what's wrong." I asked.

"I can't do it Krisha. I can't do it another day."

"Carmen?" I said astonished. "What are you saying?"

"I can't live another day like this. I gotta tell her the truth."

The first thing I could think of was, *not now*. It just didn't seem like the right time.

"I'm sorry Krisha. It just hurts so much to see her. To be this close. I've been dealing with this for years. I've got to tell her."

"Okay. It's your call." I said as I held her.

"Is everything okay Krisha?" Mia asked confused.

"No baby it's not okay." Carmen answered.

Mia looked at me then back to Carmen.

Carmen got up and went over to her purse. She sat down clutching her purse in her arms.

"Lord help me." She screamed.

Mia looked as if she were about to run out of there.

"Mia please sit down." I asked.

Sitting down she said, "What's going on Krisha? Why do I need to sit down?"

"If I die today or tomorrow my conscious will be cleared." Carmen said as she cried.

She reached in her purse and retrieved the worn documents that I'd seen before. The birth certificate and photo of her and Mia as a baby. She clutched them in her hand.

"Baby...I...Mia...I." She stuttered.

I caressed her back to console her. She couldn't bring herself to speak the necessary word to convey her feelings. Instead she shoved the documents in Mia's directions. I assisted by passing them to her.

As Mia looked them over, I began to shed tears. Confusion swept her face. Shock filled her mind as she read line for line on the birth certificate. She looked at the photo. When she laid eyes on the photo, I saw the first tear roll down her cheek.

"I'm your biological mother." Carmen spoke.

Mia sat motionless staring at the birth certificate.

"I'm so sorry but every time I see you it hurts me so bad. I had to let you know. I had to get this out."

Mia finally looked up. As she raised her head, many tears began to fall. She looked at me.

I nodded my head in approval.

"I was fourteen. I thought it would be best...Mrs. Davis...she."

"This is too much. This can't be happening." Mia said.

I ran over to her and threw my arms around her as she sat on the couch.

"How...Why...Why didn't you tell me?" She asked me showing disappointment. "I thought we shared everything."

"I just recently found out too. She was waiting for the right time. I had to respect that."

"Right time huh?"

"Mia, there are some things you must hear. You've gotta understand. I was just as shocked as you." I said.

"Krisha my mother is dead!" She screamed.

"Yes. Your mother is dead, but your biological mother isn't." I told her.

"This is a lie. Why would you guys do this to me?"

"You know I'd never intentionally hurt you. Please, just listen to her... Carmen tell her."

I held Mia as Carmen got herself together enough to tell her story. Mia remained silent until Carmen was done. Then she spoke with tears staining her blouse.

"She told me when I was twelve. I never wanted to accept it, so I blocked it out. She never said who my real mother was, because we never talked about it again. I think it hurt her just as much to tell me as it did for me to hear it. When I was younger kids would always tease me and say my momma was a dope head. I knew my mother wasn't so it didn't bother me. Guess they were right."

Now, I was the one shocked. Though we shared everything, she'd never revealed this to me. Guess she was really in denial. I can imagine if someone told me my mother wasn't really my mother, I'd block that shit out too.

"Tell her everything Carmen."

"Krisha, she might not be able..."

"Carmen get it all out. No more secrets."

Carmen told her about my father being her brother and about our ruthless family. The only thing that made her smile was when I said, "That means you're my first cousin." She smiled then burst into tears again. I showed her the pictures Carmen had of me, my parents, and me.

"How could a family keep secrets like this? This is unbelievable." Mia asked. She found it hard to keep the tears from staining her silk blouse.

She looked up at Carmen as she'd stared at the documents the entire time.

She studied her before saying anything to me.

"Everybody always said we looked like sisters."

We gave a weak laugh as I hugged her tighter.

Mia looked down at the picture of Carmen and my dad together when they were probably in their twenties.

She said, "You guys look like twins."

Carmen nodded her head in agreement.

"And I look just like you." Mia said.

I was astonished at her revelation. Carmen nodded her head in agreement while crying.

Mia hugged me tight and kissed my cheek. "I knew our bond was strong for some reason. I love you so much."

"Love you too girl."

Then she surprisingly got up from the couch walked over to Carmen fell to her knees grabbing Carmen around the waist hugging her body.

"I'm so sorry baby." Carmen cried. "I should have told you a long time ago. I've missed so much of your life."

They cried together.

"I thought I didn't have anybody. I never had anyone except Krisha and her mom after I lost my mother." Mia cried.

"She gave you a better life baby. I couldn't do it at the time. I'm grateful to her for that. But I could never stop loving you. That's why I could never let her officially adopt you. I love you as much as I did the day I gave birth to you." Carmen stroked Mia's hair while she spoke. "Over the years, you've been here with Krisha and we've all been like family. Only now it's official."

I'd never realized my friend's need for family in her life. I never knew her need to be loved. She was hurting inside and had been for years. She knew she'd been handed away by her natural mother to a stranger that had raised her and loved her, one she loved more than anything; the only person she knew as her mother. The only family she had. It was hard realizing that she had been hurting and I had done nothing to soothe her pain.

We were all bawling like someone had died. Mia on her knees with her head on Carmen's lap. Carmen bending down to hug Mia. Me on my knees on the floor embracing them both. If someone had walked in they would swear we were all crazy.

"You have to meet your brother."

"Does he know about me?"

"He knows I had another child in my youth. He doesn't know you though. He would have contacted you by now if he did."

"Where is he?" Mia asked. I could tell she was elated to know she had a sibling.

"He's in college in Atlanta. He lives there."

I sat on the floor next to Mia with my back against the sofa. We sat in silence for about five minutes. Everyone trying their best to pull themselves together.

"I think I'd better go." Mia said.

"Are you okay?" I asked.

"I will be. I need to go think about everything. I need to be alone right now."

"I understand."

I got up from the floor and helped Mia up. She got her purse and rushed out of the house. I didn't go behind her. Just let her be. I figured she'd call when she wanted to talk.

The events of the evening weighed heavily on my mind as I lay awake in bed. I was restless, so I decided to call to check on my best friend. I couldn't wait any longer for her to call me.

The phone rang about five times before she sluggishly answered.

"Hey Krish." She said.

"Hey. I didn't mean to wake you. Just thought I'd check on you before I went to bed."

"I'm good Krish."

"Are you sure? I know a lot was thrown at you all at once without warning. It's a lot to absorb."

"As shocking as it all is, I totally understand her pain. I know it must have been hard for her. She was only a baby herself. I don't hold any grudges. I'm just glad to know I have someone else out there to call family."

Her words brought a smile to my face.

"I have a lot of questions, but how can I hate her? She never really gave me up. She just allowed me to leave her care. She never turned her back on me. And I can't hate her and love you. She kept us together. If it weren't for her, I wouldn't have you."

"She did didn't she." I was starting to get teary eyed again.

"I always knew we were much more than friends. I felt it in my heart." She started to cry.

"I know. So did I."

"Now I feel like I really got a family. I love that."

"I've always been your family Mia."

"I know. But you know what I mean. A couple months ago, neither of us thought we had anymore family. Now we learned that we not only have each other, but also other family members too."

"Unbelievable, huh."

Silence.

"Yeah. Truly unbelievable."

Silence.

"Mia? Mia, are you okay?"

"Yeah."

"What are you doing?"

"Uhmm. You really wanna know?"

"On second thought, forget I asked. I guess you're doing okay then."

"Yeah. Real good right about now."

I laughed.

"Bye girl. Tell Derric I said hello."

"Who?" I could see her smiling through the phone.

"Well, tell Chad I said hello then." She giggled.

"I can do that."

"Bye."

That girl was still up to her old tricks. Her butt will never change. That's my girl though. She never lets anything get her down. I really wish I could be like that. Maybe I need to start really listening at her crazy butt.

34

When I arrived at work, I immediately began my day. There were a few things I wanted to handle personally so I could be out of there by noon. I logged onto the computer to check my emails then got right to work. A couple hours later, I got a call that altered my plans for the rest of the day. I answered the phone eager to end the call to get back to work.

"Mrs. Taylor, how may I help you?" I answered.

"Nice to hear your sweet voice again Mrs. Taylor."

"Thank you."

"Has your day been as lovely as you?"

"My day has been wonderful thank you."

"Glad to know you're doing good."

"I'm sorry but may inquire as to your identity sir?"

"By all means beautiful. This is Mr. Tyson Delaney."

I smiled.

"Tyson, how are you?"

"Good, very good. Even better now."

"What can I help you with?"

"I'm ready to do business."

"So you've decided on a house?"

"Yes, I've chosen the perfect bachelor's pad. So I wanted to put the best person on the job. And I hear you're the best."

Now I could have elaborated on that comment; in a different place and time. But I let it rest. Wouldn't have been too professional of me.

"Thanks Tyson, I really appreciate that."

"So do I need to come see you?"

"No I can get you started over the phone, but I'll be out there in a few days, so if you'd like we can complete the process then."

"I'd like that. I'd much rather be in the company of a beautiful woman if I had a choice."

"Don't flatter me too much. My head's swelling over here."

We shared a laugh.

Looking at my personal calendar. "Is Wednesday at one o'clock okay with you?" I asked.

"Is that am or pm?" He said jokingly.

"PM of course."

"I guess that'll do." He laughed.

"You are a trip Mr. Delaney."

"I'm just kidding. But, hey, one is good. Let's meet at my office."

"Fine."

He gave me the address to his office and I promised to meet him there with all the necessary documents for him to complete and sign. I had a good feeling my trip back to Maryland was going to be quite interesting as well as profitable.

Two days later, I boarded a flight to Maryland. Ryan met me at the airport and we headed for his condo. I called Sheri on my way to Ryan's. We made plans to hook up on the next day for lunch.

My flight was good and my night would be even better, but only if I could convince Ryan to drop the celibacy bull. I was as horny as ever now. Then I had to sleep next to his fine behind and keep my hands to myself. I was quite sure this was gonna be a screwed up night.

Ryan and I shared an early dinner. We took in a movie and relaxed in each other's company. I was so glad to be with him. It was late when the movie ended so we went back to his condo.

When we got there, Jace had company, as usual. A short chick with a short cut. Kinda thick, had a big behind and wore the shortest skirt I'd ever seen. The thigh high boots added to her wardrobe demise. She looked like a ten cent trick in that get up. I'm sure her way of dress is what interested Jace in her in the first place. Poor thing. She just didn't know. She'd be history in a few hours once her services were rendered. She was just glad to be there.

I wondered if she was thinking the same about me.

Ryan didn't bother acknowledging the girl or introducing us. He advised he was going to shower and went right on up the stairs. For some reason he'd been acting a little shady all night. Not his usual self.

I thought his actions to be very rude so I said hello to the girl once he scurried up the stairs.

"Hi, I'm Danielle." She extended her hand. "You must be Maican."

I briefly shook her hand. "No, actually I'm Krisha." I responded.

"I'm so sorry. I thought you were someone else... Oh! You know what? I forgot Maican is Tim's girlfriend. Wrong guy. I'm so sorry."

"That's okay." I said.

"Are you Jace's girlfriend?" I asked nosily.

"Yeah, we've been dating a couple months now."

Now I know this wasn't the girl he had at my engagement party and matter-of-factly, I don't remember seeing her two weeks ago when I was here. Now why this heffa got to lie. I thought. These guys are really wild. I can't say it's their profession and the attention they get from it. Because Todd didn't play pro ball and his ass was the leader of the southern chapter of no good mothafuckas.

"You're Ryan's fiancé?"

"Yes."

"It's a pleasure to meet you. Tell me how you did it?"

"Did what?"

"How'd you wrap him up like that?"

"Actually Danielle. It's totally up to the individual. And all I can do is be myself."

"I wish Jace was ready to settle down like that."

"If it's meant to be, it'll happen before you know it."

She seemed too young to know what she wanted. She knew she didn't want to settle down. The Gucci bag filled with Jace's change sounded more like it. And Jace wasn't about to settle down either so she could go on with that too.

"Hey Krisha." Jace chimed in as he entered the room with two glasses of wine in hand.

He gave Danielle a glass, set his down, and walked over to greet me with a hug.

"How are you?"

"Great. I see you've met Danielle."

"Yes, I have. I'm sorry, I introduced myself." I said.

"Quite alright darling. No problem…Where's your man at?"

"He went straight up to shower and I think I'll do the same."

"You're welcome to chill with us."

"No thanks. I think I better go check on Ryan. He's not really been himself tonight."

"Yeah. He has been kinda distant the last couple days. So yeah go give that dude what he needs to perk up."

"Jace!" I looked at him wide eyed.

He laughed.

"Well it's the truth." He said while laughing.

"Nice to meet you Danielle." I said as I turned to go up the stairs.

"Thank you same to you." I heard her say.

When I reached the bedroom, Ryan was done showering and lying in bed with the TV watching him.

"Hey baby." I threw out while joining him on the bed.

"What's up?" He replied not taking his eyes off the TV.

"What's wrong Ryan?" I caressed his leg.

"Nothing. Why you ask?"

"Because you're not acting right."

"I'm cool."

"Are you sure?"

"Yeah, I'm fine." He sat up and kissed me on the lips. Then quickly lay back down. "Now go ahead and shower. I'll wait up for you." He urged.

I hopped up to gather my things for my shower and retreated to the bathroom off his bedroom.

After staying in the shower much longer than anticipated, I dried off and gathered my clothes to put them in my dirty clothes sack in the bathroom.

I entered Ryan's bedroom in my birthday suit just to see if I could get a reaction out of him or not.

When he looked up at me, his eyes grew big, but quickly deflated.

"Girl what are you doing?" He asked.

I didn't answer. Instead I moved over to the bed and got under the covers next to him.

I snuggled my naked body against his warm body; lay my head on his chest as he wrapped one arm around me.

"What are you watching?" I asked.

"ESPN."

"Figures."

"I was about to turn the TV off and go to bed anyway, so you can watch what you want."

"I don't wanna watch TV Ryan. I wanna have a lil fun baby."

I slid my hand down his nicely toned chest over those hard abs down inside his boxers to locate my love interest.

"Please stop Krisha. I thought you agreed…"

"No, I didn't agree. You told me what *you* wanted to do. I don't want that, I want you."

"I'm sure you can abstain for a few months. You've done it before right?"

"What the hell is that suppose to mean?" Was he testing me or something?

"I'm not always with you. We've gone without seeing each other for several months in the past. That means we weren't having sex."

He must didn't know whom he was talking to. Little did he know nothing went undone my way. And I'm sure he wasn't lacking either.

"Why is this so important to you?" I asked with attitude.

"Krisha, we have a child together. We've done everything married folks do. I just thought our wedding night would be much more special if we waited until then to make love again."

I gently took his hand and guided it between my legs. Slid his fingers across my pearl and slightly below.

"Does this feel like a woman who gives a damn about waiting? I'm still gonna want you the same then."

I let him feel my wetness. "And that's from just touching you."

He stared at me as if he were thinking about it.

Then all of a sudden he turned on his side with his back to me.

"That's cold Ryan. Really cold."

I was pissed.

I did respect his reason for waiting; but that wasn't doing much for me right now. So I hopped up and retreated to the bathroom once again, to take a cold shower. The shower refreshed me and got it off my mind.

After a quick shower, I dressed in boy shorts and a tank and tried my best to clear my head. When I got back into the bedroom, Ryan was sound asleep. I snuggled in close, threw my arm around his waist and fell into a peaceful slumber next to the love of my life.

35

After closing on the house, we celebrated with Sheri and Steve and a couple more friends of Ryan's. I was introduced to Tim and Rodney when we made it to the restaurant. They both arrived alone; said their girlfriends would be joining us shortly.

After Jace proposed a toast to Ryan and me, Tim and Rodney's girl's showed up. Tim introduced them as Bianca and Teressa, respectively. I got a couple of fake hellos and hugs. They both looked like teenagers but I'm sure they were a little older.

I hate fake bitches. I thought.

I could see clean through both of the Jessica Simpson wannabes. They were spending their men's money and spending it big. Every dime was all over them. They were both designer from head to toe. From the stunner shades to the bags, down to the shoes, and probably the underwear underneath. Pretty but fake.

I got to thinking about what Danielle said on last night. She said Tim's girl was Maican. Something wasn't right. I'm pretty sure homegirl was makin' Tim happy below the belt and that was about it.

Anyway, they were probably thinking the same about me. But little did they know I was a different kind of woman.

Okay, stop it Krisha. You're going off inside your head for nothing. I said to myself.

I was happy about purchasing our first home together, but my nerves were bad now. I was trying to be a good girl; hadn't been touched by a man in four months, and it showed. My attitude was getting fouler as the evening grew. I was ready to call it a night. It was time for me to get my tail back home. To Louisiana.

The next day I called Tyson regarding the mortgage. He wanted to meet immediately. While Ryan was practicing, I met with Tyson at his office with all the documents he needed to get the ball rolling.

Tyson was one of the most handsome men I'd ever seen. He was definitely up there with Todd's pretty behind. Not only was he enlightening on the outside, but I found that he was a highly intelligent man. I discovered that he was a computer science major, as myself. That was one thing we both had in common. After that revelation, we had plenty to converse about. Mostly talking about our college horror stories, being stuck in the computer lab all night trying to get a program to run.

He owned TyTech Consulting firm, which had six locations in six different U.S. cities. He also owns a small restaurant in the city that he allows his mother and family to run, and few vacation homes in Orlando, Miami, and L.A. I was so surprised and amazed at his intellect. Our initial meeting in the club did nothing for his character. Very articulate and professional, but still had that swagger. That was sexy. Gotdamn sexy. But I know a successful, wealthy man like him had a few distractions. And I was taken. So what?

We completed all requirements in record time. The home he was purchasing was a two million dollar bachelor pad. I had no idea. I'd only written a couple million dollar mortgages in my entire career. Not like folks in Louisiana had that kind of money. I was thanking God for Sheri introducing us right about now. He wrote out a check for the down payment. When I looked at it, I wondered why he didn't just pay cash for the damn house. The check was way more than what was required.

I put all material in my briefcase and packed up to leave.

"Ump thank you for coming Ms. Taylor."

"No, thank you for your business Mr. Delaney. I'll be in touch shortly."

He got up to walk me out.

"How about having lunch with me?"

"Is it for business or pleasure?" I asked.

"Oh business of course." He said quickly.

"In that case, lunch would be nice." I smiled.

We shared an interesting lunch. Talked a lot about the business then he shifted the conversation toward life in general then onto relationships; mine in particular.

"Look Ms. Taylor, forgive me for being honest, if it offends you. But, I think you're a wonderful woman. If you weren't already taken, I'd ask you to have dinner with me tonight, on a different level."

"Thank you, but sorry."

"Can I ask you something?"

"Sure."

"Are you in love with Ryan?"

"Why would I marry him if I weren't?"

He just stared at me.

"Look I don't know exactly what you're getting at, but I don't *need* a Ryan Mathers in my life for me to be okay. I can hold my own."

"No, No." He put his hands up in protest. "I'm not trying to suggest anything. I can see that you're a very independent woman. You've definitely got your stuff together. I just wanted to know. I don't like interfering with happy homes."

"But if I weren't happy, I would be fair game?" I smiled and asked.

"I wouldn't say fair game. I hate to think of a woman as some type of play thing. But I would definitely show you how happy I could make you?"

"I could never be bought Mr. Delaney?"

"There's a lot more to me Mrs. Taylor. It's just that I'm mature enough to recognize when a woman deserves the world. I may have just met you, but I've met plenty women in my time and I recognize a worthy woman."

He smiled and sipped his drink.

"Well thank you Mr. Delaney, you're a wise man. But you know what this means right?"

"What's that?"

"Saying that has changed the scope of our relationship. I can't accept any more invitations from you. It must be about business only."

"So I can't take the lady who's giving me my dream home out to dinner when the deal is closed?"

"Not unless my fiancé chooses to come."

"That's cold baby. Besides, I'm sure he'll have other things to do."

"What's that supposed to mean?"

I stared at him for an answer.

"Sorry." He threw up his hands in defense. "Just being sarcastic. It's business, strictly business."

"Well, Tyson, thank you for the lunch, but I should be going."

"I can't deny the physical attraction. But I'd like to get to know you better."

"Thank you, but I've gotta go." I got up from the chair. He jumped up from his seat too.

"I'm sorry. I just speak from the heart."

"Tyson, I'm taken and very much in love."

"Trust me, I can change that."

Ignoring his comment. "Didn't you say you and Ryan were cool?"

"Yeah, he's a cool guy, but when I first met you I didn't know you were with him. The attraction was already there."

"Goodbye. I'll be in touch. About the mortgage that is." I turned on my heels and strolled out of the restaurant.

He was too much. Fine and cute. Pretty boys are nothing but trouble.

Ryan and I spent the evening together chilling, talking, and kidding around. I was bored and ready to go home. I'd done what I came here for. Now all I needed to do was finish with Tyson on tomorrow and I'll be ready to leave. I had planned to stay two more days to begin decorating the house but I was getting a little homesick. I missed my kids, Mia, Carmen, and my house. I was ready to be in the confines of my own home. This one bedroom crap was old. I loved being with Ryan but he was beginning to get on my last nerve. For some reason, he was still acting shady. And I couldn't shake my funky attitude. The 'tude he was throwing off had *me* foul. The only times I had a good time was when I was with Sheri or Tyson. I just needed to be alone and in my own space. I had a good mind to go to a hotel.

I had an idea that would get my mind off going home, so I mentioned it to Ryan.

We'd just finished eating the dinner I'd cooked and were cleaning the kitchen together.

"Ryan, let's stay at our house tonight."

"And what are we supposed to sleep on?"

"We can sleep on the floor."

"On the floor? In that big cold house."

"Ryan the electricity is on. And as long as I'm with you, nothing else matters. We don't need any furniture."

"Can't we wait until we get furniture tomorrow?"

"We won't get furniture tomorrow. I'm sure it'll have to be ordered and delivered. So we may as well go ahead tonight."

"You know I can't have my legs and back all stiff sleeping on the floor."

"Well, let's get one of those air mattresses from the store on the way over."

Pulling me close. "Baby we have a lifetime to spend in that house. What's the hurry?"

"I just want to be in my own space, with my man, in our new home tonight; with or without furniture. Besides I got something to show you." Thought I'd throw that in there just to see his reaction.

Smiling and shaking his finger. "Aw, now see. I knew you were up to your tricks."

"C'mon baby. Why not?"

He grabbed me by my waist and turned my body to face him. He gave me a peck on the lips.

"We need to wait."

Letting my frustration out of the bag. Being fed up with him and this wait for everything shit, I said, "Look, I'm sick of waiting. What's wrong with me wanting to spend the night in my new home that I just purchased with my fiancé?"

"But sleeping is not all you want to do."

"You damn right. I wouldn't mind laying butt ass naked in front of the fireplace in your arms."

"I would like that too, but…"

Cutting him off. "But what? If I came here not wanting to make love to you then you would have had something to say about that. I hear what you're saying and I think it's very thoughtful and loving. But I'm sexually frustrated right now."

"What's the difference in you being in Louisiana and my not seeing you for months?"

"The difference is that when you're not there, we're not together, and I can't see or touch you. But damn, we're here together. We sleep in the same bed. I want you. I screamed.

"I want you too, but I think with my heart and mind, not with big boy down there."

"Well got damn, I guess I think with my vajayjay cause all I know right now is that I want to have sex!" I screamed.

He just stared at me.

"Don't talk like that."

I know it wasn't lady like. But who cares.

"I'm sorry. Look, we don't have to do anything. Let's just go."

"You know you're not gonna act right."

It was clear he was on some other shit.

"You know what Ryan? I think there's another reason for your refusals."

"What's that?"

"Look, just remember, I don't get down with the bullshit."

"Girl what are you talking about?"

"I don't think I have to say anything else."

"Like hell you don't. Are you accusing me of something? If so, let it be known."

"Just forget it. You don't want to stay at the house. I've been with you three days and you don't wanna touch me, so forget it."

"Let me know what else is on your mind. That's not all you're trying to say."

"You want it? You really want it Ryan? Cause you know I can bring it."

"Say what you feel Krisha, it's just me."

He was getting pissed. He had a stern look. Eyes squinted. Facial muscles twitching.

"Okay then. You want it, you got it." I stared him directly in the eyes. "Who is Maican?"

"Who?"

"Need I repeat myself?"

"Where'd you get that name from and why are you asking me?"

"You know what? Forget it. I don't know what I was thinking. I'm wasting my time."

I turned to walk away. He jumped in front of me preventing me from leaving.

"Answer me. Where'd you get that name? Who've you been listening to?"

"What does it matter?"

"It matters a lot if someone is feeding you some crazy shit."

"Ryan you're hittin' something alright." I spat matter-of-factly. "Don't tell me you aint and it's sure not me."

"Krisha what in the world are you talking about? Where are you getting this?"

"I'm grown. Nobody has to tell me anything. I know a sneaky mothafucka when I see one."

"A sneaky motha...you must have me confused with your ex." He spat.

"Keep him out of this. He has nothing to do with this."

"It amazes me as to how you're always quick to defend his ass."

"Why are you trying to change things around? This is not about Todd or me. This is about you, your Mr. Wait, Goody Two Shoes ass."

"I try to treat you like a lady. I try to respect you and show you love, but you beat me down for that? I don't understand you."

"I'm not beating you down. And don't go to thinking you've done something another man can't do. You need a trophy for being a man?"

He looked like he could knock me to China.

He quickly changed the mood.

"Wait, wait. Let's calm down baby. This is going too far. We're gonna both end up saying things we don't really mean." He stuttered.

I looked at him and rolled my eyes. I didn't say a word.

I knew I was wrong for that last comment. I just wasn't ready to apologize yet.

He tried pulling me to him again, but I pulled away.

"Krisha don't let your past interfere with our relationship."

"Excuse me…My past?" *No he didn't.* I thought. *Now he gon' start me up again.* "My past has nothing to do with this."

"Every man is not an adulterer like your ex. I told you I would never put you through that."

Now that was low. No matter how long it's been, the realization still hurt. I was sensitive to anybody talking about me and Todd and the nature of our break up. And especially if they're trying to throw it up in my face in some foul form or fashion. He was just trying to turn things from pointing at him. He knew how to get at me. And he knew damn well not to do that shit to me.

"You know what? I don't know what's going on with you but rest assures time will tell. I'm not going to look for it either, so if you're screwing up, you better get it right before I find out because then it won't be nothing you can say to me. And I mean nothing!"

"So I only get one chance. You mean I don't get ten chances before I strike out."

That was even lower. I didn't respond. Instead, I stormed out of the kitchen. I went upstairs to get my coat, purse and keys.

As I was exiting the bedroom, Ryan came in.

"Where are you going?"

"I gotta get out of here. I need to be alone."

"We can talk about it. You don't have to go."

"No we can't talk about it tonight. You've said what you had to say and so did I. Anything else is gonna lead to an argument."

"Yah know what. You are too selfish Krisha. Why does everything have to go your way?"

I was trying to leave in peace. Now he wanna test me again.

"Oh I am huh? Let me find out who the fuck Maican is and I'll guarantee I'll be really generous when I start passing out ass whippings podnah."

I brushed past him to head out of the room. He grabbed my arm and spun me around to face him. Stared into my eyes as if his eyes would reveal the message from his heart.

He read my facial expression and let me go.

I walked away.

"So you're gonna leave me in *my* shit?"

I didn't utter a sound. I took his truck and headed out the driveway without looking back.

I drove around for about thirty minutes before my phone rang. I look down at the phone's ID to discover it was Todd. *Damn!* I thought. I didn't feel like dealing with him right now.

"Yes." I answered.

"How are you?"

"Okay."

"What's wrong?"

"Nothing."

"What's wrong Krisha?"

"Why do you assume..."

"Did you forget? I know you. That young buck didn't hit you did he?"

"No Todd."

"Then what happened?"

"Todd I don't wanna involve you in our business. It's nothing I can't handle."

He didn't know he was one of the reasons I was out here driving around aimlessly.

"Come home baby. You won't ever have to deal with drama again. I've done the shit and learned. Aint nothing' else out there for me. That young mothafucka got a whole lot of experiencing left to do. You just gonna end up going through some of the same shit I put you through all over again."

"You're jumping to conclusions."

"Am I? I know you sound like you've been crying. You're answering your phone so that means you're not with him, because lately you haven't been answering my calls. And I know he's too young for you. Maybe not so much in age, but mentally. He's got to finish growing up to get with a woman like you. He thinks he's ready right now. And in a lot of ways he probably is. But his lifestyle won't let him fully commit right now. He's got to get all of that out of his system first. Trust me, I know."

"I'm okay boo." I said softly. Swiping at the tears on my face.

"When are you coming home?"

"Probably tomorrow, if not the next day."

"I wanted to let you know that I have the boys with me."

"Why? Did they call you for some reason?"

"They said they were bored. They wanted to go to the game room. So I picked them up today. And if you'd answer my calls sometimes and talk to me, I would have told you that I'd take them anyway. I can keep my own kids if you're out of town Krisha."

"I'm sorry Todd. I know. I just don't want to bother you sometimes. I know you're busy."

"Never too busy for you guys. They're my children."

"Did you see the baby?"

"Yeah, she's getting big. She's beautiful. Looking more and more like you everyday."

That made me smile.

"Thanks."

"You know I love her like she's mine. There's no difference."

"Yeah I know." I said softly.

"And I would love for all of us to be together."

"Todd stop. Now you were doing good just now."

"I can't watch you suffer."

"What...I'm not suffering Todd. What are you...?"

He cut me off. "I will never watch you suffer with anyone. I can't do it."

"I love you too." I said trying to get him to shut up.

"He needs to grow up Krisha. You're gonna be his first marriage. Probably first real commitment. He's gonna mess up and you'll be walking the same road as you did with me, helping a grown man grow up. You've done that already. That will break you if you have to do it again. You don't need to try to raise another man. You need a full grown experienced man to grow old with at this point."

"I do agree on that note. I'm too old to be playing games."

"You do you, but always know that the door to my heart and home will always be open to you. Love you girl."

"Tell my sons that I love them and I'll call them tomorrow."

I drove around another few minutes before heading toward my new house. I realized Ryan would probably look for me there so I turned around to go to Sheri's. On my way there, my cell rang again. I was sure it was Ryan this time. However it was Tyson.

"Krisha I just wanted to apologize for my behavior on yesterday. I've been thinking about you every since. I don't want you to get the wrong idea about me."

"I didn't get the wrong impression. Not to brag or anything, but I'm used to it. I can handle myself."

"Well, I do respect your engagement and I'm very sorry if I offended you."

"Hey don't worry about it. No offense taken."

Silence.

"Well, I guess I...I..." He stammered over his words.

I cut him off.

"Tyson when you look at me, what do you see?"

The words loosely flowed off my tongue.

He let out a huge sigh. "Honestly. At first glance, I see a very attractive woman. Then when I look again, I see natural beauty that is so radiantly defined. When you speak I see an inner beauty beyond compare. In your presence, I see intelligence, strength, a loving, carefree spirit, and a very outspoken woman."

"Wow. I didn't expect all of that."

"I hope you didn't expect anything less."

"I just don't know about me sometimes."

"Whatever it is, let it ride. Life's too short to be riding around town pondering and worrying about things you can't control."

"How do you know I'm riding around town?"

"You're in Ryan's truck right?"

"Yes."

"Well I just saw you make a U-turn in that intersection."

"Are you spying on me?"

"Of course not. I saw you today in that truck with #82 on the personalized plate. So now I relate that vehicle to you."

"Well don't. You probably won't see me in this too much. I have my own vehicle."

"I love an independent woman."

"Well that's me."

"Nothing wrong with that."

"So why are you out riding around aimlessly?"

"I took some things over to my daughter that she asked me to get for her."

"That's sweet."

"Yeah well, you be careful okay."

"I will. And I'll give you a call tomorrow. I should have some good news for you."

"Thanks. I'll be expecting you."

"Goodnight Tyson."

After talking to Tyson somehow my soul was at ease. I turned around again and headed back toward my house. I still needed to be alone to think though. I wasn't sure if I was having second thoughts about marrying Ryan or what but I just needed to get myself together.

I stopped at Wal-Mart first to pick up that air mattress and other essentials. I ended up buying all types of items; much more than I went in the store for, but I was certain that one way or another, I was going to need them.

I absolutely adored my house. It was very spacious and rewardingly beautiful. All it needed was furniture and my babies.

After putting up the grocery items and setting up my temporary bed. I cleaned, then relaxed in the Jacuzzi tub. I popped Fantasia's CD into the radio and laid my head back onto the tile wall in the tub to soak. I let the mellow music calm my spirit. I don't know when I fell asleep, but the ringing of my cell awakened me. It was now after 11:00 pm, and I wondered who was ringing my line. I answered quickly in search of the caller's identity.

"How are you Krisha?"

A deep male voice sang through the phone.

"I'm good."

"It's good to hear your voice."

I was still trying to make out the familiar voice so I continued to search my mental database of sexy male voices.

Then it dawned on me.

"Craig?"

"The one and only."

Silence.

I remained quiet. Tried to figure out if I should curse him out again or just hang up the phone.

"What do you want Craig?" I said instead.

"I miss you."

"Come again?"

"I'm sorry for whatever happened between us, but I want to make it up to you."

"Craig. The only thing you can do is kiss my ass."

"You know I'll be happy to do that."

"You are one disgusting bastard."

"Let's meet somewhere so we can talk."

"Craig do me a favor...don't ever call my phone again okay. As far as I'm concerned you never existed."

"Krisha, I love you."

"Love?" I laughed. "Please kill the drama. You loved nothing but the sex you were getting every now and then. Go to hell!"

"Why are you trippin' baby? It was nothing."

"Trippin'?"

Now it was time for me to let him have it. He was perfect for releasing my built up anger on tonight.

"Why do you think I want you after getting involved with that back stabbing bitch that you knew the deal on? I wouldn't trust your lying ass or that disease infested body not another day in my life! You are just as trifling as that bitch; both of you deserve each other. You can't even smell this again so get over it, okay!"

I hung up the phone amazed. I couldn't believe that after all these months he's calling me with that crap. *Did men really think I was that simple?* I wondered.

I had to take a deep breath to calm down. Craig had really run my blood pressure up and I didn't like that feeling. As if I wasn't dealing with enough already.

I was wide awake and ready to get up out of the tub so that I could say my prayers and lay down to rest my mind and body. Oh and I have to make a mental note to pray real hard on my potty mouth and vile temper.

I stood up and reached for the towel that I'd placed on the counter to dry off, then looked up into the mirror, and almost jumped out of my skin as I covered my body and screamed. I grabbed my chest, as my heart rate instantly shot toward the ceiling. My eyes were now stretched as big as golf balls and I couldn't say one mumbling word. All I could do was stare.

After regaining composure, I managed to say, "Ryan you scared the devil out of me."

He didn't say a word. Just moved away from the bathroom door, turned and high tailed it out of the bedroom. This left me in thought. *Did he hear my conversation with Craig? How long had he been standing there? I know he had to hear me; had to. I was screaming too loudly. Was the alarm on? I sure didn't hear anything. Tomorrow morning I'm calling the alarm company. I think. Maybe I need to see what tonight is gonna be like before I start making plans for tomorrow.* My thoughts consumed me. I was nervous.

Very quickly things had turned on me. I'd acted a fool earlier and left Ryan's place for no real reason. My anger was fueled by my fiancé wanting to make our honeymoon more special for the both of us and a girl mistaking me for someone else. I read more into it than the evidence provided. In all actuality, I had no evidence of anything. All I had was a crazy name that sounded like it belonged somewhere in Georgia.

It was funny how I suddenly began to realize all of this now after I'd most likely placed myself in hot water once again. I don't like being on this side of the fence. Doesn't feel too good.

I dressed in the bathroom in a tank and underwear that I'd purchased at Wal-Mart due to my unexpected departure from Ryan's condo. It would have to do, I wasn't complaining; I had bigger issues.

After purposely taking a long time to dress, I eased out of the bathroom into the bedroom but found no Ryan. I thought about getting down on the mattress and going to sleep but, I figured I should at least go see if he was still inside the house. So, I went downstairs in search of him but didn't seem to see him anywhere. I went to the gym and peeked outside on the patio. No Ryan. I found his car still parked in the garage, so I knew he had to be around the house somewhere.

I called out his name, to no avail. Decided to go back upstairs to check all of the rooms, no luck. He wasn't inside. Maybe he was walking around outside or something. I thought. I sure wasn't going out there in the cold to look for him. I figured he'd come on back when he got cold enough.

So I retreated to the master bedroom and got down on the mattress to call my best homie, Mia. I talked to her for about twenty minutes, filling her in on my drama for the moment. This time I whispered. I'd learned my lesson.

Typical Mia told me to sit my "special ass" down somewhere.

"Don't take that humbuggish crap to Maryland ruining things for yourself. If you aint seen shit, then you don't know shit! Don't let *anybody* play you like that. Trust me she knew exactly what she was doing." Were her words.

I know I need my girl by me always. I never looked at things like that. Whatever her name, Jace's girl, is probably friends with Miss It or something. Who knows? Who cares?

I lay there trying my best to sleep but sleep wouldn't find me. Ryan hadn't come back inside so I had no idea where he was or what was on his mind. I'd just rolled over on my back to stare at the ceiling when I heard footsteps on the stairs. Praying to God it was Ryan, I pulled my purse close. If it wasn't Ryan whoever it was, was gonna meet the fate of my little chrome friend that lived inside my purse.

He opened the door, came into the bedroom and went straight to the bathroom. After relieving himself, I could hear the water running. Then the door to the bathroom swung open. He went to a corner in the room and began removing his clothes.

I spoke first, "Ryan I'm sorry for my behavior earlier. I overreacted."

He didn't bother responding.

I looked at him. He looked at me.

"C'mon baby, say something to me. I'll respect your wishes from now on. I respect you for even making the suggestion that we wait until our wedding night."

He undressed down to his boxers and walked over to my make shift bed on the floor. Never saying a word. He pulled the blanket up from the bottom of the mattress and began crawling his way up.

He crawled up under the covers until his head rested on my stomach.

"Ryan."

I pulled the covers down to expose his head.

"Ryan." I said again for no apparent reason.

I began caressing his head as he took my waist and snuggled his head into me.

"At this point, I don't care to know who, what, or when. But I did hear you say that it was over and had been for a while. I'm praying to God that's true because I don't know what I'd do without you, to you, or to him." He gripped my waist tighter and caressed my stomach with the side of his face. "I'm just scared Krisha."

"What is there to be scared of?"

"I love you too much. I'm afraid of what I'd do if I ever lost you to anybody. I don't know how I'd react to that. I have never felt like this about anyone."

"You won't have to do anything baby. I'm not going anywhere; there is no other man in my life."

We didn't speak.

As we quietly marveled in holding each other, out of the blue he said, "I should have told you before, but Maican is someone I used to date."

"Guess you would have never told me if I didn't ask."

"Probably not. Didn't think it was anything important."

"It's not. Forget I even mentioned it."

"I'm never leaving you. You know that right?"

I figured that was a rhetorical question so I didn't say a word.

"I love you Krisha."

I massaged his head and shoulders.

"You're not gonna tell me you love me back?" He asked.

At that moment I realized that something had changed. He seemed so different than the Ryan that I'd just left at his condo. Right now he was so sincere. He seemed so needy. Hung onto me as if his life depended on it. I got a feeling that something was eating at his heart. Something like, regret.

"You know I do."

He kissed my stomach. "I want to hear it."

"Oh you do huh?"

I decided to lighten the mood being playful. He was being too serious almost as if death was knocking at somebody's door.

"Yeah, I wanna hear you tell me you love me. Say it like you really mean it, but don't say it if you don't feel it." He tugged at the rim of my panties with his teeth.

"Don't start anything you aren't willing to finish."

"You know me, if I get the fire started, I'm gonna let the motha burn. Besides, you said oral wasn't included. But I gotta know how much you love me." He kissed my crotch.

"Let me show you." I panted.

"You're not playing fair."

I placed my hand on his head. Caressed his head and face as I spoke. "Mr. Mathers. You are my world. You have a significant place in my heart."

He pulled at my crotch with his lips. "Awww." I screamed. "Baby...I love you like I've never loved before. I'm so sorry. I love you man!" I said really fast.

"That's what I'm talking 'bout", he said as he slid my panties over to the side placing his tongue on my pearl. He pulled the blanket back over his head and trailed light kisses down my thighs. Parting my legs to his satisfaction he then indulged in my sweetness making love to me.

I was willing to settle for the pleasure he was offering me just to keep him happy. Besides he was good at it. I didn't want a minor issue to ruin what we had because all issues can be resolved. I had the perfect resolution to mine. I'd already decided that when I get home, Todd was gonna be my own resolution. Hell I was still Krisha Taylor. Technically Ryan and I aren't even married. And what he didn't know wasn't going to hurt him.

36

Ryan and I left for his place early the next morning. I awakened later, dressed, and gathered my things. I met Tyson for a couple hours to close the deal on his mortgage. We both walked away with smiles on our faces.

Tyson offered lunch, but I had to decline. Sheri and I had planned to go shopping for furniture and other household items today. Just like that I'd forgotten all about going home. All was well. All I'd asked was for my baby to give me what I wanted. I was taken to a heavenly land of soft carnal pleasure a couple times last night, so I was okay for a minute.

I decided to stay in Maryland a few more days. Sherri and I decided to take a trip to New York to shop on the next day. We would spend a couple days there. I just needed to check in with my people back in Louisiana. I had to call Carmen to see if that was okay with her, but first I called Todd. It was going on five days that I'd been away and I was just beginning to have a good time.

Todd advised that I could stay in Maryland until "Jesus came back", he didn't "give a shit." He said he would take care of his kids regardless of where I was. He was livid. I think he enjoyed it when he thought Ryan and I were on shaky grounds. Guess that gave him hope. I didn't argue with him. I politely said thank you and hung up the phone. He was on a serious trip. Pissed that I was still here with Ryan. Oh well, he'd better get his mind right.

On our trip, it was nonstop with Sheri. The girl was like the energizer bunny when it came to shopping. I liked nice things, but darn it Sheri lived expensive, designer things.

Our New York trip was very productive and entertaining. We met up with a couple of Sheri's friends and had a blast. By the time I left New York, I had all types of designer, custom made and imported goods being shipped to my house. And for every package I had, Sheri had two. I'd never in my life spent money like that in one trip. But I think there were gonna be more trips like that. I kind of enjoyed the freedom of splurging for once; something different for me. Besides my fiancé told me to have fun and spend as much as I needed; money wasn't an issue.

I ended up staying in Baltimore another week. For somebody who was bored as hell and ready to go home a few days ago, I stayed another whole week.

Once we moved into our house, I felt more relaxed. I was more at home and comfortable being in my own space. We took the week to move in Ryan's things, and I wanted to be there when some of the furniture arrived. I decided to hire Sheri as my interior decorator because there was no way I could do it all myself, and it was time for me to go. I needed to get back to Louisiana for my children and my business. Since a lot of the furniture was imported, Sheri promised she would accept all deliveries and get everything set up in my absence. At least Ryan did have a bed to sleep in now.

After arriving home, I went to take some things to Ryan's mother then went to get my children. I was so happy to see my baby and she was just as happy to see me. My little men were just as glad to see me too. They loved being with their dad, but I know they missed me.

It took a week to finalize all the wedding arrangements. My wedding was a month away and I had everything in order. I was glad to be finally putting one responsibility behind me.

I talked to Ryan every morning and night while we were apart. His team was in the playoffs so his season was even longer. I wished the team much luck, but at the same time I was ready to have him all to myself. Mia, the kids and I were to fly to Baltimore next weekend to check on the house. I wanted to see the progress Sheri had made.

My kids and I had planned to have a nice quiet dinner at home. They insisted I make their favorite dishes, fried catfish and macaroni and cheese. TJ insisted on inviting his dad to eat dinner with us. He said his Dad doesn't have anyone to cook for him and often eats alone. I agreed. Mainly due to the fact that they were going to be several miles away from Todd in a matter of weeks. I wanted them to spend as much time with him as possible.

We had dinner, put the kids to bed, and Todd and I talked for a couple hours. Our conversation was nice. Just like old times. For a moment, I felt as if we'd never been apart. Like we'd never experienced any of the drama that ruined our marriage. Todd was becoming a good friend and I welcomed that.

I told him about my father and the things Carmen revealed to me. Surprisingly, he said he'd sensed there was a personal relationship between my mother and Carmen. He said they always seemed as if they knew each other. As we sat side by side on the couch, he shared some things I never knew before. He talked about the many conversations he and my mother had over the years. He told me about a conversation a couple years before my mother's death where she asked him to always be there for me.

We talked about the Kyra thing. When I thought about how things were at that time, it still angered me a little. I no longer hated him for what he did to us. Though, it still hurts when I think about it because I was blatantly betrayed by two people I loved to death. But time heals all wounds. I've forgiven both of them for what they did. I just can't stand Kyra for doing it again with Craig. There was no doubt that I loved Todd.

As he sat, talking about my mother and our past. I became overwhelmed. Memories are so good to have, but at times they're too much to bear. I shed tears. I believe the tears were more for the undying love that my mother had for me rather my loving her. I'm still seeing, feeling, and hearing about the love she had for me though she's been gone almost three short years now. She knew I'd lose Todd. She knew I'd lose Kyra, and she knew I'd lose her. Our last conversation rang so clearly in my head now. Every word now made sense. She was telling me my future. I just didn't know it. She was preparing me for it. Giving me strength. I cried. Todd wiped my tears. He held me in his arms. Kissed my forehead.

Through the monitor I heard the baby crying.

Todd went to get her. He came back, went into the kitchen and grabbed her juice cup from the fridge. He gave her the cup and rocked her in his arms until she fell asleep. He insisted on caring for her himself as I watched. He looked at her as if she were his own. *What if she were?* I thought. *Would it have made a difference? How would Tamia have affected our relationship? He wasn't faithful with two kids. Would three have set him on the straight and narrow?* These questions flooded my mind as I watched him rock my baby girl in his arms.

"I can take her." I offered.

"No. She's okay." He held her as she slept. Looking down at her tiny frame with a loving smile.

"She should be mine you know."

I didn't answer. Wasn't sure if he wanted an answer. He'd said those words before. Considering the way he looked at her, I knew he meant them. He absolutely adored her.

I wiped my tears, cleaned my face, and watched him watch her for a while longer before speaking.

"I guess it's time for us to go up to bed." I softly said. Referring to the baby and myself.

"Yeah. I'd better go. It's getting late."

I got up to turn the CD player and lights off in the room.

"I'll put her back in her bed." Todd said as he turned to go back upstairs.

I went to the kitchen to double check everything, and then went up the stairs to my bedroom. Since Todd hadn't come back down, he would have to let himself out.

When I got up the stairs, Todd had already placed Tamia in her crib and was in the boys' bedroom. I headed to my bedroom to start my bath. I gathered my things and began to undress. I was down to my bra and panties when he came to the door.

"I'm gonna go Krisha." He said as he stood in the open doorway of my bedroom.

"Okay. You can let yourself out."

"Are you okay?" As concerned covered his face.

"Ummm...yeah. I'll be fine." I stuttered.

He walked inside my bedroom. Wrapped his arms around me comforting me with sincere affection. *Damn! I love this man.* I thought. *My chest hurts so freakin' bad.*

He didn't say a word. Just held my body tight as my head lay in his chest and strong hands caressed my back.

His love was so different than that with Ryan.

But then again, I was so confused when it came to Todd. He always brought me back.

"I would give up all that I have to be here with you again."

"I love you." I had to say. The sensation and feelings surrounding me allowed me to admit it without thinking.

He pulled away and looked at my face.

"Are you okay?"

"Yeah. I just felt the need to say that."

"You already know how I feel." He kissed my cheek.

I kissed his lips.

We stood silently staring at each other.

"I wanna hold you all night." He whispered.

"I'd like that. I don't wanna be alone."

He kissed me. This time with more meaning.

We bathed together. He washed my body. I washed his.

We dried each other. I lay across the bed. Todd got the oil and massaged my entire body, front and back. I was exhausted mentally and physically.

His lips found the places his hands had just left. From head to toe, one side to the other. His lips graced my body. Soothing. Relaxing. Mixed emotions. A confused spirit. An undying love.

Our lips met. His body told me he was happy to be with me. Told me he would always be mine. An unconditional love that I could never deny. And will never admit. I don't think I'll ever rid myself of Todd; ever.

As we kissed and caressed, my phone rang.

My heart immediately started its wild rendition of beating. I knew who it was. We hadn't had our evening conversation, so I picked up on the third ring.

I looked over at Todd and used my eyes to dare him to say a word.

"Hi babe." Ryan's strong masculine voice rang out.

"Hey baby."

Todd sighed heavily, but stayed on top of me with his head in my chest. I wrapped my legs around him.

"What's up?"

"Nothing."

I was short. Trying to sound normal.

"Are the kids asleep?"

"Yes. Tamia just got down."

"I miss my baby."

"I know. But, hey we'll see you next weekend remember?"

"I can't wait. Wish I could just hold you right now."

When he said that, I felt a load of guilt come over me.

Trying not to sound suspicious. I said, "I wish I were in your arms too, baby."

As soon as I said that, I realized those might have been a bad choice of words. Hell I didn't know what else to say.

Todd immediately shot me a glance and rolled off of me.

Initially I'm thinking, *why is he trippin' when he knows I'm engaged to Ryan?* Then the thought popped in my mind. I remembered I'd just told Todd that I wanted him to hold me all night.

I stroked Todd's arm as I talked to Ryan trying to reassure him.

"What are you wearing?"

"Nothing."

"Damn!" Ryan screamed.

"Boy stop, please." I laughed at his silliness.

"Hurry up and get back to me. I'd gotten used to you being here."

"I will."

"I love you."

"I know."

"What's wrong?"

"Nothing, why?"

"I don't get one back."

"I love you Mr. Mathers."

"I love you more Mrs. Mathers."

I smiled.

"Call me when you get up."

"You know it."

"Goodnight."

When I hung up the phone, Todd was sitting on the side of the bed with his back to me.

I ran the tips of my fingers down his bare back.

"Why are you getting married?" He asked coldly while refusing to look at me.

"What?" I said knowing good and well I heard him.

He repeated the question.

"Why are you asking me that?" I asked.

"You don't love him."

"Yes I do."

"Why am I in your bed then?"

"I told you, I don't want to be alone tonight."

"Then why were you with me a few weeks ago?"

"It was the moment Todd."

"So you're using *me* now?"

"I'm not using you."

"Two men can't hold you at the same time. You want me to hold you, and then you tell him you want him to hold you. Krisha, you need to be honest with yourself and get yourself together."

"It's not like you don't know about my relationship with Ryan. I can see him trippin' but why are you?"

"You just don't get it do you? Stop being so damn blind and selfish and look at this picture."

"I'm not being selfish and I'm not blind to anything."

"You're either one or the other. Or you just don't give a damn. You were never like this before. What's gotten into you?"

"Just what are you trying to say Todd?"

Getting up from the bed, "I'll tell you what. You think about it. You figure out what I'm saying. You're a smart girl." He began gathering his clothes.

"Todd don't go. Talk to me."

"Krisha I can't be here with you. Not after what I just heard. I've never actually seen or heard you interact with him on that level. You know how much that hurts me. Though I love the hell out of you, I don't have any claim to you. Other than being your children's father, I mean nothing to you. It's obvious to me now that you love him, or you're a good actress. Which one is it?"

"I don't believe you Todd."

"At one time in your life, you wouldn't ever look at another guy. Especially not in my presence. Now you're telling him you love him as if I'm not even here. I see now Krisha. It's really over. I saw it all over your face. Your body language. Heard it in your voice. If you love him, I have no business here."

"I do love him. I'm in love with him, but I'll always love you. I've said that to you several times before."

"So it's okay with you to marry him and sleep with me whenever we end up falling into each other's bed. Is that the woman you've become?"

"I know that's not right as far as me and Ryan are concerned. But you and me go back much farther than what he and I have. It's hard to let go of the past sometimes."

"Baby, you've gotta decide. Either you're gonna be his wife or you're not. You can't have it both ways because then I get my hopes all high."

"I never said I didn't want to be his wife."

"No, your mouth didn't, but your actions are sending mixed signals."

I knew he was right. I just didn't want to accept it. I was dead wrong. But, I couldn't help it. I didn't feel like I was being unfaithful being with Todd. He *was* my husband. Once.

"As soon as you get to him and get away from here, you won't think twice about me."

"I always wanted you Todd. You had the problem, remember? I want you now."

"Tonight right? But what'll tomorrow be like. You'll go back to being Ryan Mathers' fiancé and my ex-wife. What's in it for me? I don't need sex if that's what you're thinking."

"I never said that. I never thought of us together as being just quick sex. I can get sex if that's what I wanted."

"Yeah, but you know this one. You already know what you're getting. Don't try and play me." He tried to look serious.

I grinned. He knew damn well I wanted him.

I seductively strutted toward him with open arms. "Just come here baby, we'll talk about it later. I don't want you to leave tonight."

Todd looked at me with amazement.

"Haven't you heard me Krish? As much as I want to be with you, I can't do that."

He finished putting his clothes on.

This time I looked at him in amazement. "I'm sorry, but you know I don't beg." I rolled my eyes.

"That's a good thing. Keep it up okay."

"You don't have to be mean Todd."

"If I didn't love you so much. If I didn't see my faults. If I weren't trying to right the wrongs I've done. I wouldn't be. I'd jump in that bed, love you down, get up, get dressed and go home with no conscious. Just like I used to. I'm man enough to admit I was wrong for that. For all of it. That's why I'm trying to show you the old Todd; the man you fell in love with. "

That attitude that's been hard to suppress lately had kicked in and I was beginning not to care anymore.

He finished dressing and left without saying goodnight.

After I heard him drive off, I went to set the alarm and check on the kids. I brought Tamia to my bed. I just simply didn't want to sleep alone.

I was pissed at Todd when I should have been upset with myself. It was easier to be mad at him though. He was right in many ways. But he was messed up in so many others.

He said I needed to decide. Would I have to if he hadn't had his philandering ways? I had already decided. I was in love with Ryan and I was going to marry him. No questions about that. Guess I was just being a little slick getting it in with him. Guess I *was* using him; in a way. Oh well, so what, he used me plenty.

37

On Saturday night, Mia and I went out clubbing for the first time in ages. We were really having a good time until we ended up running into Todd and his date. I hadn't talked to him since that night he stormed out my house about a week ago. I tried my best to ignore him and his lil hoochie.

I'd already talked to Ryan twice throughout the night. He knew Mia and I were out and he was good with that. He'd even spoken to Mia so I was good with him for the night.

After Todd saw me out and all the attention I was getting, guess he had a change of heart about our little non-situation, or shall I say all that bull he talked.

He started blowing up my cell.

After somehow getting rid of his date, Todd quickly made his way over to me and commenced to being all up in my grill. I couldn't catch a breath without him.

Although he was buying too, he had stopped my drinks from coming from all over the room.

Mia still couldn't stand the sight of Todd. She was cordial, but didn't have much to say. Instead she got her party on and ignored him.

He was suave. Dressed to perfection, and as handsome as ever.

The more I drank, the better he looked. Though he'd made himself a part of my night out, he didn't stop our flow. Mia and I had a good ole' time as usual. We danced a little, drank a lot, and flirted even more.

Next thing I knew I was spread eagle on Todd's kitchen table with him giving me the serious business. I don't even remember how I got there. I was messssssed up! More than I've ever been in my entire life.

Around 8:30 am, I woke up with a headache out of this world.

After coming to my senses, I found that I was on the hard tiled floor. Todd was asleep with his head on my thigh. His arms held my legs tightly.

"Todd get up." I said groggily holding my head.

The side of my head felt heavy, and I could only squench to focus. My back and everything else ached without reservation. I was as stiff as a board. I tried to move him but didn't have the strength.

"Todd, get up." I repeated a little louder.

"Huh?" He replied.

"What the hell happened?" I asked looking around the room.

I meant, how did we end up on the floor by the doorway? I already knew some of what had happened. Something like...the wild sex, magnificent orgasms, loud noise of the bed hitting the wall, and being bent over the tub getting it real nice from the back. I got small visuals of those incidents in my mind.

"Huh?" He said again.

"Would you please move? I need to get up."

He was gettin' on my nerves.

He rolled off my thigh. So, I got up slowly aching from head to toe.

I went straight to the bathroom to take a warm bath to soothe my bones. Soon he joined me and we cleaned each other up real good.

I went back into the bedroom to find some of my clothes. Todd went into the kitchen to find the rest. I dressed in silence. Reality trying to set in.

"So when are you leaving?"

"Next weekend."

"I mean, when are you leaving for good?"

"A week after we return from the honeymoon."

"Are you sure?"

"About what?"

His eyes told me what he was referring to.

"C'mon let's not go back there." I said watching my toes.

"This is the last time I'll ask you."

"Yes, I'm sure." I answered annoyed.

"If it's the baby, you know I'll take care of her."

"You know as well as I do that I can take care of my own children. I wouldn't marry someone because of a child. I'm marrying Ryan because I'm in love with him and I want to be with him."

"Are you sure it's love Krisha?"

"Positive."

"Then what was last night?"

"You know what? I haven't had time to think about last night yet, but the way it looks, I'm leaning toward it being a big, alcohol induced mistake."

"Really? Is that the way you see it now?"

"Look. I've told you times before. I love you and I always will. I've told Ryan that, he knows that too. No one can ever take your place and

I'm not trying to replace you. I just want to be happy and Ryan makes me happy."

"I can make you happy Krish. I made you happy for many years."

"Yes, but you also…" I stopped it short because he was about to work my nerves. "Look we're not gonna go there. I'm sorry if I've confused you. This will not happen again." I said sincerely.

"I'll be here. You know the deal."

"Thanks."

I kissed him and gave him a big hug. He kissed me back and slipped me his tongue. I took it in. He found mine and loved it. Caressed my body as he probed my mouth. I abruptly pulled away.

"I gotta go."

He engulfed me in a tight bear hug.

"You're my heart." He said softly in my ear. "Don't stay away from me. I'll take you whenever and however you want me to have you. I'll never deny you again. You're mine and will always be mine. But if it makes you happy, I'll let you go on with him. He just better not ever mess up."

He kissed my ear. "Love you girl." Began a soft nibble. "I'll never stop loving you." We stood embraced.

"Stop please." I whispered resisting his advances.

"Let me love you goodbye."

I grinned.

"No." I said softly.

"Why not?"

"I never say goodbye unless the end is here." I whispered with a smile.

I kissed his lips.

He smiled.

"So, see ya later." I said.

I broke away from him and felt my pockets for my phone. *Time for me to check in with my family.* I thought.

"Todd, have you seen my cell?" I said looking around the room.

"No. You were on it last night."

"Here? In this room?"

"Yeah, you had it in here. So it should be here somewhere."

I searched for my phone. Found it on the floor on the other side of the bed.

I stuck it in my jacket pocket.

"I gotta go Todd. Carmen is gonna kill me. She was supposed to go to church this morning."

"I can take you home or you can take my truck."

I decided to take his truck since him taking me home would mean I'd have to wait for him to throw on some clothes. Besides I was ready to get rid of him.

When I got inside his truck, I pulled out my cell to call Carmen to let her know I was on my way and she could start dressing for church.

When I looked at my phone the screen looked funny. I couldn't determine why the counter was still ticking and the screen didn't have my babies' picture on it. It dawned on me that the phone was still on.

I held the phone to my ear. "Hello." I said.

No one answered, so I looked back at the phone then put it back to my ear.

"Hello." I repeated. No one replied so I hung up.

I looked at the call counter.

The counter revealed that the phone had been on for six hours and eighteen minutes. I immediately went to my recent calls and clicked on dialed calls. I hadn't dialed anyone since I called Mia to let her know I was on my way. And that was another thing. I didn't even remember riding with Todd last night. Where the hell was my car?

I clicked on received calls. Ryan's name was the last one on the list. I clicked on his name and there was his number. Call time at 2:21 am, the date and call counter time, six hours, 18 minutes, and 10 seconds. Lord have mercy!

I started the truck up and moved out of Todd's driveway. My heart beat fast. Oh my Gosh! was all I could say. *Did he hear anything? Did he hold the phone all those hours? Was he asleep? Did he forget to hang up?* I didn't know. He was at his game out of town. I know he had to be by the phone.

I called Mia. She told me she and Derric had dropped my car off at home. I explained what happened. Mia hung up the phone in my face. She was pissed at me as usual when it came to Todd, so I left her alone. I had to focus on Ryan.

I was a nervous wreck. Tears made a dash for my cheeks. I had to pull over to the side of the road to get myself together. Words Mia spoke a while back played in my head. *"Don't let Todd ruin things for you with Ryan."*

My phone rang as I was approaching my house.

"You are the silliest bitch I know!" Mia screamed through my cell.

"Why'd you hang up in my face?"

"I couldn't really talk. I was still at Derric's. I had to leave *my* man to get in *yo'* shit. When are you gonna wake up Krisha? You are not a teenager. You are a grown ass woman. Act like one. If you done fucked up with Ryan, I just don't know what to tell you."

"I know. I can't even find a lie to tell if he was listening all night."

"What in the world were you doing messing with him like that anyway? I thought that was all over."

"Why'd you let me leave with him?"

"You're grown hoe!"

"I know, but you remember how hard it was for me to let him go. He's hard to resist Mia. I swear he got some tricks no other man can even get wit. I *cannot* get rid of him Mia. I just can't."

"Sex doesn't make a relationship Krisha. It doesn't define love. And it doesn't make a man respect you."

"I know Mia, but it's not all about sex. It's our past. It's our kids. I just can't shake him completely. If I leave here, I believe I could. But being around Todd is hard."

"Either your ass is just the stupidest bitch I've ever met, or that fool got a magnum pole and gold tongue tips."

"It's not about all that. He's just mesmerizing."

"You got probs cuz."

"I know. But I want to be with Ryan, but I must admit that I gotta be with Todd every now and then until I can forget him completely…He loves me Mia. He just screwed up."

"That's his problem. He's a manwhore Krisha!"

"Mia!"

"Mia my ass. He needs a woman. When he has a woman, you're fine because he's occupied. It's easy for him to forget about you when he has a woman."

"You're right, but you know he can get somebody. He just doesn't want them. So he says. You see how he took that girl home once he saw us out."

"Fuck him Krisha! That bitch just wanted to block. Did you suddenly forget about all the crap he put you through? Make shit right with the man who really loves you; who hasn't caused you a lifetime of headaches and heartache. Todd just doesn't want anybody else to have you. If he gets you back, eventually he'll start his stuff again."

"I wish I could go to rehab for sex addiction."

"Bitch, they aint got no rehab for hoes. That shit is just in you. You gonna have to get it right yourself." She said laughing.

"You wrong for that one cousin. Dead wrong."

I laughed hard too, but that wasn't funny. That was the truth. I felt like a cheap whore.

38

After getting home and getting settled, I called Ryan but got no answer. I knew he was getting ready for the game so I figured I'd call him later. Speaking of game, that's where I should have been in the first place. Supporting my man instead of laid up with another. I used the excuse of not being able to get away from the kids or bring them out to Denver's freezing cold weather which were both tired excuses.

I went to watch the game on TV with Ryan's family. My boo made one touchdown but his team still lost. At first I was selfishly thinking if they lost I could go be with him without him having to work, but now I don't know what's gonna happen. Ryan's mother insisted on keeping the kids with her so I burned rubber out of her driveway. Took a long ride to clear my head.

When I arrived home, it was late. I called Ryan again. I know they were probably back in Baltimore by now, being the game was earlier in the day. His phone kept going to voicemail. I called him up until after eleven p.m. but to no avail.

I would have called all night, but I was exhausted from the events of last night and today. I fell asleep with the phone in my hand.

Startled awake by the ringing of the phone, I jumped up from the bed as if Jason were on my tail. The fact that I had the phone lying on the pillow next to my head didn't help either, so I had to gather my senses before I answered.

"Hey sweetheart." I said softly.

"Hey."

"I needed to hear your voice. I've called you all day. Why didn't you answer?"

"Honestly. I didn't want to talk to you then."

I didn't say word one. That statement told me what I already knew.

The next thing he said was, "Why'd you do it?"

Still at a loss for words. I let him speak. I wanted to be certain of what he was talking about. Wasn't gonna incriminate myself.

"So is that your way of telling me to get lost? Come on tell me, what's up?"

And there it was. My heart beat so fast. I had to swallow six or seven times before even attempting to speak.

"Talk to me Krisha. What is it that he has? He can screw over you with your best friend, divorce you, disrespect you and you still fuck with him? What is it?" He was so calm with his words that it scared me.

Tears found my cheeks.

"You know how bad that hurt me. You know what it was like listening to you with him? About like you felt when you found out about him and your friend. Or did you forget all of that?"

I could feel his hurt through the phone.

"I could barely concentrate on my game for thinking about you. You got my head so messed up right now Krisha. I should just tell you to go to hell right now."

"I know baby."

"You know? Then why? To intentionally hurt me? Do I really deserve that?"

"No. No baby. I made a mistake. I was drunk."

"You made the mistake of not hanging up the phone. Is that what you mean? Because if I wouldn't have called you. You would go on like nothing happened."

"No." I lay there in a ball with my head covered and phone to my ear. "No, that's not it."

"You don't know how hard this is."

He held the phone without speaking.

"Where are you baby?"

He refused to answer.

"Ryan. Where are you?" I said again softly.

He hesitated before speaking. "Does it really matter Krisha?"

"I wanna be with you. I'll come right now."

"No."

"Why not baby? I wanna be close to you. We need to talk face to face."

He hesitated. Didn't say anything for about thirty seconds.

"I'm outside."

I didn't speak. Instead I jumped up and did my thing with the steps, two at a time. I know one day I was gonna bust my tail on those steps. I would have just slid down the banister if I didn't know any better. But I made it to the bottom of the stairs safely.

I knew he was there. I didn't bother to look out the window. That was how he did it. Just show up.

I nervously opened the front door to the house and exited. Feeling the wet grass on my feet, it was then I realized I wore no shoes; however, I didn't let that stop me.

Ryan didn't see me coming from the side. He sat still in the car staring in front of him with the phone still to his ear. I held the phone as I went toward the driver's side of the car. I could see Ryan wiping his face with the front of his shirt.

"Open the door please." I said as I approached the car door. He immediately looked up at me and clicked the lock open.

I opened the door and gave him a sincere look. I didn't know what to say. So, I sat in his lap with my legs still outside on the ground. Wrapped my arms around his neck, embraced him for all it was worth. Leaned back to look into his eyes. I whispered, "I'm so sorry."

He gave me a hard stare. I know he was hurting. I was all too familiar with the feeling.

Suddenly, he pushed me back against the steering wheel. Pulling my arms from around his neck. He held my arms tightly preventing me from touching him. He stared into my eyes. Face showing signs of hurt and anger.

Physically pushing me away wasn't kosher with me, but in many ways I understood his anger. This was not an acceptable way of showing it, but I felt the pain. I'd been there several times before.

"I'm sorry." He buried his face in my neck. One hand on the back of my neck, the other around my waist.

I mimicked his movements. My chest to his. I poured my heart out. Everything I should have said in the past, I found the courage to say then. All the being hard crap was thrown out the window. I had been softened. Softened by shame. Softened by the heart that was breaking right in front of me. Softened by the love that he had for me. Softened with the love that I had for the man that I held in my arms. One who has an unconditional love for me.

When did I become the hurter instead of the hurtee? And, why? I asked myself.

Though in my heart, nothing was intentional. My actions indicated that of a selfish, uncaring, sex addicted woman. I was hurt and didn't think that my actions would hurt someone else.

"Come inside with me." I said.

"Krisha, I don't ..."

"Shhh." I covered his lips with my finger.

I rose up from his lap, took his hand and led him inside.

Once upstairs in my bathroom, I started Ryan a warm bath. Slowly undressed him, admired every lovely inch of him, and then led him to the Jacuzzi tub. Washed his body without a word being spoken. Softly kissed his forehead. Felt the heat escape his body as my fingers roamed his delicate parts.

I embraced him from behind. Gave love to his neck until my lips found his. I tried kissing away the pain. Make him forget.

I dried his body and pulled the sheets back for him to get into bed. Catered to my man. It was the least I could do.

"I love you Ryan." I repeated. I wanted to reassure him. Wanted him to believe me. Wanted him to forgive me.

While lying in my arms, staring at the ceiling, he said, "I don't know about the wedding."

"I made a mistake."

"Krisha." He turned to look at me. "We both need some time."

"I don't need time. I know where my heart is. It's with you and only you."

"You told him you loved him." He said.

"I've told you that also. I'll always love him, but it's not the same. I'm not in love with him."

"Then why would you give yourself to him?"

"In all honesty, I was drunk. I don't even remember getting there."

"So he took advantage of you?" He searched my face.

"Ryan I'm just as responsible. I'm a grown woman. I shouldn't have put myself in that position."

"I'll kill him."

He'd heard what he wanted to hear.

"Please don't blame him. This is about me."

"I heard you tell him you wanted me."

"So you heard everything?"

"Everything." He assured.

"Why didn't you say anything to me then?"

"What was I gonna say?"

I didn't have an answer for that. There wasn't anything he could have said. I probably would have died right there if I'd heard his voice.

"Please forgive me." I begged planting soft kisses on his face. I held him tight until he fell asleep in my arms.

The next five days were the most difficult. Ryan physically stayed with me at my home, but mentally and emotionally, he wasn't there. He was very distant and seemed unmoved by anything I did or said. He'd responded more the night he came back than over the last few days. He hadn't touched me and didn't seem interested in showing any type of affection when I approached him. I think he was only there for the baby because the kids and Carmen were the only persons he would talk to in the house.

At the end of the week, it was all really beginning to weigh heavily on me. I hated rejection. And it was like he was only sharing my bedroom to keep an eye on me. He damn sure didn't want to be bothered; acted like he really hated me. I understood how a wounded heart felt, so I tried my best to be all I could possibly be to him and still give him his space.

On day six, he began coming around a little and suggested we go out and unwind. I agreed. So, we took the kids to his mother's for the night. We started our evening with dinner on the river and a walk along the levee. We didn't want anything elaborate. Just simply us. We had a long conversation and he explained that he had no intentions of leaving me. But he had to, as he said, "get his mind right." He stated that he loved me unconditionally and refused to let someone as low as Todd, stand in the way of our happiness.

"You're a special woman Krisha. A good woman but I made the mistake of thinking you were perfect. I understand that no one is without fault. I know some of it was my fault too. I guess if I would have given you what you wanted, none of this would have happened."

"Don't even try to blame yourself for anything. You were doing what you were supposed to do. It was me that messed up."

"I'd like to start over Krisha. We have about three weeks before our wedding. Let's forget about it and move on from here." He took my hand in his. "I know you still hurt behind him, but if you say you love me, you gotta let *me* make you happy. Leave your past behind. He knows your heart and he knows your weaknesses. He used you Krisha. He wants to own you. But I'd die before I let that happen."

"He could never own me baby. My heart is for you." I kissed him. "I'd like to start over too. I knew I loved you for many reasons."

"Oh yeah?"

"Yeah."

He kissed me. For the first time in six days, he showed some affection. It was nice.

With a newfound understanding we had a very romantic evening. After all was said and done, we wanted to celebrate. We joined Mia at Club Vibe. She claimed to have a surprise.

Club Vibe had a calmer, adult atmosphere than the clubs Mia and I usually frequented. It was upscale and mellow.

Ryan and I had been there about twenty minutes before Mia and Derric joined us.

They shocked us by announcing their engagement. Mia grinned from ear to ear flashing a rock bigger than the knuckle on her finger. I was truly happy for them. But also surprised because I know a couple weeks ago that heffa had Chad all up in her crib.

It was definitely time for the both of us to stop. Oh well, who was I to say a mumbling word. I know she and Derric had sincere love for each other. And Derric seemed ideal, so I shared in their excitement.

Our night turned out to be a big celebration for all of us. We shared bottles of Moet one after the next. We talked a little, danced a little, and drank a lot. As usual.

39

We left Club Vibe around one am for Club 21.

Derric was to meet his brother Troy and some more guy who played for the Thunder so we tagged along. Now this was the spot where everything went down. If you really wanted to party, this was the place. One thing I failed to remember was that this was Todd's spot and the club where I got drunk and left with Todd just last weekend.

Everything was going so good that I'd totally forgotten those things until thirty minutes later when a tall, caramel, flawless model of perfection made me have instant flashbacks. I felt in my gut that my good night was about to end.

Mia and I were at the bar talking to some friends when I spotted him.

"Mia." I immediately said in a panic. "Look." I glanced Todd's way. She followed my gaze.

"Just great. Double trouble… Ignore him please Krish."

"I know but I don't know if Ryan will."

"He'll be okay, you just be cool. Ignore him and don't even look at him."

"I'll never disrespect my man for Todd or no one else."

"Good…now let's go be with them before Todd sees you and marches his slimy ass over here."

We did just that.

We'd been there an hour having the time of our lives when Troy's date and I went to the bathroom. When I came out, Todd was posted outside the door. He caught me off guard, grabbed me around my waist and tried to kiss me.

"Excuse me." I said with serious attitude while pushing him away.

He seemed tipsy. My eyes instantly went in search of Ryan. He wasn't at our table.

"Good to see you Krisha." Todd said taking his lips to the back of my hand.

I snatched my hand back. "Please Todd I'm here with Ryan." I pleaded.

"I don't care. I'm just saying hello to my wife."

I shot him a glance. "Don't start no shit." I snatched away and stormed off.

Ryan wasn't back at the table when I returned.

"Where's Ryan?"

"Think he went to the bar." Troy said.

I looked around for him, but didn't see him.

"Wanna dance Krisha?" Troy asked.

I looked at Kharysma, his date. She shrugged, so I agreed.

Troy and I danced two songs. During the second song, I looked out into the crowd to see Derric pushing Ryan in his chest. Whatever was going on, Derric was trying with all his strength to pull that 6'5" steel frame back from whatever the commotion was.

Troy, who was doing his best at dancing, didn't notice.

I tapped him on the shoulder. "Troy, isn't that Ryan?" He looked up in the direction I was pointing.

"Hell yeah!" He rushed off the dance floor with me following close behind.

Troy did a better job at getting Ryan out of Todd's face than Derric. How did I not know that this had to have something to do with Todd?

I'd already gathered our things from the table. It was time for us to go home.

They were walking Ryan outside the door when we caught up to them.

"Baby, what happened?" I asked.

"That mothafucka don't wanna see me. I promise you. He don't want that."

"What did he do?"

"I saw what he did to you. I asked him why he would disrespect me like that. I'd seen him watching you all night. I know he saw us together. He popped off and told me some bull, then said you were still his wife and he would do what he wanted."

"Man, you know what you got with your lady, so fuck him." Troy said.

We talked as we walked to our vehicles.

"Forget it Ryan, don't let him do this to you." I said.

Instead he started to rant. "Krisha I don't disrespect him. I take care of his kids like they're my own. I don't trip when you interact with him. I don't fuck with him. He gon' show me some respect!"

"Man yall gotta get along. His kids gotta live with you. Try to let it go." Troy suggested.

"I'm cool with that. But he gotta understand, Krisha is my woman not his. He can't pull no shit like that when he sees her. Talking about she still his wife and kissing on her and shit. Man I'll hurt that mothafucka."

No sooner than he said that Todd braces his ass around the building walking toward us. *No he's not coming over here. Is this man crazy?* I thought.

I looked around to see my old BMW parked right next to us. *I'll be damn.* What did I ever do to deserve this?

Come to think of it, the picture is pretty clear.

Ryan and the guys noticed them coming as they neared us.

"What the...?" Ryan said.

"Ryan!" I stopped him. "This is his car right here. "Just be quiet please. Matter of fact, let's go." I motioned toward the car.

Todd knew he was parking beside us when he brought his tail up here. He knew exactly what he was doing.

"Let's just go." I said. I took his hand to lead him to the car.

We all started moving to our cars, but before we all could get inside the car. Todd approached his car. I could tell he was tipsy, not drunk, but feeling cocky. Guess he thought Ryan was a punk ass Craig.

"What's up Mia?" Todd said.

"Hey." Mia replied dryly.

"Krisha where the hell my babies at while you out partying all night?"

I wanted to ignore him but I had to reply. That comment struck a nerve.

"I see you're out too, so you tell me?" I replied sarcastically.

He grinned.

"I'm tripping. Good night baby." Then blew me a kiss.

Now what did he say and do that for. Oh my goodness.

Ryan came around the car like lightning. Before I knew it he was in Todd's face.

"Don't ever address my woman by anything other than her name. You're gonna respect me lil bitch!"

"I don't have to do shit." Todd spat. "I'm giving you a little time so enjoy it while it lasts lil man."

I tried getting between them. "Just shut up and go Todd." I screamed.

Ryan was trying to get at him, but Troy and Derric were holding him back. Trent was trying to get Todd into the car. They were both yelling profanities and insults.

"She will always be my wife; learn to respect that. You can't handle a real woman anyway; keep trying to be like me, you might get there one day dog."

"Step up like a man." Ryan replied.

I interjected; got in the middle of the drama.

"Todd just go. And why are you saying all that? That is so disrespectful."

"Baby you know I'll never disrespect you. It's this lil punk I don't give a damn about."

Ryan broke away from Troy and lunged at Todd.

His right connected with Todd's face. Todd came back with a good one to Ryan's face as well. The brawl was on in the parking lot of the club. Two guys couldn't hold Ryan and one damn sure couldn't hold Todd. Mia and I tried to help Trent get Todd into the car, but we only got knocked around. I tried talking to and yelling at both of them, but they weren't listening. They were only interested in whipping each other's asses. Something they both wanted to do for a long time I'm sure.

When Troy and Derric finally got Ryan away from Todd, Todd had more to get off his chest. He laid a good one to Ryan's eye. Ryan's head went down as he grabbed his eye. When he came back up, he ran up on Todd and in one motion laid a jab and a black automatic against Todd's head. Troy and Derric backed up. I almost passed out.

While Todd was laid out on the hood of the car with the gun to his head, Ryan used his other hand to surround his neck.

"Ryan let him go." I said softly. The words clogging my throat.

The guys and Mia also encouraged him to put the gun down. He wasn't listening.

I went to his side to look at his face. I begged and pleaded with him while he threatened to take Todd's life.

"It's not worth it Ryan. He's my kids' father. Don't do this to them." I saw a rage I'd never seen before in Ryan. Didn't know he had it in him. He still wasn't listening.

He was choking the life out of Todd and listening to the devil telling him to let him feel a bullet.

"Ryan please just let him go." I pleaded.

Todd gasped for air.

"His ass gotta respect me Krisha."

"I know baby but this is not the way. I don't care about any of this. Just please let him go."

Todd's face had turned absolutely red. That beautiful face that I could have once stood to look at 24/7 was planted with fear.

Ryan was not letting up regardless of what was being said. Nobody could stop him. He was in control with the gun in hand.

"Baby please. Please. You're gonna kill him if you don't let him go."

"I'm calling the police." Trent said as he moved to reach for his cell.

"No Trent!" I screamed. "Please don't."

"Baby your career, your life, your daughter, our lives together is way more important than any respect from Todd. Forget him Ryan. I love you. He's not important. Just let it go. Let him go."

"Why are you defending him Krisha? You want him or something? Huh? Krisha you want him?"

He was turning it on me.

I looked at him in disbelief

"What? How the...? He's the father of my children Ryan. Just stop!" I screamed.

Trent pulled out his cell again. "Forget that Krisha. I'm calling the police."

Troy knocked the phone from his punk ass hands. I could see Mia smirking.

I massaged Ryan's face with one hand attempting to calm him while I wiped the sweat from Todd's with the other. I looked into Todd's beautiful eyes. He pleaded with me. His eyes were red and he was giving up the fight. I didn't want to see them closed. I had to do something.

I took a good look at Ryan and I knew he wasn't crazy. I gently took the gun from his hand and handed it to Derric. But he still refused to let Todd's neck go. Instead he put the free hand around his neck also.

I began yelling like a maniac for him to let him go. This was going too far. He was gonna choke him to death. Derric and Troy began pulling at his arms. Everyone else was talking to him. Telling him to just let him go.

Trying to make him release the hold, I went off. I pushed him, slapped him, punched him and fought him like I was street fighting. All done with uncontrollable tears. That gave Troy and Derric the strength to both pry his hands away from Todd's neck while talking some sense into him.

Mia held me while I screamed and cried.

They finally got him to release Todd's neck. Because he definitely wasn't gonna do it on his own.

"You want him? You stay with him then." Ryan screamed as he turned his back to me to walk away.

"I don't want him, Ryan. I had to do something. You weren't listening."

He turned to me. "I'm out here because of you and you turn on me for him! Stay with him!" He yelled.

I turned my back to him, ignored him and went to see if Todd was okay.

His neck had quickly begun to bruise. I told Trent to take him on home.

That enraged Ryan even more.

"See what I'm saying man." His words directed at me but looking at Derric.

"You make me wanna whip your ass and I don't get down like that." Ryan spat. "You 'bout a confused bitch!" He yelled.

I turned around like the exorcist.

"What?"

No this man didn't just call me the b word. I thought. I walked toward him. Still in disbelief.

Now everything had turned again. It was he and I. All within me, I tried to suppress it. Lord knows I tried.

But I couldn't.

I ran up on him. But before I could get to him, Mia lifted me up off my feet. I knew he could knock me out cold if he wanted to but who cares about pain or consequences when they're mad.

"Calm down." Mia kept saying in my ear as she held me.

"I'll remember that. You're gonna curse me like that in front of all these people and you talk about respect? At least Todd never did no foul shit like that." I said that to get back at him. "I was trying to stop you from doing something that would be life altering for you and our family. I told you it was all about you. That should've been enough. But if you want it like that, fuck you and this elementary bullshit! Both of yall can go to hell!"

He looked to the ground. Regret already over him. He knew he didn't want me to leave him. I was irreplaceable.

He stepped toward me with open arms. "Look baby I'm sorry. I was just…"

I took a step back.

"Grow the fuck up!" I threw out. "Get me outta here Mia."

"Let's go boo." Mia said as she opened the door for me to get in the car.

I heard Ryan say my name as I was getting inside. I ignored him as I lay back in the seat.

Mia burned rubber out the parking lot.

"He'd better not come back to my house tonight."

"He's living with you. Where else is he gonna go?"

"I don't care. He got a mama."

"Todd got what he deserved but Ryan was dead wrong for coming at you like that."

"God knows I'm trying to do things right. No matter how sneaky and dog Todd was, he never ever disrespected me in public. Never called me out of my name and definitely wouldn't in front of anyone. Never."

"None of them are perfect. They're all different. All got their faults."

"You should have let me get him."

"Girl please. You'd already got in a few good ones getting him off Todd. He probably would have knocked you out cold that time. Then I would have been in the shit."

"I let him slide the other night, but if he ever hits me, he's as good as gone, promise."

"What you mean let him slide?"

"Nothing Mia. Don't worry about it." I didn't care to share.

"Well that last statement tells me you aint through with his ass." Mia smirked at me.

I rolled my eyes. Then closed them.

40

Two days later, I was preparing to go to Baltimore as planned. Ryan had left the day before without even saying goodbye. I almost changed my mind, and said to hell with him, but I decided to have a kind and forgiving heart. It really was all my fault anyway. Maybe the change of atmosphere would do our relationship some good. I didn't think it could get any worse.

I was packing my bags when Carmen arrived to be with the kids. When she walked in I could tell something was wrong. She had a perplexed look on her face.

"Can we talk a second?"

"Sure, T. What's up?"

"Well." She stuttered. "I have something for you."

"Okay"

"A few months ago after I told my son about our family and background, he took it upon himself to contact your father. Turns out he's been going to visit him. He sent this to my address."

Carmen handed me a small white envelope.

"I don't know if I want to read that."

"Just take it. You don't have to read it if you don't want to. Take your time and decide. "There's no rush."

"I've got too much going on to deal with another issue."

"I know baby, but you've got only three weeks before your wedding day. You've gotta get things together."

"I will Carm. Somehow, I will."

The doorbell rang.

It was Mia coming to take me to the airport.

"Hey Carm. How are you?" Mia said while embracing Carmen. That by itself made my day. It was so good to see her accepting Carmen as her biological mother.

"Did Krisha tell you the news?"

"News. Good news?"

We laughed.

"Yes." Mia said.

"Well I gotta ask with you two."

Instead of telling her Mia flashed her rock in her face.

"No way!" Carmen screamed.

"Yes way." Mia replied.

Carmen screamed. "Thank you Lord the girl is finally settling down. My prayers are being heard."

We all laughed. Carmen hugged Mia again.

"Congratulations. We gonna have one of those fancy parties like Krisha did."

"I don't need all of that."

"Well you're gonna get it. Now I don't wanna hear another word about it."

Mia acted as if she were thinking for a second, and then said, "Okay."

Carmen screamed again.

The boys came running into the kitchen.

"What's wrong T Carm?" They were puzzled.

"Your Aunt Mia's getting married."

TJ and Malik smiled. "Congratulations T Mia." They both said.

"Wait a minute." Carmen said. She leaned in close to Mia, "Who's the groom?"

We all screamed in laughter.

"That's a crying shame. You know you wrong for that one Carm. You know its Derric."

"Hell, I don't know. You two aint nothin' nice."

We all laughed. But I knew where she was coming from.

"It's a shame I don't have anyone to give me away."

We thought for a minute.

"Your brother." Carmen said.

"I haven't even met him yet."

"You will. He'll be coming home this weekend, so you'll meet him then. He knows all about you and he's excited about meeting you."

"That'll be great." Mia sang happily.

"And I'm gonna miss it?"

"When you get back, he'll be gone. But I'm sure he'll be at your wedding."

"Cool." I replied.

"Come on Krish, let's get going. Don't want you to miss your flight." Mia said gathering her keys from the table. "And Carm I'll be back to holla at you."

"Thanks. You two be careful."

I kissed my babies and was off once again.

Ryan was cordial but standoffish. Pouting like a big kid. It got on my last nerve, so by day two, I couldn't take it anymore. So to the best of my ability, I asked him upfront.

"Ryan, please let me know where your head is. Is there gonna be a wedding or not? Do you still want me as your wife?"

"Just because I'm still pissed doesn't mean I don't want you to be my wife." He replied looking everywhere but at me.

"You told me to stay with him remember."

"I was angry at him and ended up taking it out on you. I apologized for that. You're the one who ran off."

"What?...I...okay, okay." I just stopped it short. Arguing all over again wouldn't help.

"Can we take this and put it behind us?"

"Sure baby but you can't put me in those type situations."

This man was really trippin'. I thought.

"I can't help if Todd was there Ryan. I can't control what he says or does. I'm with you. That should be the only thing that matters. And why all of a sudden are you so jealous of Todd?"

"I'm not jealous. Just a little cautious. And do you have to ask why?"

"Okay. I'm sorry, I shouldn't have asked. But that's behind us, and so is the club episode from the other night. Just always remember who I'm coming home to…It'll always be you baby." I said.

I walked over to him and embraced him. He hugged me back.

He whispered. "I will kill for you girl."

Well, hell, he didn't have to tell me that twice. I believe you cuz. Yes sir.

"We got three weeks left. What you wanna do?" I said with a smile. He knew what I was getting at.

He whispered in my ear all the things he wanted to do to me. A grin plastered across my face a mile wide.

"I'll race you to the tub." I threw out.

We raced up the stairs.

Guess he figured he'd better go head and break me off before I got it from somewhere else. I felt bad thinking that he thought that way. But why else would he break his months of celibacy and we only have three weeks left before marriage?

Whatever reason he had was fine with me because after a good two hours, I got put to sleep and was sleeping something lovely with a big smile glued to my face.

In reality, I needed help; and in more ways than one. Being in my early thirties was really getting the best of me; my hormones were in overdrive. I had to get it together.

Around one am, I got up to use the bathroom to discover my boo wasn't in bed with me.

I called his name several times but he didn't answer. Went to the restroom and peeked downstairs. Didn't see or hear him.

I was still naked, so I had to go back inside the room to dress. I quickly dressed in a T-shirt, jeans, and slippers. As I was attempting to exit the bedroom, I thought I heard noise outside the window.

I moved back over to the bedroom window and peeked outside. There was Ryan trying to grab the arm of a girl who was jerking away from him.

I studied the scene from the window a while longer before deciding to go down.

I exited the house through the front door to the driveway where Ryan and the girl stood. He looked back to see me coming then looked away. Obviously aggravated.

"What's going on honey?" I said as I approached.

"Honey?" The girl mocked me with attitude.

"You should go back inside. I can handle this." Ryan said to me.

"I thought you said your sister was in there. She don't look nothing like you."

"Who are you?" I asked her.

"His girlfriend that's who."

I let out a little laugh. "Oh really? Then why are you outside? You should be inside with us." I said to her then turned to Ryan. "And you never told me you had a girlfriend."

"I didn't even know I had a girlfriend."

"Oh you didn't huh? You're a no good liar Ryan. I knew you had a bitch up in there you lying bastard!"

"Bitch huh? Watch your mouth lil girl." I said.

"It's cold, go on inside. I got this baby." Ryan interjected.

"When I go in, you're going in."

"Ryan you make me sick!" The girl yelled.

"Go on before I call the police. I'm trying to be patient with you."

"What's your girlfriend's name Ryan?" I added.

"She's not my girlfriend."

When he said that, she tried to swing on him.

He grabbed her wrists.

"Look, you can stay out here acting a fool if you want to, but if you're not gone by the time I get inside my house, I'm having you arrested for stalking and trespassing."

"Ryan, I can't believe you'd do that to me. You'd really do that to me?" She stared him in the eyes.

Ryan gave her a mean stare. But didn't answer.

"And who did you say you were?" She asked me with an attitude.

"I didn't. Ask him boo, I don't owe you nothing." I said giving her eye contact.

I wanted to tell her so bad, but I wanted to hear what he had to say more. At that point I didn't know who I was to him.

"Who is this Ryan?" She directed the question to him.

"Go on home girl. I don't have to tell you nothing."

"I think you better answer her baby." I interjected. Looking at him like I could tear his ass to pieces; in a bad way.

He looked at me, then at her. I was waiting for some more hesitation or resistance. I was ready to go off.

"This is my fiancé. So take ya' ass home."

"Fiancé?" She looked from me to Ryan.

"You told me last night you got rid of some chick that was baggage. Is this who you were talking about?"

I turned to look at Ryan.

"He said all that? Last night?" Laced with sarcasm.

Ryan stood there with fire coming from his eyes. He was ready to blow his top. The same look I saw a couple nights ago.

"Get off my property." He spat.

She screamed. "Why are you doing this to me? Why are you *always* doing this to me?" She began to plead. That desperate love starved look in her eyes. I knew it all too well.

"Girl you crazy." He shot her down.

"You said you loved me." She cried.

"He told you that so you could stay on your knees."

I just had to throw that in. I was pissed.

"Shut the hell up! If you were on yours, he wouldn't need me then would he?"

I had to chuckle a little. She really thought she was saying something.

"Ok, well thanks boo. But I don't think your services are needed anymore." I said with a smile.

"That's what you think. I don't go nowhere. I've been around long before you. He don't ever get enough of me baby, neva too much Suga."

I had to take my eyes off her and look at him in amazement.

"Suga?" You call this simple trick Suga." I laughed.

"Simple and sweet missy." She threw out.

"Suga, you a sorry excuse for a woman if you can stand by and watch a man put other women first over you and be content with that. Stop dreaming hoe you'll never be first, so assume your position on the side. And go 'head with all that drama. It's almost two a.m. Too late for this type crap!"

"You saddity bitches think yall all that and can neva hold on to your man."

"Looks to me like you aint never had this one." I pointed at Ryan.

"If he would tell the truth, your ass would be ashamed bitch!"

"Imma tell you who's shame. Your cold ass when *we* go inside *our* home. Remember he told you to get your ass off the property… And furthermore, your three strikes are up for the bitches, but Imma give you the benefit of the doubt because I see that you're young and ignorant." I turned to Ryan. "Come on let's go inside, leave this triflin' slut out here in the cold if she's dumb enough to stay out here."

I turned around to walk away.

Like lightning and before I could turn around ole' girl had ran up on me and grabbed my ponytail. Pulling it with extreme force.

Ryan pried her hands off my hair, and then manhandled her, pushing her to her car.

"Ryan you gonna let her talk to me like that. I thought you loved me. That's messed up." She said.

"You went too far. Now go on before you get that ass tapped." He slammed her car door.

"I'll show you. I got something for her prissy ass too. It aint over."

"Are you threatening me?" I asked while smirking at the silly lil girl.

"Call it what it is." She cranked her Toyota and pulled off screaming profanities while crying.

I was glad we had no close neighbors yet. I'm sure we'd all be in jail by now.

I turned around and stormed inside with Ryan on my tail. I was so exhausted physically and emotionally until I really didn't have much to say to him. I'd just witnessed just about everything I needed. I'm not slow. Not the least bit.

A cheating bitch!

He did all the talking and pleading.

Talk about new to me. Always so reserved, nonchalant, and caring.

None of what I experienced this weekend seemed to be of Ryan's character at all. Now I see why he was able to forgive me so easily. He was guilty of his own stuff too and figured I may have to do the same.

I undressed and lay in silence. I know my silence was killing him. Nothing good was going to come out of my mouth at that point so I tried my best to block it out of my mind. He pulled me into his body from behind. My skin felt so dirty with him touching me. I could just put a dagger through his rapidly beating heart. I tried my best to let it go.

Eventually, I fell asleep with him cradling me and whispering, "I love you" in my ear.

Two days passed, and neither he nor I had said another word about what happened. I was definitely going to address the issue in my own time; however, I'd already decided that if he could forgive me for sleeping with Todd, I could put that little episode behind me.

I didn't want to know the details of his relationship with her, or anything. I just wanted peace in my life and for things to get back to normal. Besides, I was never really completely faithful anyway. There was first Craig, then Todd every now and then. I couldn't hold him to the same things that I knew in my heart I was guilty of. It all felt like a swift kick in the chest. Every time I imagined him with someone else, I felt that kick that knocked the wind out of me. I knew I had to suck it up and find forgiveness in my heart as he'd done.

41

"Are you ready Krisha?" Ryan asked.

We were on our way to a dinner reception with the team members and their companions. It was a formal affair. I was extravagantly lovely as usual. My boo was as handsome as ever too. Together we made a power couple in the looks department. We were just made to be together.

Being in the city where he played made me love Ryan Mathers even more.

I guess ole girl the other night made me realize the depth of my love for him also.

I'd gotten complacent with our relationship; never really took it too seriously from the beginning. Guess his age had a lot to do with that and the fact that I was always playing on my own turf. But I see now, my baby's a well-known ball player in the city of Baltimore and the state of Maryland. I guess I gotta get my stuff together and get with the baller's wife status. I really didn't know what it all meant at all.

I had been kidding myself. *Who wouldn't want a man like Ryan?* At first glance you would have already decided to spend the rest of your life with him, if for nothing other than to just look at him day in and day out.

Our night was going great. I'd met a lot of other team members and their companions. Everyone wished Ryan and me the best in our marriage. Most promised to make it to the wedding in a couple weeks. We smiled and accepted all congratulations and well wishes. Knowing full well there was trouble in paradise. But, there was no way anyone could tell from the way we carried on. Actually, Ryan was being a little too convincing.

He has never been a "show your feelings in public" person. But tonight, he openly kissed and embraced me more than ever before. I think it was a whole lot of makeup and "please forgive me, don't leave me" too. I wasn't complaining though. I enjoyed every bit of it. I took it all in with a smile. I knew he wasn't trying to prove anything to anyone there. He was trying to prove himself to me. He'd been doing that for the last two days.

I did love him and I wasn't going to leave him; however, I didn't tell him that. I'd decided on going home on tomorrow. He and I both needed some time to tie up loose ends, and I wanted him to suffer a little. I needed to see where his head and heart was.

After the reception, we met with Sheri and Steve and others for drinks and conversation. I was surprised at how the other wives were so sweet and down to earth. I could tell some were designer freaks like Sheri. You could tell how much they were worth at first glance. On the other hand, with me, it was always a guessing game.

While moving around the room of the nice and cozy establishment, mingling with others, I felt the presence of a body close to mine from behind. Warm breath on my neck, and a hand that touched the small of my back. I thought it was Ryan being overly affectionate again, but the voice told me otherwise.

"Hey beautiful." I heard in my ear in a deep sexy tone.

I turned around and thanked God for my eyes beholding such a gloriously, beautiful sight.

It was Tyson.

His face made me smile.

"Hey, how are you?" I said as I embraced him in a quick friendly hug planting a kiss on his cheek.

"I'm good. I don't have to ask how you are. I already see it."

If he only knew. I thought.

"Thanks." I said shyly.

His eyes roamed my body.

"Didn't know you were back in town."

"I came back a couple days ago."

"How's everything going…with the wedding and all?"

"Everything's good. And how's the new house? Have you moved in?"

"The house is magnificent. I'm in the process of decorating and moving in."

"I'm sure you already know the best woman for the job."

"Yeah, she's already on it."

We laughed.

"I must say she's doing a beautiful job with mine."

"I must see it sometime."

"And I must see yours."

"In due time." He smirked.

"What's that supposed to mean? Don't start nothing up in here."

Smiling, he said, "Hey, I'm cool." Throwing up his hands in surrender.

I smiled.

Ryan suddenly appeared from nowhere.

"What's up man?" Ryan sang. Tyson turned to greet Ryan with a brotherly hug and handshake.

"What's good Mr. Superstar?"

"Tryin' to be like you that's all." Ryan said.

"Naw man, you got it. You've far surpassed me in the game."

"Yeah, but you da man though."

"C'mon, you're marrying this lovely lady. Naw, you da man."

"Thanks man." Ryan said smiling at me. "I *will* see you at the bachelor party here right?"

"I'll definitely try my best to make it."

Taking me by the hand. "Alright now, I'll see you then. Oh! And congratulations on the house."

"Thanks man."

Ryan quickly led me away from Tyson. I looked back. He was still looking in our direction watching us walk away.

It's just something about Tyson that makes me feel as if I've known him for years. He has a certain calm about him. His nature is peaceful. Just what I needed in my life. Had I not been with Ryan, it would have definitely been on with Tyson and me. He was a sweetheart fo sho'.

After the Tyson encounter, Ryan stuck to me like glue. I knew he'd been somewhere watching me the entire time.

Tonight is cool; I could really get used to this life. I thought.

I liked everybody I'd met so far. Sheri was so busy running her mouth with everybody; I didn't get to spend much of the night with her. It was all good though. It just gave me the opportunity to meet others.

It was getting late and the crowd was thinning. Ryan and I had just slow danced and were taking our seats when Tyreek, one of Ryan's teammates, came to the table where we sat with Sheri and Steve. Whispered something in his ear that made Ryan jump up real quick.

"C'mon man." He told Steve.

"Ryan what's wrong?" I ask franticly.

"Just stay here. I'll be right back."

"He and Steve shot toward the exit door."

"What the hell is going on?" Sheri asked.

"We'll wait for a minute then I'm going to find out."

"I'm with you." Sheri replied.

We sat at the table for a good hot minute.

"I'm going to see what's up?" I said to Sheri.

Sheri followed as I got up from the table. I passed by Tyson who was at the bar paying his tab. He winked. I smiled as I sashayed toward the door.

As we exited the building the cool breeze from the night air surrounded my body.

"Where are they?" Sheri asked.

"We parked in the back. Let's see if they're back there."

Before we could get half way to the parking lot, we heard yelling.

The building was long, so there was a long walk to the back through the side parking lots.

Then, a car came out of nowhere speeding from the back of the building. When the car lights hit us, we jumped back against the building to get out of the way. The car suddenly came to a stop.

Out jumped the girl from the other night.

It all happened so fast, I didn't even see the other two girls exit the car.

All I heard was, "that's the bitch!"

Before I could even blink, someone had struck me in my head, and then I caught a lick to my mouth.

"That's for talking shit the other night bitch!"

Before I could make a move, I got another hard blow to the face. I crunched to cover my face.

By the time I started to swing, it was cut short by someone knocking me off my feet from the side of my head.

"This for messing with my man." Was what I heard next.

Two or three of them were on me. I really couldn't tell. I couldn't see. My head was spinning. I was on the ground. Getting my ass tore up.

I couldn't tell which one of them was doing it to me worse. Pain was just plain ole' pain at the moment. All I kept thinking was, 'If they just let me up, I'm gonna do some real damage to her lil ass.'

But, that was not an option.

They did their thing, but it took three of them to do it.

All of a sudden, I could see Suga being snatched up off me and somebody was holding the other two girls. Sheri was trying to help me up, but I had to gather my senses.

It was Ryan, Steve, Tyson, and the others.

Tyson was holding Ryan back who was trying to reach out and touch Suga.

Steve was trying to put her in the car while screaming at her to leave but she fought him and cursed Ryan and me.

I got up to no shoes, no purse, and no jewelry, a jacked up dress and pain from top to bottom.

"They stole my things." I screamed.

I think I was more concerned about my belongings than anything.

"We aint got shit for you." One of the girls said.

"I want all my things from them before they go anywhere."

"I saw them taking it." Sheri said.

That statement told me right there that Sheri would not have my back in situations like this. She was definitely no Mia. Me and Mia woulda cleaned the whole block with these girls.

"If yall won't let me whip ass, then call the police. They ain't gettin' away with this." Ryan screamed angrily.

"Just calm down man." Tyson told Ryan. "You know how this will turn out if we do. You and this will be the talk of the city."

"They can't get away with this man." Ryan said angrily.

I walked toward their car. Sheri holding onto me. Her scary ass.

"Just give me my shit." I said.

"Bitch please. This girl deserves this and a whole lot more from that dog." One of the girls said.

I was pissed.

I looked at Suga. "I tell you what. You keep it all. Now you can finally say Ryan gave ya ass something. Cheap trick."

I was on my feet and ready to act a bigger fool than they just did. They wanna whip my ass *and* steal my shit. And then bully me like I couldn't get it back. They got me twisted fo sho. They really didn't know this Louisiana hood rat on the slick.

"Oh no, she aint worth an ounce of that. I want everything back. Hell naw!"

Ryan tried to get away from Tyson and Tyreek again.

Suga and her crew got riled up again. They started cursing Ryan. If words could kill, I'd have to bury him tomorrow.

I went to Ryan and hugged and kissed him to calm him down. "You know money aint no object baby. Let her keep that. Tell the bitch thanks for her services."

Suga tried to get at me again. I knew that would set her off. But Steve held her back.

"Go on home girl. This is unnecessary." Steve said.

"Shut up Steve. You no good bastard. All of you are no good. When are you gonna start claiming your baby Steve? Sorry deadbeat!" Suga threw out.

"Just go home before you go to jail. You're already gettin' away with enough tonight." Ryan said.

"Ryan you know you love me. When you get tired of this ole' hoe, get at me. You know you can never leave this." She said as she slapped her butt.

Shameful. I shook my head.

"You're already left. You should have realized that years ago." Ryan said.

"You know you don't want her Ryan. She can never give you what I have."

"Let her go Steve. Let me whip her ass so she can kill the drama." I threw out.

These people obviously didn't know me. I thought with evilness all over my face.

"No." He pushed her to the car and tried to force her in.

"Let's go baby. I don't have time for this." Ryan said taking my hand in his.

"Steve, will you give me a ride? The wrecker service should be here any minute."

"Sure man."

We all began walking back to the parking lot where the cars were parked.

"Ignore them. Let's go." Someone said.

Suga and crew hopped in the car and began driving in reverse along side of us.

They just wouldn't give up.

"Ryan. Ryan, you wrong for how you doing me. You can't marry her." There she was pleading again.

"Yeah, you know you're wrong." They all sang from the car.

We ignored them and continued to walk at a fast pace.

"Why are you doing this? You know you love me."

"You are no good Ryan. Long as you been with her, now you disrespecting her like this. I thought you was a real man." The driver said. "Now you wanna marry this skinny bitch over her."

Poor girl was crying her eyes out.

They were badgering a hole in his head though.

As we continued to walk, they continued to drive alongside of us talking sporty.

Ryan had had enough. I think his patience was gone and his emotions had run over. He suddenly stopped and ran to the side of the car. The driver stopped the car. He looked Suga in the face.

"Listen!" He yelled. "Please leave me alone. Go home and leave me the fuck alone! I don't want you. I never did. You were a good lay while it lasted. Now go on bitch and leave me and my wife alone before you get hurt!" He spat.

He kicked the car with a vengeance. Put a big dent in the passenger door.

I kept my mouth closed. This was his show.

"You don't mean that baby." She yelled out.

"Forget him. Let's ride." The driver screamed to Suga. "And you're paying for my door playa!" She yelled while putting the car in drive. She drove off with Suga shedding tears.

Once we reached the back parking lot, I took a big gasp of air.

She had spray painted Ryan's car, busted the windows, and set that baby on all fours.

Then they had nerves enough to come back around the building through the parking lot laughing and screaming out the window. Suga sure had perked up rather quickly.

On one side of his black Benz was "DOG", and on the other side was "I EAT SUGA." And on the hood and trunk was "Ryan Mathers aint shit."

I was mad, but he had the right to be pissed. I see what he meant by she'd gotten away with too much all night. This was more drama than I'd experienced with Todd. With Ryan it would be publicized drama which was totally embarrassing. So we had to let it go.

I fumed all night long. I just could not seem to stop the twisted thoughts that rambled through my mind.

I lay awake until around two-thirty a.m. thinking about the events of the night and how I'd gotten my purse but I let them keep my diamonds, shoes and all. I believe that pissed me off more than anything.

I felt so helpless. I wasn't sure if helplessness suited me at all. *Could I really deal with this lifestyle?*

Ryan was definitely about to see my true colors. There would be no more sugar coating, Mrs. Nice girl.

The way I looked at it, he deserved it. He seemed to be just as triflin' as the next.

While he lay sleeping, I continued breathing fire and thinking. This just wasn't right. *Do I really want to travel this road again? How had things changed so fast?*

I needed to get away from him. Just looking at him made me have evil thoughts.

So I slid out of bed and into a sweatshirt and jeans. Left him in bed snoring like all was good.

I took a ride around the city to clear my head. I needed peace so I picked up my phone to find peace at the only place I knew.

The phone rang three times.

"Krisha?"

"How did you know it was me?" I spoke softly.

"I have your number programmed in my phone…Are you okay?"

"I don't know. I shouldn't have called you. I just…I just needed someone to talk to."

The tears started. I tried not to show my weakness.

"I know. You don't have to explain anything to me. I know."

"This is beginning to be too much for me to handle."

"Where are you?"

"Driving."

"Where are you going?" He said softly but very masculine.

"I don't know just driving."

"That's not safe."

"I know. I just couldn't sleep. I needed to get away."

"Does he know you left?"

"No."

Silence.

"What do you need Krisha?"

Sniffling. I said, "Peace for once in my life".

"Come to me. Let me see if I can help you."

I slept peacefully on the couch in Tyson's arms. He gave me rest. For a moment, I forgot all about Ryan and his mess. Tyson gave me the calmness that I saw in him. I saw strength. I saw maturity. I saw experience. He stroked my skin. Told me not to worry. Told me I was in control of my life. Told me to take it slowly, one day at a time.

I made it back home around 6:30 am and climbed into bed with Ryan who was still snoring hard. He never even knew I'd left.

It took me a few minutes to doze off, but as soon as I closed my eyes, the ringing of Ryan's cell phone awakened me. He was sleeping so hard and snoring so loudly that he didn't hear the ringing so I got up to answer it, but by the time I got to the phone on the dresser, it had stopped.

When I sat it back down it started to ring again. This time I answered but the caller hung up.

I went to use the bathroom but kept the phone in my hand. Somebody wanted to play games.

I got back into bed and sat the phone on the nightstand. Two minutes later a text came in. The message was from the same phone number. The message read. "I'm sorry. Please forgive me."

I didn't have to guess who that was from. I put the phone down and dozed back to sleep.

It was 7:15 am when the phone began ringing again. I grabbed the phone from the nightstand.

"Hello." I answered. Voice laced with aggravation.

Silence. Then a heavy sigh. "Can I speak to Ryan please?"

"Who is this?"

"I think you know."

"What do you want?"

"My man."

"Look I don't know the nature of your relationship with Ryan but it appears to me that whatever it was, it's over and has been for a while now. Didn't he tell you that?"

"The question is, did he tell you that?"

"I really don't care. I'm not going through this with you again."

"Then let me speak to Ryan."

"Okay. Hold on."

I put the phone on speaker and shook him hard to wake him up.

"You have a phone call." I rang loudly.

"Huh? What time is it?"

"After 7 am."

"Who is that? Who the hell…?"

I cut him off. "Just answer the phone." I held the phone up where we both could hear.

"This is Ryan." He said groggily.

"Ryan we need to talk."

"Who is this?" He said with a frown.

"Your woman."

"My woman is right here with me. Who the hell is that Krisha?"

"You know who that is."

"Krisha hang up the phone." He said as he turned over in bed.

"Ryan I just wanna talk to you. I'm sorry." She cried out.

"Girl don't call my phone no more. You must be crazy."

"Why are you doing this? You know you don't want her."

"Hang up the phone Krisha." He yelled.

"Nope talk to her."

"Woman hang up! I don't have anything to say to her. She better be glad I'm a real man. I wanna put my foot in her ass."

"Ryan I don't want it to end like this. I'm sorry. I'll pay for your car."

"Look it aint all about my car. I'm engaged to be married in a few weeks, so leave us alone!"

"Don't say that Ryan. I told you I'm sorry."

"Oh since you're sorry give me the diamonds back. I bought those for my wife, not you."

"Okay. I'll give them back. Whatever you want me to do."

"Leave 'em with Tyreek. And don't call me again. Now hang up the phone Krisha so I can sleep."

I hung up.

I lay there as he slept with his head on my chest trying to figure out how to handle this. Ryan didn't look so attractive to me at this point. Nor did his words of love mean very much. The way I saw it, if I gotta get jumped and cursed out about a man by a female, he must be doing some serious breaking her off. She aint actin' a fool for nothing. You need gas to fuel a fire.

I said I didn't want to know, but after last night, I gotta find out something. I figured I'd postpone my trip home by another day or two at least until I get to the bottom of the situation.

"Ryan, get up." I shook him awake.

"Yeah."

"Wake up."

"What is it now?"

"I need to know some things."

"What?"

"Why didn't you tell me about her?"

"I did. I just never gave a name."

"Why is she tripping? Do you still have a relationship with her?"

"No. I don't know why she's trippin'. We were over before I met you. I've had other women before you. She never tripped this hard on any of them."

"Well, she picked the wrong one to clown with."

"Don't take any of this too personally. I'll put her in her place."

"How? By keeping her bed warm? Give her what she wants huh?"

"No. I don't know what she wants."

"If you were through with her, she wouldn't be clowning. You're still involved with her aren't you?"

"No!"

"Then why? It doesn't add up."

"I always told you I'd never bring you drama and I meant it. I don't know why she's trippin'. Guess she heard I was getting married and didn't like it."

"Okay Ryan. Since you don't wanna come clean, I'll be catching you later. Tell your family and friends the wedding is off."

I got up from the bed.

He jumped up behind me.

"You can't be serious."

He was on my trail.

"Yes, I'm serious. I'll be gone in a few hours, so you can carry on as you like with Suga or whoever else.

"Krisha. Baby it's not what you think."

He was talking fast.

"I asked for the truth. You wanna play games. I'm too old for this Ryan. I've been through this same stuff before. I promise I won't do it again. Now, I love you, but I love myself even more."

"So you're gonna just leave me? You're gonna let her win?"

"Since when did this become a game? And for the record, I don't care about winning when it concerns my heart."

I went into the bathroom and slammed the door. Jumped into the shower and let the tears fall with the water. The hot water stung my skin on my side and legs that were bruised from all the kicking I endured. Guess payback is real. That's what I get for always putting my feet on somebody.

My body ached. I'd felt like that before, but it had been so long ago. I hadn't had an ass whipping like that in a good minute. Matter of fact, I don't think I've ever had an ass whipping' like that.

The shower door slowly opened. Ryan stood in silence watching me. Wanting to speak but at a loss for words. My tears flowing so freely. I couldn't stop them. So emotional. So embarrassed.

He looked down at my body and suddenly realized the severity of the entire ordeal. He saw the black and blue bruises that covered the light skin on my naked body.

Ryan stepped into the shower with me. Eyes on my body. He reached out to take my arm. Turned me around, checked me out thoroughly. Without warning, he took my body into his arms.

"I'm so sorry for this baby." He began kissing the bruises on my arms while I cried. He followed the patterns of bruises over my entire body with kisses.

"I didn't know they did this to you." He said as he continued planting small kisses on my bruised skin. Please don't leave me."

"I gotta go." I whispered.

He embraced my waist. Cheek against my stomach. Massaged my aching body. He turned me around and kissed the bruises on the side of my small frame from one side to the other.

"I can't let you leave; not alone. You're going to be my wife Krisha."

"Please stop Ryan."

He tasted the water on my skin.

From my waist to my knees. Strong hands massive and comforting. Tongue slowly massaging the water into the skin on my bottom one at a time.

"Please." I managed to whisper.

"Say you'll stay with me."

He turned me around to taste the water that surrounded my V.

"I can't say that." I said in one big pant.

Ryan slowly rose to his feet engulfing my body into strong arms.

"You better hope that I drop dead in the next few minutes...that will be the only way you'll be able to leave me."

We gave each other a longing stare. The stare really meant that he meant every word he'd just said. Mine meant, you're my heart but I can't stand you right now!

"I wanna make love to you." He said in my ear.

I shook my head as I threw my head back.

"Please Krisha. Please." He whispered between kisses to the ear.

Needless to say, I gave in. We made love in the shower then finally on our huge bed.

We both slept five hours straight. Sex induced sleep was the best sleep in the world.

I pulled myself up to try showering again. This time I was stepping out of the shower when Ryan came into the bathroom.

He hopped into the shower after I got out. While he was showering, I started throwing my things into my Louis Vutton bags.

"Where are you going?"

I turned to see him drying off in the doorway that separated the bedroom from the master bath.

"Home."

"How...I mean, do you even have a flight?"

"Not yet."

"I asked you to stay. I thought you would."

"I've done what I came here for. I've got children to care for remember?"

"Are you coming back?"

"For what?"

"What do you mean, for what?"

"I mean if we're getting married why come back and the wedding is in Louisiana in two weeks."

"Why are you saying *if*? We *are* getting married, or are you having second thoughts?"

"Baby, sex doesn't solve anything. We have issues we need to address."

"We don't have issues. I don't consider anything that happened in the last few days a hindrance for us getting married. You are the only one who can keep me from marrying you."

"You know how I feel about you, but this thing with whatever her name is, is far more serious than anything I've ever experienced."

"It means nothing to me Krisha. It really is nothing."

"Because I don't feel like you're telling me the whole truth. We have no foundation for a marriage if it's based on a lie."

"I don't know why you feel that way. I've always let you know that you're the woman I love."

"You never volunteered any information regarding her. Everything I learned I learned from the run-ins with her or by prying little pieces out of you."

Ryan sat in his birthday suit in silence on the side of the bed as I packed. He was in deep thought.

He suddenly hopped up. "Don't worry about a flight."

"And why not?"

"We're driving."

"We?"

"Yes, I'm going with you. I'll fly back in a few days for my bachelor party."

"I didn't anticipate getting home in eighteen hours."

"It'll give us time to talk."

I pondered the suggestion. We did need to talk. Maybe he would really open up and tell me something to make me feel good about the marriage. At this time, I just wasn't feeling it. I didn't want to make the same mistake twice; marrying an adulterous man. *But how can you tell?* When in love, the writings of infidelity are usually on the wall, but it's so hard to see. The difference this time is that I see perfectly well. If I marry him, I'm marrying him knowing the possibility is there that he is being unfaithful. If I chose to do that, I get what I ask for. I know the rules to the game.

After thinking for a minute, I said, "Let's get moving then."

The trip home was very therapeutic for our relationship. We talked about the Maican, better known as Suga, incident as well as the Todd situation. We discussed our relationship and anticipated marriage. We argued. Cried. Laughed. Shared. At one critical point in our discussion, I'd told Ryan to forget it all. There wouldn't be a wedding. I was frustrated and angry and felt as if he wasn't being totally honest.

He pulled the car over at the next rest area and poured his heart out to me.

He opened up and explained how he'd dated Maican a few years ago and how they'd broken up because he'd discovered her love for his fame and money and the fact that she'd cheated on him with a guy that she now has a child with. He confessed that throughout his dating experiences and women over the years, he'd never totally stopped seeing her. He also confessed that during the first year of our relationship he continued to see her on a friendly basis. Through snot and tears he told me that it took him to lose me for more than a year for him to be true to himself and finally leave her alone. He claimed that when he came back to me, after he found out about Tamia, he broke it off with Maican for good. He said she hadn't been considered his girlfriend for years, but to quote him, only a "side piece" used for late night cravings.

It seems that she can't accept the fact that he's truly moved on and is marrying someone else. She blames him for her child's father leaving her, as he'd found out about their secret relationship. She feels Ryan has betrayed her and owes her his heart after all the years of messing around.

What could I say? In the position again where the pot couldn't call the kettle black. He knew about Todd and me. Maybe not everything and certainly not every sexual encounter, but I'd always tried being honest when it came to Todd. He didn't know about Craig, so I kept it like that. Something told me to tell him, but then again I aint nobody's fool. Men look at cheating totally different than women. Women will forgive their men time and time again, but one time and we're history. I was lucky. I'd gotten my one time and I definitely wasn't gonna push it. Though I loved him, I wasn't blind or naïve to anything that was going on. I wasn't surprised by what he told me. I'd always said he was getting it from somewhere while not in my presence. Experience has been a very good teacher for me. And I've never been a dummy. I loved my boo too much to cancel our relationship over this. And he'd already made it clear that he wasn't letting me go.

Once we reached Louisiana, we were good. My love for Ryan had increased another 30% at the least. We arrived at my home around 3:15 am. Talk about dog tired. We didn't bother waking the kids. We were out like lights as soon as we reached my bedroom.

42

The next evening while Ryan and the boys went to a basketball game, I decided it was time to take a peek at my past. The letter Carmen had given me was still in my dresser drawer where I'd placed it before I left. So after the baby and I bathed, I put her down to bed then retrieved the letter from the drawer.

I was nervous about reading it, but I told myself I had nothing to be afraid of. I didn't even know the man; he was an absolute stranger to me. I never knew he existed until a few months ago.

As soon as I climbed into bed and slowly ripped the envelope open, the phone rang. Caller ID told me it was Todd. I almost didn't answer but I figured he might want something important.

The first words out of his mouth were, "Can I come over?"

"Don't start, please."

"Start what?"

"What do you want?"

"You."

"Sorry. You already know Ryan came home with me."

"So what? Come over here then."

"You've gotta stop this and respect him."

"I don't have to do a damn thang."

"Let's be adult about this."

"You know how I feel about you and you know I can't stand his ass."

"You have no reason to hate him. He loves your kids and me. He only wants to make us happy."

"You're a trophy for him. He wants to own you."

How ironic, this is exactly what Ryan says about him. I thought.

"He knows he has a good woman, but he's young. He aint through playing yet."

"I guess you would know huh?" I threw in.

"Exactly. That's why I can tell you better than anyone."

"He does love me Todd."

"No doubt I'm sure he does. You are absolutely loveable. But I love you too."

"We've been through this before. And please tell me why you said those disrespectful things about me that night."

"I didn't mean anything by that. Just came out wrong. I was trying to get at lover boy."

"Don't you ever disrespect me like that again."

"I won't. I called to apologize earlier, but you were out of town. I didn't try reaching you. I do respect you when you're away with him."

"Thanks for that much."

"I just can't stand the fact that you're with him. You should be with me."

"You're right. I should be with you. But you messed it up didn't you?"

"Yeah I did." He said softly.

"By the way, where is the little back stabbing whore that stole my husband?"

I laughed at myself.

"Who?"

"Kyra, who else?"

"She did not steal me Krisha. And last I heard she was in Atlanta in jail."

"Get out! Are you serious?"

"She and her ghetto lovers moved there and started stealing and committing all types of fraud. She called me to bail her out of jail a couple months ago."

"Did you?"

"I aint gonna lie. I bailed her ass out…"

Cutting him off. "Bye, Todd."

"No, no wait a minute. Let me explain."

"Uh huh." I sighed.

"I got her out because her daughter was there in Atlanta with practical strangers when she was in jail. She'd already been in there two days before she called me. I did it for Paige, not her. Despite what all went on between us, we were all friends once, and I always did love Paige. I would have been crushed if something had happened to her."

"On that note, you were right. I miss Paige. Bet she's so big now. But her dumb ass mama needs her ass whipped."

"She called a day later and thanked me and promised to follow through with all her legal requirements. That's the last I heard from her. I haven't had any issues yet so I guess she's handling her business."

"Anyway Todd. Enough drama for tonight. It was really nice having a decent conversation with you."

"Love you boo."

"Love you too, boo."

We laughed a little.

He held the phone.

"I won't allow you to marry him. I'll stop the wedding."

"Go 'head Todd. Bye."

He became quiet and serious. Didn't say goodbye. Held the phone.

"I'm serious. I can't let you do it. If I can't have you, I can't live anymore."

"Todd please don't, we've discussed this over and over."

"I'm sorry. I'll live the rest of my life with regret. I can't stand by and watch my family live happily ever after with another man. I just can't do it."

"Why can't you be happy for me? We're good friends. Good friends are happy for each other."

"My heart aches. I try my best to give you your space and respect your relationship, but I can't watch you marry him. If you marry him, my blood will be on your hands."

"Blood? Oh my God! Don't do this to me. I can't believe you said that!"

"Come back to me then."

"I can't."

"You can. I promise it'll be different. Can't you see I've changed?"

"Yes, a little, but I love him Todd."

"You love me too."

"It's different. I love him the way I used to love you before you betrayed me. Before you hurt me. Before you tore my heart away from my chest and trampled all over it."

Ignoring every word I'd just said. "Come be with me." He uttered.

"No! I'm tired of discussing this. If you leave me alone, I'll be fine. Just please leave me alone."

"You're *my* wife and the mother of my children. I can *never* nor will I *ever* leave you alone."

"Ex-wife...and c'mon be for real. I gotta move on with my life."

"If both of us are still breathing, we're forever man and wife. Your marriage to him will be wrong."

"Your adultery was wrong. Look, I gotta go."

"Wait Krisha."

"What?" I screamed. He was trying my patience.

"I need to say something."

"Save it please."

"No, you need to hear this."

"What?"

"He's cheating on you."

"C'mon Todd."

"I didn't want to tell you. I don't throw salt in another man's game, but this is you. I had to make the decision to let you know."

"Stop lying Todd. You're just saying that to mess my life up some more."

"You know I wouldn't intentionally hurt you."

"Then why are you saying that?"

"Because it's true. I've checked him out and..."

"Wait. What! Checked him out?"

"You know I have friends and connections."

"You had no right."

"Oh yes. If he's around my children, I have every right."

He did have a point, but that wasn't cool.

"I can't believe you Todd."

"Krisha the man has another family in Baltimore."

"Please. He damn sure don't see them when I'm there."

"Krisha he's a man. You should know, we find ways."

"God, you're desperate."

"You know me better than that. I wouldn't lie to get you or anybody else."

"If you know so much, then who is she?"

"Her name is Maican Rogers. He's paying for the house she and her son lives in in Baltimore. She's a travel agent."

I laughed when he said that name.

"Is that the deranged woman you're talking about? I thought you had something."

"You know her? How? Actually, I just happened to stumble upon her through business which started my probing."

Oh did I know her. If I didn't before, I did now.

"Let's just say I've come to know Ms. Maican over the last few days."

"Didn't I tell you this young buck was gonna bring you drama? He's not ready for what you need."

"I know about his past with Maican."

"Past? What past?"

"Thanks Todd. I got this one. And find you something else to do other than play around in my business. You wanted the other women when we were married, now what's the problem?"

"I grew up."

"I'm sorry it took you so long but I have to go."

"Alright I'll go, but call if you need me."

"Thanks, bye." I eagerly hung up.

I wish he'd told me that before I went to Baltimore and got my behind kicked. Maican aka Suga, whoever she was, was old news to me. I thought not to even dwell on that again.

The way I saw it, Ryan and I were moving in a new direction, there was no need in dwelling on the past. In a few days I was to be Mrs. Ryan Mathers. I'd successfully accomplished my triumph; I'd succeeded in letting Todd Taylor go. I had finally moved on.

43

After hanging up the phone, I picked up the letter again. The letter was addressed to Twink.

I hadn't been referred to as Twink since I was about twelve years old. I felt I was grown then so I begged my mom to please call me Krisha or Krish instead of that baby name. I was surprised that this man, who I never knew as a part of my past referred to me by my nickname.

When I was done reading the letter, I was in tears. For the first time in thirty-two years, I had a real father. I wanted to understand how a parent could leave their child's life for twenty-seven years and never once look back. I felt he could have done something to find me.

He didn't mention what he'd tried to do to me in the letter, but thanks to Carmen I knew the painful details. As per Carmen, he was definitely a beast. The lifestyle and drugs had transformed him into an unrecognizable person without a conscience. Nonetheless he was my father. We shared the same genes, same DNA, same blood, same name. However, biological factors were all that we share. We were complete strangers. Different in so many ways. I lay and wonder who this man was. I was curious. I had to see him. Had to know.

The next day I awakened to Ryan doing sit-ups on the bedroom floor. I threw the letter on the floor by his head. Wanted him to read what I'd read last night.

After reading the letter, he came to sit on the bed next to me.

"Baby, you're a grown woman now. Your mother did the best she could at protecting you when you needed her to do so. Your mother is not here anymore and you're the strong woman that she raised you to be. You can protect yourself now and if you should ever fall short, I'll always be there for you."

"I know but truth is, I'm scared and angry. I have mixed feelings about him. No one made him travel the road he did. He knew he had a family."

"Sometimes the strongest people fall victim to drugs and the pressures of society. From what I've seen and have been told, drugs are very powerful and mind altering substances. Yes, he is accountable for his actions, but when you have no support system it only makes overcoming more difficult."

"He had my mother."

"You don't know the entire situation from the inside. The most you know is what Carmen has told you. Talk to him. Listen to his side of the story."

"I'll never know the truth. My mother is gone. It'll still be one-sided."

"But that's all you have to go by baby. What else can you do?" He asked. "I won't pressure you, but if you're curious, go see him. I'll support you."

"You're a sweetheart."

"You have a family right here that loves you, and a man that can't see living life without you. Whatever happens, I'll love you regardless. We're all we need."

I kissed him. "Thanks love. I needed to hear that."

"I know exactly what you need."

"Really?"

He kissed me.

"Yep?"

"Well what do I need right now?"

"Want me to tell you or show you?"

"How 'bout both?"

"Early in the morning? Girl you should be ashamed." Ryan said playfully.

We shared a laugh.

I playfully pushed him out of the way to get up from the bed.

"Move Ryan I gotta get dressed."

"Where you going girl?"

"I do have a business to run or have you forgotten? I need to go to work some times."

"Tonight we need to discuss you and this work thing. My wife doesn't need to go to work. I want you to rest your pretty head and be home waiting for me. You need to enjoy life for what it is."

"I like what I do, and I've never been dependent on anyone."

"I know. I wouldn't ask you to change that. Maybe you should do something with your creative side that allows you to have fun too. Something less mentally and physically demanding."

"It's not as bad as you think. I have a lot of freedom and I really enjoy my career."

"We'll discuss it later, but keep it in mind. You don't have to do a damn thing as long as you're with me. I only want to make you happy."

"Thanks baby. I love you for that. And in that case, I think I'll make you happy this morning."

"Now ya talking." Ryan said with a smile as he leaned in to kiss me.

44

The next couple days were very busy days for me at work and home. Just when you think you have it all laid out for a wedding there's always last minute things to do.

Mia helped tremendously, so I didn't stress too much about that. But work and the situation with my father were like thorns in my side. Ryan made me promise that tomorrow would be the last day in the office before the wedding, which was now ten days away.

After receiving reassurance from Carmen, I decided to visit my father. I was to travel to the prison on Saturday, a week before my wedding.

The week went by too fast.

I awakened around five thirty am. I was nervous about my visit to the prison. The visit was at 11:00 am, but Ryan and I left around 7:00 am to allow time for travel and thought.

I'd never been to a state penitentiary before and just the thought scared me. Seeing the many acres that surrounded the prison and the razor wire fence that stood high around the perimeter, did me in.

Meeting my father for the first time at such a strange and depressing place as a prison, made me more doubtful that I'd made the right decision in coming.

Ryan sat in the waiting area, while I checked in. The guard seemed surprised when I said the name. He checked his list and ID'd me, and then okayed my visit.

"Mam, forgive me for being nosey, but, would you happen to be his daughter?"

Though the question sounded funny for someone to ask, I'd never really admitted to being anyone's daughter other than my mother's.

I nodded my head.

"I knew it." The guard said ecstatically.

I smiled, but the sound of the steel doors closing diminished the smile and made my heart skip two beats.

I was led to my destination and shown where I needed to sit.

No sooner than I sat down, out of the corner of my eye, I saw this tall figure approaching. I was too afraid to look up. Instead I picked up the receiver to hear his voice.

"Hello Krisha."

I found the courage to pick my head up and look at this person who claimed to be the man who gave me life.

When my eyes focused on the man on the other side of the wall that divided us, immediately the tears I'd tried so hard to suppress during my entire ride dampened my face. I pulled out my handkerchief and wiped my face. He didn't have to say anything else to assure me that he was my father. From the sound of his voice, I knew it in my heart. Looking at his face, it was written all over it. It was like looking in a mirror. The picture from Carmen did no justice for his apparent physical features. His hair in long braids. Skin the same exotic light caramel complexion as mine. Eyes same color. Same full lips. It was clear to anyone that this man was indeed my father.

"Don't cry baby." He said while losing a few tears himself. "I'm so sorry."

He paused to regain his composure. "You're beautiful…Just like your mother…I loved her very much." He said with a smile.

Our conversation consisted of a lot of confessions, apologies, family history, and tears. Through it all, I enjoyed every minute. It was a very enlightening, informational experience.

Ryan sat in the waiting area eagerly anticipating my arrival. He jumped up when he saw me exit the steel doors.

"How'd it go?" He said in my ear.

"It was…it was interesting."

"He wasn't mean was he?"

"Absolutely not. He was pleasant, very regretful. He seems lonely and miserable."

"Twenty three years in here, I'm sure will do that to you." Ryan said as we walked hand in hand out of the prison.

"I felt as if I've known him all my life. In my heart I knew he was my father from the first words he spoke."

"At five years old, you should still have some memory of him. Even if it's vague."

"I know. But for some reason, I don't."

"I want to take you somewhere to relax and unwind. Get your mind off this visit for a while."

"That sounds nice babe. Where do you want to go?"

"Today is your day. We'll have lunch first, then you can shop or whatever you care to do. Then we'll have some quiet time. And I know the perfect place for all of that."

"Do you love me Mr. Mathers?"

"Of course, why?"

He eyed me suspiciously.

"Just thought I'd ask?"

"Don't second guess my love for you because of what you just experienced with your father. I'm not him. Every man you know is not gonna just walk out of your life."

"Well I'm up to two out of three right now." I said as I felt tears swallow my eyes.

"Krisha please don't do that to yourself."

"I've always had that fear. I've lived with it all my life. I took unnecessary drama from Todd that I shouldn't have had to deal with because of that fear. He was *that* man in my life. I didn't want him to leave me like my father did so I dealt with it. Though I did have strong love for him, my relationship was based on fear of not having a male figure in my life."

"Didn't you realize you could have had any man you wanted? You didn't have to deal with him."

"You don't understand."

"Yes I do Krisha. Remember we have something in common. I used to cling to any male figure that took up time with me. Wishing he was my father. So I know what you mean."

"I'm sorry. I didn't mean to imply…"

"No, nothing to be sorry about. Just let it rest for a while. Don't worry your pretty head about it."

I'd fallen asleep in the car on our way to our unknown destination. When I opened my eyes to see where he'd brought me, I smile and hugged his neck.

"Thanks Ryan. This is nice."

We were at Lake Essence. My last memory of us being here wasn't too pleasurable but I loved being on the lake nonetheless.

After reserving a cabin, we took a ride into the city.

First we had a quiet lunch then Ryan insisted on me going to the spa. After being pampered, I shopped a little. Shopping always did rehabilitate me. I was very pleased when we were done with our day out and about.

We returned to the cabin where we took a long hot bath together, then relaxed with a glass of wine. Ryan massaged my feet while I read a magazine. We talked while lying in front of the fireplace. Then fell asleep in each other's arms.

I couldn't tell how long we were asleep but the ringing of Ryan's cell startled us awake.

The next thing I heard was, "What? What do you want…I told you to chill?"

I took a big sigh before continuing to ear hustle on the conversation.

"Stop calling my phone." He continued. How many times am I gonna have to tell you that?"

He slammed the phone shut.

"I hate for you to turn it off. Your mother may try to call."

Soon after that was said, his phone rang again.

"I'm not answering that. I'll switch it to vibrate."

"Please." I said.

That damn phone vibrated all night. He didn't hear it. He was snoring too loud. After about the fifteenth time, I turned it off.

While driving back home the next morning, I thought I'd be a little nosey and ask.

"What did she want?"

"Nothing." He replied unmoved.

"What did she say?"

"Same ole, same ole."

"Like what?"

"Can we talk? Blah, blah, blah."

"She must really love you."

"Naw." Was all he had to offer.

"The girl is obviously obsessed for some reason."

"Just crazy. But I'm getting a new number today. She just doesn't get it."

"I agree with you. But I still say she's trippin' for something. And if you haven't been totally honest with me, I'm gonna kill you. Just wanted you to know that."

He smiled.

Since when was death funny? He really didn't understand that I was serious.

45

Todd called me every single day and night up to the day before my wedding. He said the same ole things every time. "I want you, I love you, don't marry him, can't live without you." Same ole things Maican was saying to Ryan.

I had been still sleeping with Todd, so I knew what fueled his fire. So I knew Ryan had to be giving her the business too. But it's funny how things turn around. I remember saying some of those same words to Todd.

Ryan had been in Baltimore for the last three days. At this hour I guessed he was enjoying his bachelor party and having the time of his life.

I was definitely having a hell of a time at my bachelorette party. This was the night before I would be Mrs. Ryan Mathers; my second, and last, time around in the marriage department, so the way I saw it, I wanted to party my single life away.

I started the night with glasses of wine and ended it with several mixed drinks and a few shots. I tried my best to refrain from drinking too much so that it wouldn't show the next day at my wedding, but for some reason the urge was bigger than my ability to just say no.

Sheri had done a fantastic job with planning everything from the shower to the bachelorette party. She had that baby seriously off the chain. She'd invited everyone I knew; the room was packed with friends and associates with an abundance of well wishes. I appreciated every bit.

Sheri had reserved the hotel ballroom for both the shower and bachelorette party, and six rooms upstairs for guests and us. She'd hired two male dancers and a DJ, and there was an open bar and an atmosphere for ladies only.

Dancers were never my thing but I threw caution to the wind and went with the flow of the night. The drinks had me in the right mind for it; therefore, I really didn't have a care in the world.

The dancers were beyond impressive though. I wasn't disappointed at all. I had never seen tools of that magnitude on a man in my whole life. I couldn't believe that they were real. The both of them knew their jobs very well, but they were just too much for my hazy, squinted up eyes to see. They almost caused a few women to go into cardiac arrest; they were just that great.

After their unique performances and while on their way out of the hotel lobby, Black Jack, the dancer with the most talent, slipped me his card and said "holla at me if you ever get lonely."

I smiled, but immediately threw that card away when he was out of sight. I didn't trust myself. That boy had it going on.

As the party was thinning, Mia advised that she was on her way to go meet Derric but would be back. She questioned my ability to carry on at the party without her, as it was clear that I was toasted. I assured her that I was a big girl and could handle the rest of the evening on my own even though my head had begun a horrific pounding.

The remainder of the ladies was still getting their party on, so I exited the ballroom after Mia left. I needed to get the scent of those two sweaty strippers off me and freshen up, so I went in search of the elevator in an attempt to get to my room.

As I searched for the elevator, I silently regretted consuming as much alcohol as I did as an aura of sickness quickly covered me from head to toe. I began to feel extremely bad. I felt myself incoherently struggling to make tiny step toward the elevator while holding my head in one hand and my stomach with the other.

Why did I have all those drinks? I thought to myself.

I was certifiably drunk. More than I'd ever been before.

"Mrs. Taylor do you need some help?" I remember hearing.

I remember the room spinning. My destination far away.

I remember a weakness coming over me.

"Right here, Mrs. Taylor. I'll take care of you." I thought I heard.

I was tired.

"Just lie back Mrs. Taylor. Everything will be okay."

I remember balling up into a fetal position.

I opened my eyes to voices, but I couldn't see a thing.

I was so tired. I was too weak. I just wanted to purge and sleep.

I remember sleep finding me.

46

Ryan wore a tux that suited him very well, and my white dress was flawless on my toned body. Mia was beautiful and my kids were absolutely adorable.

My wedding day was here and I could not stop smiling. The internal feeling of love and excitement had caused a collage of butterflies to flutter aimlessly about my belly.

Happy was an understatement.

I was elated for more reasons than anyone on the outside looking in could ever guess.

My biggest triumph was done. And my grandest mission was accomplished.

I'd loosed the strength of captivity from the hands of Todd Taylor and had married another man. Something I never thought I could do regardless of the words that I said.

The beginning of my life with Ryan would prove to be confirmation that it is possible to love again, no matter the brutal beating the heart may have endured.

I reminisced upon the incidents and the road that I'd travelled over the last several months due to my break up with Todd and new relationship with Ryan. I wasn't exactly pleased with who I was when I was going through the trials but I can look back, see my faults, change some things and move on to be a better person.

Lessons were learned and growth occurred. What more can you ask for in life? As long as I'm living, I will continuously be learning. When learning takes place, you are armed with something that no one can erase.

My heart is full and I shed tears because I have overcome some of my biggest trials; although the roads were bumpy, I persisted to move on with my life. No one will ever know how hard that was for me. And I'm a firm believer in the fact that anytime there is a will there is a way. No one should ever allow people or circumstances to hinder them from being who they know they are inside or from being the best person they could possibly be.

Today I was Mrs. Ryan Mathers. I wore the name and the smile that came with it very well. I couldn't wait to see where the road with Ryan would take me, but I would persist to move on; no matter what.

Mission Accomplished. Those words of satisfaction perused my mind on cruise and settled into my heart.

With closed eyes, I felt the warmth of security around me; something I'd long forgotten. A feeling of importance that went beyond vanity, status, or material possessions.

As these thoughts continued to invade my mind, I was becoming more coherent as reality insisted on making its presence.

"Mission Accomplished."

The words became clearer in what seemed to be a vocal utterance of sounds in an unvaried tone, instead of the thoughts in my head. The depth of the sounds stirred me in my haze.

Did I think the words into existence? I thought.

As that thought popped into my head, I quickly opened my eyes and answered myself. I struggled to sit up.

"What tha…?" I said frantically as I looked around.

As my eyes focused, they also grew as big as fifty cent coins.

Confused, I looked around to see unfamiliar faces.

"Who the hell are yall?"

I could feel movement under my body.

"And where the hell am I going?"

Discussion Questions

1. Did you think Krisha would ever get over Todd?
2. Was it okay for Krisha to continue sleeping with Todd even though she shared a relationship with Ryan?
3. Do you think Todd was being selfish in constantly trying to get Krisha back?
4. Should Krisha have given Todd another chance to prove himself? When should a woman allow a man another chance?
5. Does Ryan really love Krisha or does he want a trophy?
6. Why do you think Ryan forgave Krisha for sleeping with Todd? Why was he so forgiving of the things that she did?
7. How do you think Krisha really feels about her friendship with Tyson? Do you think it could have developed if she wasn't engaged?
8. Why do you think she confided in Tyson? Is it okay for a woman to confide in another man?
9. What do you think about Krisha's behavior throughout her ordeal? Do women really go through such transformations when hurt from a relationship?
10. What was Krisha's biggest issue that she sought to address in the story?
11. What do you think was Krisha's biggest accomplishment in her story?

Visit the author at

www.mickimichelle.com

For information on booking the author for book signings, interviews, and other speaking events, contact:

MickiMichelle at <u>mickimichel@live.com</u>

www.ingramcontent.com/pod-product-compliance
Lightning Source LLC
Chambersburg PA
CBHW031119030726
47496CB00002BA/596